THE GILGO BEACH SERIAL KILLER CASE

DOES *REX* HEUERMANN REIGN *KING* OF MURDER AND MAYHEM?

A Comprehensive Unfolding of

the Long Island Serial Killer Investigation

Robert Banfelder

BB

~

Broadwater Books
Riverhead, New York

Robert Banfelder

Broadwater Books
141 Riverside Drive
Riverhead, New York 11901

ISBN: 978-1-7326025-2-6

Printed in the United States of America
10 9 8 7 6 5 4 3 2 1

Cover Image: Rex Heuermann at the Peconic River Sportsman's Club in Manorville, Long Island, New York. The remains of two of seven victims were found near the club's property, linking Heuermann to the area, early 2000s. Credit: Peconic River Sportsman's Club

DEDICATION

Once again, I dedicate this book to Donna Derasmo, my life's partner, muse, graphic designer, researcher, editor, and savvy advisor. I would add "chief cook and bottlewasher," except to say I do most of the cooking and, arguably, clean up after myself. To avoid any dispute concerning the latter; that is, *cleanup*, I shall simply state that we, unarguably, make one hell of a team!

Assisting me over the course of 52 consecutive years, not once has Donna complained about the workload . . . . Well, maybe just once or twice.

ALSO BY ROBERT BANFELDER

FICTION

<u>Trilogy</u>:

Dicky, Richard, and I
The Signing
The Triumvirate

<u>Tetralogy</u>:
[A Justin Barnes Four-Book Series]

The Author
Award Winner for Best Suspense Novel from NewBookReviews
The Teacher
Award Winner for Best Suspense Novel from NewBookReviews
Knots
The Good Samaritans

FICTIONAL/FACTUAL ACCOUNTINGS

Trace Evidence
Inspired by and based on the Robert Shulman serial killer trial,
Riverhead, Long Island, New York. As a spectator at the Shulman trial,
Banfelder spent fifteen (15) months in the courtroom before penning
the story.

Battered

Inspired by and based on the murder trial of Sylvia Flynn, Brick Township, New Jersey. Banfelder spent two (2) years corresponding with Flynn prior to her release from prison before penning the story.

NEW JOURNALISM
An admixture of Fact ~ Fiction ~ Supposition

The Long Island Serial Killer Murders ~ Gilgo Beach and Beyond
A well-received fictional/nonfictional account of one of the most notorious serial cases of our time ~ books purchased in the United States, Canada, United Kingdom, Germany

Snuff Stuff
Gilgo Beach/Oak Beach/Manorville/Atlantic City Serial Killer Murders
Sequel to *The Long Island Serial Killer Murders ~ Gilgo Beach and Beyond*

NONFICTION

The Long-Awaited Arrest of Long Island Serial Killer Rex Heuermann ~ Past "Administration" to Blame

The Essential Guide to Writing Well and Getting Published with
Bonus Feature: *Making Decent Dollars Writing Plus Little-Known Reward-Reaping Benefits*

The Fishing Smart Anywhere Handbook for Salt Water & Fresh Water
Spin Casting, Baitcasting, Fly Casting ~ Lethal Lures & Live Baits ~ Kayaking/Canoeing ~ Seafood Recipes ~ Smoking Fish

The North American Hunting Smart Handbook with Bonus Feature:
Hunting Africa's Five Most Dangerous Game Animals

Robert Banfelder

Bull's Eye! The Smart Bowhunter's Handbook with Bonus Feature:
Bowfishing on a Budget

On Your Way to Gourmet Cooking
A Unique Guide for both the Beginner and Veteran Cook ~ 50 Outstanding Recipes

Gourmet Cooking with Confidence
A Unique Guide for the Beginner and Veteran Chef
Plus Budget-Friendly Tools & Equipment for Making Life Easier in the Kitchen

Additionally, Robert has written hundred of articles for local, regional, and national magazines, including co-hosting YouTube channel "Special Interests with Bob & Donna." Bob and Donna cover numerous topics. Robert has been interviewed by the *New York Post* as well as for a Peacock documentary, both referencing the Long Island Serial Killer Case.

A complete listing of the author's works may be viewed on his website: www.robertbanfelder.com.

FORWARD

Rampant corruption within the elite Suffolk County Homicide Squad and District Attorney's office can be traced back to the late 1970s, escalating through the 1980s, and culminating in 2021: threats of violence and\or blatant acts of violence directed toward a suspect; coercing and\or exacting false confessions from suspects; disregarding evidence that would tend to exonerate a suspect; willfully blocking a murder investigation. I will be briefly addressing these egregious acts in subsequent chapters.

Though the focus of the book is primarily on Rex Andrew Heuermann, it is important for the reader to understand the underlying facts that led to this travesty of justice. Corruption is the catchall.

As there is a lengthy list of characters covering a span of 45-plus years, an alphabetical listing has been provided for easy reference. Victims' names for which Rex Heuermann has been formally charged, likely to be charged, and suspected of abducting and murdering are listed separately below. Since there is a plethora of such names and places, only those leads that proved the most promising have been included in the listing. Other victims' names and locations have been addressed throughout the text.

CAST OF CHARACTERS

Bellone, Steve ~ Former Suffolk County executive.

Beyrer, Kevin ~ Detective Lieutenant Suffolk County Police Department Homicide Section. Narrates Shannan Gilbert's 911 call.

Bissett, Jimmy ~ Wealthy businessman and co-owner of the Long Island Aquarium and Exhibition Center, including the Hyatt Place Hotel in Riverhead ~ supposedly committed suicide ~ purportedly connected to the LISK case on several levels.

Bittrolff, John ~ Known as the Manorville Butcher. Convicted for the 1993 '94 murders of sex workers Rita Tangredi and Colleen

McNamee. Bittrolff was also a suspect in the Sandra Costilla Long Island Serial Killer case, the latter of which was proven not to be true and for which Rex Heuermann has been charged.

Bombace, Detective Kenneth ~ One of several cops involved in the former Chief of Police James Burke cover-up, including participation in the Christopher Loeb beating.

Brennan, Barbara ~ Oak Beach resident, one of whose door Shannan Gilbert knocked on the morning of her disappearance.

Brensic, Robert ~ One of four youths found guilty in the 1979 murder trial of 13-year-old Johnny Pius; later acquitted.

Brewer, Joseph ~ Owner of the home at number 8 The Fairway, Oak Beach, Long Island, from which Shannan Gilbert fled, screaming for her life.

Burke, James C. ~ Disgraced and convicted former chief of the Suffolk County Police Department.

Coletti, Gus ~ Oak Beach resident who tried to help Shannan Gilbert by calling 911 on the morning of her disappearance.

Cottingham, Detective Thomas ~ Suffolk County Police Department. One of several cops involved in the James Burke cover-up.

Cuff, Patrick ~ Suffolk County police commander whom James Burke, after being made chief of police, went after with a vengeance and retaliation referencing an internal affairs investigation into Burke and known prostitute Lowrita Rickenbacker.

Draiss, Officer Brian ~ Suffolk County Police Department. One of several cops involved in the James Burke cover-up.

Ellerup, Asa ~ Estranged wife of Rex Heuermann (kept her maiden name.)

Giuliani, Rudy ~ former New York City mayor and childhood friend of clergyman priest Alan Placa.

Hackett, Peter C. ~ Former police surgeon for Suffolk County's Emergency Services; neighbor of Joseph Brewer, Oak Beach, Long Island.

Harrison, Rodney ~ Newly appointed Suffolk County, Long Island Police Commissioner, December 21, 2021. Created the Suffolk County Gilgo Beach Homicide Investigation Task Force.

Hart, Geraldine ~ Former FBI Agent; former police commissioner, Suffolk County; presently, Director of Public Safety, Hofstra University, Hempstead, Long Island.

Hayden, Michael Edison ~ American writer.

Heuermann, Craig ~ Rex Heuermann's younger brother.

Heuermann, Rex Andrew ~ age 59 when arrested on July 13, 2023, charged with the murders of Megan Waterman, Amber Lynn Costello, Melissa Barthelemy, Maureen Brainard-Barnes. Later charged with the murders of Jessica Taylor, Sandra Costilla, and Valerie Mack.

Heuermann family ~ Asa Ellerup ~ age 60, estranged wife of Rex Heuermann [children: Christopher Sheridan, age 33 (by Ellerup's previous marriage) & Victoria Heuermann, age 26.

Hickey, James ~ Former Suffolk County police lieutenant and star witness for the prosecution who testified against former Suffolk County district attorney Thomas Spota and the former head of the Anti-Corruption Bureau, Christopher McPartland, in the trial of convicted former chief of police James Burke.

Kelly, Sergeant Michael ~ Suffolk County Police Department. One of several cops involved in the James Burke cover-up.

Lanieri, Robert ~ Food services executive for the Long Island Aquarium who committed suicide ~ see Bissett, Jimmy.

Leto, Detective Anthony ~ Suffolk County Police Department. One of several cops involved in the former Chief of Police James Burke cover-up, including participation in the Christopher Loeb beating.

Macedonio, Robert ~ attorney for Asa Ellerup (Rex Heuermann's wife).

Malone, Guy ~ Insurance fraud investigator whose wife (Heather Malone) was purportedly working as a 'sporting girl,' protected by, and part and parcel to, then police sergeant James Burke's prostitution network.

Malone, Heather ~ Whose husband (Guy Malone) brought to light the nefarious dealings of then police officer James Burke.

McCready, K. James ~ Detective who railroaded Marty Tankleff.

McNamee, Colleen ~ Victim of convicted killer John Bittrolff.

McPartland, Christopher ~ Disgraced and convicted former chief prosecutor of the Anti-Corruption Bureau for the district attorney's office, Suffolk County.

Mitev, Vess ~ attorney for Asa Ellerup-Heuermann's two adult children.

Murphy, Michael ~ Suffolk County Police Sergeant. Early suspect in the Colleen McNamee and Rita Tangredi murders.

Namm, Judge Stuart (Retired) ~ Author of *A Whisteblower's Lament: The Perverted Pursuit of Justice in the State of New York*.

Nealis, Detective Christopher ~ Suffolk County Police Department. One of several cops involved in the James Burke cover-up.

Pak, Michael ~ Shannan Gilbert's driver/bodyguard on May 1, 2010.

Paulino, Lorraine ~ Testified that she attended a swinger's meet-up at Rex Heuermann's home along with her boyfriend and Karen Vergata.

Placa, Alan (Monsignor) ~ priest of the Diocese of Rockville Centre; defrocked then reinstated with limited duties.

Quartararo, Michael ~ One of four youths found guilty in the 1979 murder trial of 13-year-old Johnny Pius; later acquitted.

Quartararo, Peter ~ One of four youths found guilty in the 1979 murder trial of 13-year-old Johnny Pius; later acquitted.

Ray, John ~ Attorney for the Gilbert estate: Mari Gilbert (mother); Sarra, Sherre, Stevie, Shannan (daughters).

Regensburg, Detective Kenneth ~ Suffolk County Police Department. One of several cops involved in the James Burke cover-up.

Rickenbacker, Lowrita ~ Known prostitute with whom then Sergeant James Burke, Suffolk County, was sexually involved.

Ruggiero, Francine ~ Christopher Loeb's probation officer.

Ryan, Thomas ~ One of four youths found guilty in the 1979 murder trial of 13-year-old Johnny Pius; later acquitted.

Schaller, Dave ~ Friend/roommate/pimp of Amber Lynn Costello ~ Gilgo Beach murder victim.

Sinclair, Detective Keith ~ Suffolk County Police Department. One of several cops involved in the James Burke cover-up.

Spota, Thomas ~ Disgraced and convicted former district attorney, Suffolk County.

Stephan, Vincent ~ Homicide Detective spokesman for the Suffolk County Police Department who initially announced and pushed the narrative that Shannan Gilbert was not murdered, that she died as the result of a "misadventure."

Tangredi, Rita ~ Victim of convicted killer John Bittrolff.

Tankleff, Martin ~ Convicted for the murder of his parents, the innocent young man spent 17 years in prison for a crime he did not commit.

Tierney, Ray ~ Newly elected Suffolk County District Attorney, 2022.

Toulon, Errol D., Jr. ~ Suffolk County Sheriff, Riverhead Correctional Facility.

Varrone, Dominick ~ Former chief of detectives, Suffolk County, re Gilgo Beach serial killer case ~ removed from case by former chief of police James Burke.

Note: "Leanne" [actual name withheld]. The woman identified as "Leanne" signed an affidavit before her attorney John Ray, stating that she was paid for sexual relations with then Inspector James Burke of the Organized Crime Bureau, Suffolk County, at a cocaine-fueled house party in Oak Beach, Long Island.

LONG ISLAND SERIAL KILLER VICTIMS FOR WHICH REX HEUERMANN HAS BEEN CHARGED

Barthelemy, Melissa ~ 24 years old, 4 feet 10 inches tall. Disappeared 2009, found by police December 11, 2010. (One of the "Gilgo Four").

Brainard-Barnes, Maureen ~ 25 years old, 4 feet 11 inches tall. Disappeared 2007, remains found by police December 14, 2010. (One of the "Gilgo Four").

Costello, Amber Lynn ~ 27 years old, 5 feet tall. Disappeared September 2010. Remains found by police December 13, 2010. (One of the "Gilgo Four").

Costilla, Sandra ~ 28 years old when she went missing. Her body was found November 21, 1993 by hunters near Fish Cove, a hamlet of North Sea, town of Southampton on Long Island's South Shore.

Mack, Valerie ~ 24 years old, living in Philadelphia when she went missing in 2000. On November 19, 2000, her partially dismembered body (torso) was found close to the Peconic River Sportsman's Club near a utility path on an adjacent parcel of woodlands in Manorville. On April 4, 2011, eleven years later, Valerie's remains (head, hands, and right foot) were found within plastic bags in the vicinity of Ocean Parkway near Gilgo Beach.

Taylor, Jessica ~ 20 years old, working as an escort in New York City. Her torso was discovered on July 27, 2003 in a wooded area off Halsey Manor Road in Manorville. On March 29, 2011, Jessica's additional remains were discovered almost eight years later along Ocean Parkway in the Gilgo Beach area, 47 miles away.

Waterman, Megan, 22 years old, 5 feet 5 inches tall. Disappeared June 2010, found by police December 13, 2010. (One of the "Gilgo Four").

LONG ISLAND SERIAL KILLER VICTIMS FOR WHICH REX HEUERMANN MAY POSSIBLY BE CHARGED

Gilbert, Shannan ~ Craigslist sex worker victim whose remains led to the discovery of the "Gilgo Four." No one has been charged with her death to date because police, to this day, have ruled it an accident.

Mack, Valerie ~ Identified via genetic genealogy. Heuermann not yet officially charged with her murder.

"Peaches" and her 2-year-old toddler remain unknown. See "Peaches & Her Daughter, pages 44 and 228 for full details. Also, see below info re .

Vergata, Karen ~ Last seen by a witness on February 14, 1996, running from the Heuermann home in Massapequa Park. Karen's partial remains were first found in a plastic bag at Fire Island's Blue Point Beach on April 20, 1996. Fifteen years later, on April 11, 2011, Karen's subsequent remains (her skull) was found near the remains of "Peaches," not far from Gilgo Beach.

LAS VEGAS, NEVADA WOMEN (MISSING OR FOUND MURDERED), WITH POSSIBLE TIES TO REX HEUERMANN

Brewer, Jodi Marie ~ On August 29, 2003, 19-year-old Las Vegas resident Jodi Marie Brewer's torso was found wrapped in cloth and plastic, discovered across the state line in San Bernadino County, California. Her torso had been cut with precision using a surgical saw.

Camara, Victoria ~ On August 11, 2003, 17-year-old Victoria Camara's body was found near a desert haul road in Bolder City, Nevada. She had been dumped like trash 26 miles southeast of Las Vegas. Victoria and her family lived in New Jersey; she had moved to Las Vegas.

Foster, Jessica Edith Louise ~ On March 28, 2006, 21-year-old Jessica Edith Louise Foster was last seen in Las Vegas, Nevada. Jessica last had phone contact with her family while she was at home in the 1000 block of Cornerstone Place, North Las Vegas.

Harris, Lindsay Marie ~ On May 4, 2005, 21-year-old Lindsay Marie Harris disappeared from her home in Henderson, Nevada. She was last seen at a nearby bank making a deposit.

Saens, Misty Marie ~ On March 12, 2003, 21-year-old Misty Marie Saens disappeared from her home in Henderson, Nevada.

SOUTH CAROLINA WOMEN MISSING WITH POSSIBLE TIES TO REX HEUERMANN

Bean, Julia Ann ~ On May 31, 2017, 36-year-old Julia Ann Bean, a pretty, petite, 5-foot 6-inch, 110 to 120-pound South Carolina woman, suddenly vanished.

Bell, Aallyah ~ On November 26, 2014, two days before Thanksgiving, 18-year-old Aallyah Bell of Rock Hill, South Carolina disappeared.

Note: Superseding indictments for which Rex Heuermann has been charged may tend to confuse the issue. For example, Heuermann was not charged with the murders of Jessica Taylor and Sandra Costilla until June 6, 2024. Also, the defendant was not charged with Valerie Mack's murder until December 17, 2024. However, for the sake of clarity, I indicated early on that we are addressing the fifth, sixth, and seventh murders, respectively, which Heuermann allegedly committed.

CHAPTER ONE

Shannan Gilbert, a 23-year-old sex worker, disappeared from a client's home, Joseph Brewer, at number 8 The Fairway, Oak Beach in Suffolk County, Long Island, New York during the early morning hours of May 1, 2010. In mid-December of that year, in the adjacent community of Gilgo Beach (7½ miles away), police inadvertently discovered the bodies of four young women that the newspapers dubbed the "Gilgo Four": Maureen Brainard-Barnes, Melissa Barthelemy, Megan Waterman, and Amber Lynn Costello. After a 19-month search for Shannan Gilbert, her skeletal remains were eventually found in a marsh approximately ¼ mile from client Joseph Brewer's home in Oak Beach (not Gilgo Beach as is sometimes reported).

Excerpted from my first nonfiction book, *The Long-Awaited Arrest of Long Island Serial Killer Rex Heuermann ~ Past "Administration" to Blame*, I have a small bone (pun intended) to pick: The hyoid bone. I will explain.

Authorities do not believe that Shannan Gilbert was the victim of foul play but rather the victim of a so-called "misadventure," that she became disoriented and drowned in the marsh near Joseph Brewer's home. The police made that determination *prior* to the Suffolk County medical examiner's autopsy report. Skeptics disputed that claim, particularly Shannan's family and their estate attorney John Ray. Suffolk County's medical examiner's findings clearly stated that Shannan Gilbert's cause of death was "inconclusive." Shannan's family hired their own independent medical examiner, world renowned Dr. Michael Baden (former medical examiner for New York City). Baden also found that Shannan's cause of death was "inconclusive," but he also noted that Shannan's hyoid bone had been fractured, pointing out that a fractured or broken hyoid bone is typical of someone who has been strangled. However, after a period of nineteen months of being subjected to the elements, the hyoid bone *may* have been the result of animal infestation, he added.

Two medical examiners had ruled that Shannan Gilbert's cause of death was "inconclusive." Yet, to this day, the Suffolk County police maintain that Gilbert's death was an accident, that she became disoriented and drowned. What we must keep foremost in mind are the three notorious men who originally spun the narrative of Gilbert's so-called "misadventure." Namely, disgraced Police Chief James Burke, disgraced Suffolk County District Attorney Thomas Spota, and his equally despicable cohort Anti-corruption Bureau Chief Christopher McPartland, all three convicted felons. We will be covering James Burke, Thomas Spota, and Christopher McPartland, along with several other unsavory sorts, shortly.

Attorney John Ray for the Gilbert family stated, "I don't believe that the authorities believe their own story. Their story is that Shannan became crazed by some unknown cause, ran into an almost impenetrable marsh as daylight approached, and found her way into a marsh, a relatively narrow marsh, and just managed to drop dead. And the other theory they espouse, equally absurd, is that she died from drowning, where she was found face up in the brush, and there is no [collected] water even close by [where she was found]. She would have had to swallow water [soggy, spongy groundwater] to drown. And yet they adhere to their absurdity."

Both past and present administrations adhere to this claim; that is, the *old* regime under James Burke and Thomas Spota as well as the *new* administration under District Attorney Ray Tierney. Police Commissioner Rodney Harrison handed in his resignation on November 2, 2023 before retiring, having served as commissioner for almost two years. The pair created the Suffolk County Gilgo Beach Homicide Investigation Task Force in 2022 and have done a remarkable job. Still, there is this bone of contention existing between attorney John Ray and District Attorney Ray Tierney, but more on that later.

Keep in mind that Police Commissioner Harrison would not have been standing alongside attorney John Ray at his Wednesday, October 18, 2023 press conference in support of John Ray if he did not take the attorney seriously.

CHAPTER TWO

Fifty-nine-year-old architect Rex Andrew Heuermann of Massapequa Park, Long Island was arrested outside his Manhattan office on July 13, 2023 for the murders of the "Gilgo Four." Heuermann has been indicted by a grand jury and charged with first- and second-degree murder of Melissa Barthelemy, Megan Waterman, and Amber Lynn Costello; second-degree murder of Maureen Brainard-Barnes. First-degree murder is intentional; that is, premeditated. Second-degree murder could still be intentional; however, it might have been unplanned.

On June 6, 2024, Heuermann was charged with two additional murders in the second-degree: Jessica Taylor, and Sandra Costilla. Sandra's murder dates back in time to November 20, 1993. It is likely that Heuermann has been committing these murders for a period of several decades. We will be delving into serial killers and their probable time frame for committing these violent acts in a later chapter.

The partial remains of Jessica Taylor were discovered on July 26, 2003 by a dog walker in Manorville, Long Island. Approximately 13 hours before the dog walker discovered Taylor's partial remains, another witness reportedly saw a dark-colored Chevrolet pickup truck backed into the wooded area where the mutilated torso was found. Jessica's head and arms below the elbows had been removed, and her tattoo was mutilated to thwart identification. Her skull and hands were found eight years later, on March 29, 2011, along Ocean Parkway, just east of Gilgo Beach. It is believed that Taylor was killed sometime between July 21 and 26, 2003.

Internet search data later revealed that Heuermann had shopped for a new light-colored pickup truck in the days shortly after Jessica Taylor's remains were first found by the dog walker, despite that

Heuermann's dark-green Chevy pickup truck was only four months old.

Excerpted from my nonfiction paperback book published in 2023, titled *The Long-Awaited Arrest of Long Island Serial Killer Rex Heuermann ~ Past "Administration" To Blame*, is the unfolding of another victim who more than likely fell prey to Rex Heuermann. I say "likely" because Heuermann has not yet been charged for the murder of Karen Ann Vergata. The accusation has been made by attorney John Ray, who has been following the investigation for years and has in his possession signed affidavits from witnesses who told the attorney a series of shocking stories.

Here is but one story — with detailed information involving other victims to follow in subsequent chapters:

A 34-year-old Manhattan woman who worked as an escort at the time of her disappearance was identified as Karen Vergata, brought up in Glenwood Landing, a hamlet on Long Island. Known initially as Fire Island Jane Doe #7, missing from February 14, 1996, when she last called her father, was later identified via genetic genealogy. The partial remains of two severed legs were first discovered on April 20, 1996 by residents Robert and Andrew Ragona, who were walking along the beach when they came across a pair of severed legs in a black plastic garbage bag floating in the water along Blue Point Beach, approximately one mile west of Fire Island's Davis Park.

Karen's right leg had three scars as reported by police: a three-and-a-half-inch scar on the lateral mid-leg area, a one-inch linear scar on the lateral mid-to-lower leg, and a half-inch scar on the inside of her ankle. Karen's left leg had a two-inch surgical scar and adjacent suture scars on her left ankle. It was subsequently learned that Karen had been hit by a truck in the late 1980s, which would help explain the scars. Fifteen years later in April of 2011, a second set of remains, inclusive of Vergata's skull, was found near Jones Beach along Ocean Parkway.

A retired homicide detective had contacted authorities and told them about the severed legs that had washed ashore in 1996. Vergata's remains had been safely stored away in a freezer at the medical examiner's office for more than fifteen years. In July of 2011, DNA testing revealed that the skull and legs belonged to the same person; however, it would be more than a decade before the victim could be positively identified. Eleven years later, in September of 2022, genetic genealogy was used to home in on the woman's identity. We will talk more about genetic genealogy later.

Karen Vergata

Back to Shannan Gilbert:

Shannan Gilbert

Another witness for attorney John Ray, a female banker by day and a taxi cab driver by night, signed an affidavit stating that she picked up Shannan Gilbert in the fall of 2009. The woman said that Shannan had been hiding in a Sayville Lodge motel bathroom from the man whom she later recognized as Rex Heuermann. He fled the scene, Ray explains, relating the taxi driver's story:

"Suddenly, a giant man who fits the description of Rex Heuermann comes out of the motel, covering his face with his arms so as not to be identified. He runs to a van or an SUV that is parked nearby. The taxi driver continues to flash her lights and beep her horn as part of a prearranged signal with the [taxi driver's] dispatcher until Shannan runs out, crying, shaking, very upset, and gets in the taxi.

"The witness is certain that the woman was Shannan Gilbert because she had a 'drooping eye' and other features that she immediately recognized from media reports of Shannan's 2010 disappearance," Ray relates.

"What had happened in the motel room, the pretty, petite young woman told the cabbie, is that she met the man on Craigslist, and he convinced her to come to Long Island with promises of financial assistance for her family. Upon Shannan's arrival, he handed her an envelope that he said contained $1,000 and told her she could keep it regardless of how their evening went. She said she opened the envelope when the man went to the bathroom and discovered that it was stuffed with papers, not cash. Fearful, she ran toward the bathroom after the man exited, locked its door, and called the cab company, the witness had said. The young woman told her driver to take her to the Ronkonkoma train station so that she could return to the city," Ray continues to explain.

"The witness said that she had told several people about the encounter at the time and left messages on a police tip line after Rex Heuermann's arrest.

"During another incident, the same taxi driver witness said that she had picked up the man she is certain was Rex Heuermann several weeks or months later, refusing to drive him out to a distant location 'in the woods' because he changed their original destination. Enraged, he threatened to kill her and flashed a gun before getting out of the vehicle."

Here is where it is important to realize that there is a distinct dichotomy between attorney John Ray's assessments concerning certain victims and witnesses compared to District Attorney Ray

Tierney's take on such matters. We will explore these inconsistencies in later chapters.

Attorney John Ray

It is also important to note that Ray Tierney was and is quite upset when John Ray held a joint press conference alongside the newly appointed Suffolk County Police Commissioner Rodney Harrison. Obviously, Harrison saw merit in investigating John Ray's witness' testimonies; Ray Tierney did not.

Suffolk County District Attorney
Raymond Tierney

No sooner than I was about to put my first nonfiction book referencing Gilgo Beach to bed on October 18, 2023, attorney John Ray held that press conference with Rodney Harrison. Immediately, it should tell you that the commissioner of the Suffolk County Gilgo Beach Homicide Investigation Task Force is taking John Ray seriously referencing the allegations the attorney made concerning witnesses who could shed new light on the police investigations. And what a light John Ray cast. In a word, extraordinary!

Police Commissioner Rodney Harrison confirmed that they are, indeed, interviewing four new witnesses who could connect more cases to suspect Rex Heuermann. "When it comes to Miss Karen Vergata," Harrison said, "and when it comes to Miss Shannan Gilbert, they're the ones that we are going to take a closer look at and see if they are connected to our defendant [Rex Heuermann]."

Police Commissioner Harrison has since retired in November of 2023. His leadership was credited in the arrest of the suspected Gilgo Beach serial killer. Harrison spent 32 years in law enforcement, including serving as NYPD chief of the department. Although now retired, we will hear from him earlier in time, May of 2022, when he released new information on the "Gilgo Four," which included previously unreleased information "in the hopes of eliciting tips from the public and providing greater transparency about the victims," Harrison said.

I will cover that information in a later chapter.

**Former Suffolk County Police Commissioner
Rodney Harrison**

Subsequently, John Ray has opened Pandora's box concerning Rex Heuermann's 27-year-old daughter, Victoria Heuermann, strongly suggesting that she may be more involved than first believed. It is interesting to note the eerie similarities between her art and the murders for which her father has been charged. Ray dramatically presented a dark side to Victoria via a series of pictures that he displayed at a press conference held on June 13, 2024, depicting disturbing demonic images of a macabre, gruesome, and sadistic nature. Victoria obviously has a fascination with torture, murder, brutalization, mutilation, amputation, and death as you will note in the following chapter.

CHAPTER THREE

Presenting at John Ray's June 13, 2024 press conference, the attorney displayed a series of artwork that was retrieved from Victoria Heuermann's computer before being deleted. There are eleven images, plus a few more she missed before deleting others. Apparently, Victoria has a certain fascination with the macabre. Where applicable, the artists are credited in the upper left-hand corner of each image.

Naked woman impaled by a set of deer antlers, backdropped by a marsh.
Credit: exOskeletal-undead.tumblr.com

**Hangings. Note the victim's right shoe is off
in foreground, like how Sandra Costilla's, Rita Tangredi's,
and Colleen McNamee's bodies were posed.**
Credit: exOskeletal-undead.tumblr.com

Note: Rita's and Colleen's murders were charged to convicted killer John Bittrolff.

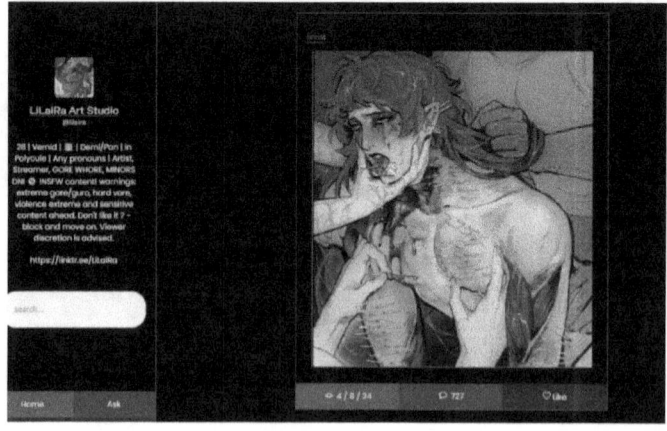

Brutality. Note: Three pairs of hands attacking victim ~ torturing woman with pins. Credit: LiLaiRa Art Studio

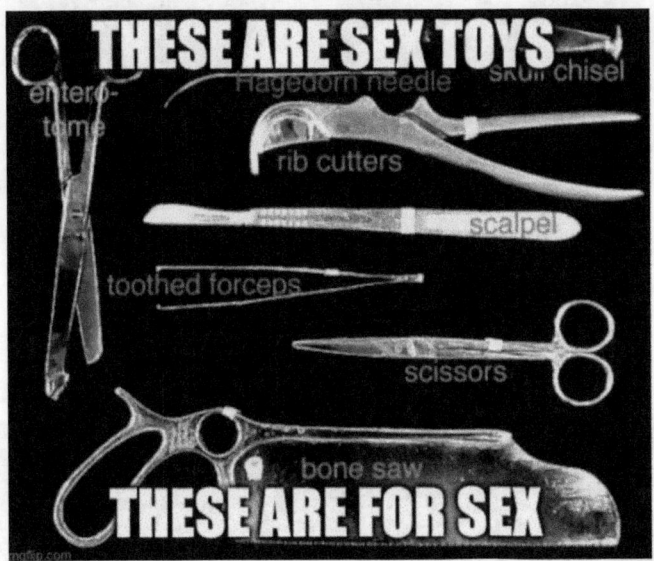

Tools of the trade: Upper left corner. enterotome (a surgical cutting instrument for opening the digestive tract, especially the intestines); Immediate right. Hagedorn needle (a surgical suture needle for joining up or closing wounds; skull chisel, et cetera. The rest of these items are self-explanatory.
Credit not available

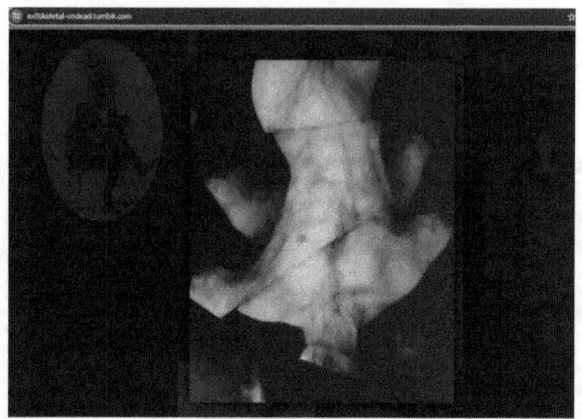

Bloody, dissected body
Credit: exOskeletal-undead.tumblr.com

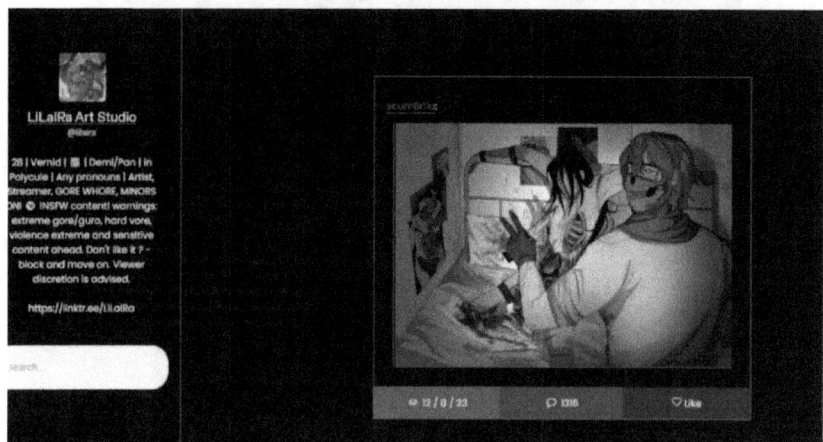

Evisceration. Note body in background, knife in assailant's gloved hand, and exposed entrails. Credit: LiLaiRa Art Studio

Amputation and perhaps meal-packaging preparation for transport. Credit: LiLaiRa Art Studio

Cannibalism depicted. Credit: not available.

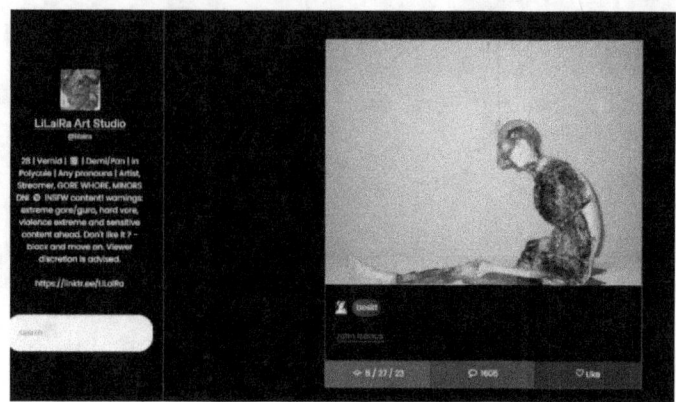

Cannibalism; parts of body eaten away.
Credit: LiLaiRa Art Studio

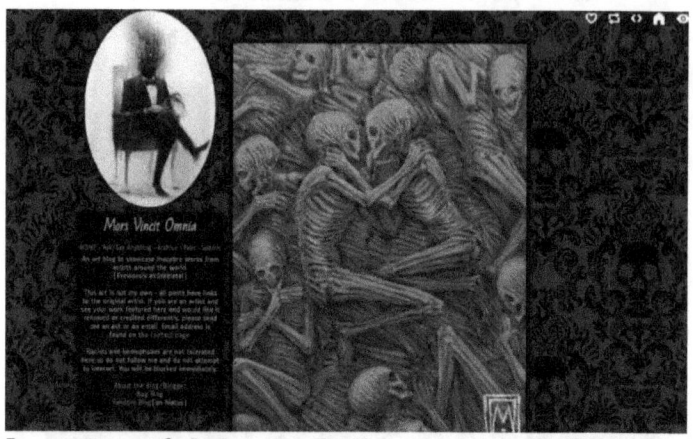

**Mass grave of skeletons. Perhaps a sort of RIP (Rest in
Purgatory) statement within a sadistic murderer's mind.
Latin phrase: Mors Vincit Omnia ~ "Death Conquers All."**
Credit not available

vinnandimadtur Follow
Jun 10, 2018

Another image Victoria Heuermann posted on her blog before deleting them. According to Attorney John Ray, the image of the woman is Victoria Heuermann. Credit: vinnandimadtur

These are but several images John Ray shared with viewers at his press conference concerning Victoria Heuermann's area of interest. There are other images that he said are far worse. Rather than have Ray specifically spell out its implications, he asks the audience to draw their own inferences of the images Victoria was watching referencing her Tumblr account themes (a micro-blogging service). She has subsequently deleted *all* her sites, all her social media. "She just missed these [eleven]," Ray said. He sent *Newsweek* approximately twenty-seven pictures.

Victoria's mother, Asa Ellerup, had deleted her own social media site.

CHAPTER FOUR

Also present at John Ray's June 13, 2024 press conference was Dr. Gary Brucato, clinical forensic psychologist, researcher, and author in the areas of psychotic illness and violence. Dr. Brucato earned his Ph.D. at the New School for Social Research in New York City. He has over two decades of clinical experience, having trained at Creedmoor Psychiatric Center, Beth Israel Medical Center, Bronx Lebanon Hospital Center, Long Island Jewish/Zucker Hillside Hospital Center, and Mount Sinai Services/Elmhurst Hospital Center, including work on the Riker's Island female prisoner unit at EHC.

Dr. Gary Brucato

Dr. Brucato said of Victoria Heuermann: "There is potential that she was surrounded by the murders and thought nothing of it, referring to this as 'normalization.' Victoria also could have suffered from Stockholm Syndrome," he added. [The phenomenon is a reaction to developing a psychological bond between captor and abuser.] "The jury is out on what this was about," Brucato said.

Victoria Heuermann, Rex Heuermann's daughter

Christopher Sheridan, Rex Heuermann's stepson

**Asa Ellerup ~ estranged wife of
Rex Heuermann**

About 20% of serial killers operate in groups, according to Brucato. "Hairs on some of Rex Heuermann's victims could have been directly from Victoria rather than transferred by her father," John Ray said. "This goes against what District Attorney Raymond Tierney announced," Ray added. "He [Tierney] has no way of knowing that for certain."[that the hairs were transfer hairs].

Brucato pointed to similar cases as Rex Heuermann's, "who potentially worked alongside his daughter Victoria," he stated. including the case of David Parker Ray. Known as the "Toy-Box Killer," Parker Ray is accused of torturing and killing approximately 50 women in his basement, who were sometimes brought by Parker Ray's own daughter, Brucato added.

Brucato also noted the case of John Wayne Gacy, who is now thought to have worked in a group. Gacy murdered and raped over 30 young men and boys in Chicago.

Brucato believes there are other multiple individuals who have been harmed, killed, or kidnapped by Rex Heuermann.

"Until recently it was thought that he [Heuermann] was a lone wolf," Brucato said. "There is a tendency to think that these people are lone wolfs that cannot have connections with other people."

Taken from the Bail Hearing

Gilgo Beach murder suspect Rex Heuermann kept meticulous notes on his kills — including reminders for future murders like "hit harder" and to "get more sleep to have more play time," prosecutors revealed — as he was charged with two more slayings.

Heuermann, now 61, who is accused of killing multiple women and leaving their remains scattered along Long Island's Ocean Parkway, appeared in court on Thursday June 6, 2024, and pleaded not guilty to second-degree murder charges for the 1993 murder of Sandra Costilla as well as the 2003 murder of Jessica Taylor.

Rex Heuermann "nodded" along as Suffolk County prosecutors read aloud from an alleged "planning document" recovered from the accused's computer found in his Massapequa Park home that they say served as a "blueprint" for his twisted crimes and showed his "obvious" intention to kill women.

The married father of two — who was arrested in 2023 for the murders of four young women dubbed the "Gilgo Four" — was linked to both Costilla and Taylor through DNA from male and female hairs found on their remains, prosecutors said in a court filing.

The prosecution's case had relied mostly on evidence that showed Heuermann was in the same location as burner phones used to contact some of the victims and taunt their families, as well as DNA found on several victims that was linked to him. But in March of 2024, investigators discovered a damning trove of "planning documents" that Heuermann allegedly used to "methodically blueprint" his kills, the new filing alleged.

The shocking evidence was found on a hard drive taken from Heuermann's basement during a search in the wake of his arrest in July 2023, prosecutors said.

"The task force believes that this is a 'planning document' that was used by Heuermann to plot out his kills with excruciating detail," Suffolk County District Attorney Ray Tierney told reporters after the arraignment. "His motivations, meticulous planning, and clear intent were obvious. His intent was nothing short but to murder these victims."

Heuermann's lists included notes on potential or past dump sites, as well as supplies that he used to try and evade detection as he allegedly targeted, tortured, and murdered the young women.

One of Heuermann's list marked "POST EVENT" included reminders to "change tires," "burn gloves," "dispose of pics [of victims]," and "have story set," while another list titled "PROBLEMS" noted the potential pitfalls of DNA evidence or fingerprints.

Another list titled "BODY PREP" included notes to wash the "inside and all cavities" of his deceased victim and to remove their "head and hands" and "marks from torture."

Still, another list detailing post-crime cleanup referred to strategies for hanging drop cloths from the ceiling and concerns about how sound travels, leading investigators to believe that the torture "likely" took place inside Heuermann's home.

Rex Heuermann even noted that "getting more sleep" was important to having "more play time" — the sick euphemism he used to refer to torturing and killing the victims.

Heuermann listed his preparation for his victims. Credit: Suffolk County District Attorney Raymond Tierney:

Planning Document Found by Police in Rex Heuermann's Massapequa Park Home Basement

BODY PREP:
- WASH BODY INSIDE AND ALL CAVITIES
- REMOVE TRACE EVENDICE [FINGER PRINTS/HAIR]
- REMOVE TRACE DNA
- REMOVE ID MARKS [TATOOS, MARKS.....]
- REMOVE MARKS FROM TOURTURE
- REMOVE HEAD AND HANDS
- PACKAGE FOR TRANSPORT

DISPOSE OF THE FOLLOWING:
- TOOLS AND DEVICES
- T-1 CLOTHES AND PERSONAL ITEMS
- DROP CLOTHES
- WIPES AND TOWELS
- PROPS, TOYS, WOOD ITEMS.......
- ANYTHING THAT TOUCHED T-1
- WHAT YOU WORE
- DISTROY BOOK AND COMPUTER FILES.
- BURN GLOVES
- DISPOSE OF BOX OF PLATIC BAS TO AVOID TRACE.

THINGS:TO REMEMBER
- SOUND TRAVELS (IE: BIRD OUTSIDE) CONTROL THE AMOUNT OF AIR IN AND OUT TO CONTROL THE NOISE MADE.
- GET SLEEP BEFORE HUNT TOO TIRED CREATS PROBLEMS
- HIT HARDER TOO MANY HIT TO TAKE DOWN. CONSIDER A HIT TO THE FACE OR NECK NEXT TIME FOR TAKE DOWN.
- MORE SLEEP & NOISE CONTROL = MORE PLAY TIME
- USE PUSH PINS TO HANG DROP CLOTHES FROM CEILING – NOT TAPE.
- USE HEVEY ROPE FOR NECK-LIGHT ROPE BROKE UNDER STRESS OF BEING TIGHTEND.

TAKE DOWN/PICK UP:
- HUNT TOO LONG SEEN IN AREA TOO LONG.
- REMEMBER DON'T CHARGE GAS.
- RECON FOR VID.CAMS. IN PICK UP AREA NEXT TIME.

Authorities also found Heuermann's "significant collection" of torture porn, including images of breast mutilation and vaginal torture.

The architect had also compiled what appeared to be notes from a first edition paperback of *Mindhunter* by retired FBI agent John Douglas, the prosecution noted.

Heuermann also had a copy of Douglas' *The Cases That Haunt Us*, which included analyses on victimology and other evidence in some of the United States' most infamous crimes.

CHAPTER FIVE

Earlier in time, on Tuesday, January 30, 2024, John Ray held a symposium at St. John's University in Queens, New York, where he introduced witnesses who have given sworn affidavits detailing their alleged encounters with Rex Heuermann. Five women claimed they had met Gilgo Beach serial killer suspect Heuermann and spoke out about their encounters — one of them saying that she barely escaped with her life. At the event, John Ray spoke on behalf of a woman using the pseudonym Mary Poe, who did not attend the symposium. Here is her terrifying story per her affidavit:

"In 1994, I was a sex worker. I had a pimp who worked as well with other sex workers. On or about Sunday, August 24, 1994, a customer pulled up next to me about 3:30 a.m. to 5:30 a.m. while I was on the corner of 24th Street and 11th Avenue in Manhattan."

Mary Poe explained that he asked her for oral sex, and after entering his Chevrolet pickup, she claimed she heard a loud explosion on the left side of her body.

"I smelled gunpowder. I was stunned. I felt a stinging in the back of my neck. I turned back toward him and saw that he was pointing a gun at me as he was driving. I grabbed his hand with both of my hands and threw my body upon and across him as I tried to exit the vehicle out the large driver's side window," the affidavit read.

"I was screaming words to the effect of 'God, someone help me, he is trying to murder me!' I tried to get his car keys. He put his foot on the gas. I told him to just let me out."

Mary Poe said she managed to jump out the driver's side of the moving vehicle and dropped to the ground.

"His vehicle ran over my feet with the rear tire. One of my shoes was crushed. My feet were not injured. I don't know why. I remained lying in the street. I realized I had been shot in the back of my neck," the affidavit added.

Mary Poe said other female sex workers called an ambulance, and she was taken to a hospital.

In her affidavit, she said the driver who attacked her had on a large flannel shirt with a dark t-shirt underneath it.

She said: "He was a man of enormous size. He was very fat with a large gut. He had dark, curly, wavy hair. His brow and face were unusually wide; his brow was thick. He had fierce blue eyes. His face was full of observable hatred.

"When I saw Rex Heuermann on a video screen, I recognized him as the man I described."

John Ray said Mary Poe has filed a police report and that her case is still under investigation.

Lorraine Paulino, who testified at the symposium, is a psychiatric nurse. She claims in her affidavit that she met Heuermann when she was 26 years old during a swingers' meet-up.

Lorraine Paulino

Ms. Paulino, of Belizean nationality, who is now age 54, said that she and her police officer boyfriend were swingers, belonging to La Trapeze, a club based in Midtown Manhattan, close to where Heuermann worked as an architect. The psychiatric nurse said that Heuermann in 1996 had posted on the wall of La Trapeze a notice asking for a sexual encounter at his Massapequa Park home. The witness's swinger boyfriend, a NYPD narcotics detective, was referred to in the affidavit as R.W. In February of 1996, R.W. and she picked up Karen Vergata in New York City, on their way to the Heuermann home. "Karen had just gotten out of jail; she was disheveled, hungry, and homeless," said the witness.

R.W., Karen, and the witness entered Heuermann's home and met Heuermann's wife [Asa Ellerup], who was not only privy to the situation but was to be a participant, until seeing that the female witness is African American, to which Asa Ellerup declines.

"Karen went downstairs," Paulino related. "I stayed upstairs. My partner, who is bisexual, kept disappearing. I believe he was elsewhere in the house, having sex with Rex. I had sex with Rex as well. I never went downstairs."

The witness said that she had serviced Rex Heuermann many times in the past and that he was a serial user of sex workers.

Ray related that Heuermann would sometimes have them come to his house two at a time while his wife was home upstairs.

The witness said they left Karen Vergata playing "swinger games" with Rex Heuermann.

Once outside, the witness questioned her detective boyfriend as to why they were leaving Karen behind, who was seen frantically waving from a window before running naked outside the house and crying. "He told me not to worry about her, that she was okay, that they were only playing a game. We left without her. I felt uneasy that we left without Karen."

Most interestingly, Lorraine Paulino noted that she and her detective boyfriend left together in a different vehicle from the one in which they arrived.

That was the last time Paulino ever saw the woman.

Though Paulino described Heuermann as "the best sex she ever had," she claimed that at one point he put a hand around her neck and started to choke her, but that he backed off when she asked him to.

She said she also remembered that Heuermann had made a fire in a barrel in the backyard at one point during the night.

Her affidavit read: "I saw Rex on TV recently, and a picture of Karen Vergata. I recognized her as the woman who R.W. and I brought to Heuermann's home. I was shocked and deeply sorrowful for having left her behind at Heuermann's house."

Another witness, Taylor [no surname shared], spoke at the symposium. The woman, now 32 years old, was 18 at the time and addicted to cocaine when she first met Rex Heuermann. He called himself John. In her affidavit she said the pair did cocaine at a hotel in New Jersey, but when she suspected she was in danger, she ran out of the hotel to a nearby gas station for safety.

Taylor

John Ray stated, "In her affidavit, Taylor said she had come forward because she is concerned about what happened to the victims and wishes to state the truth as to what Heuermann did to her."

Taylor said she was selling liquor shots at a club in Center City in downtown Philadelphia, when a man approached her and invited her to his place to do cocaine and earn some fast cash.

"I was addicted to cocaine at the time and took the man up on his offer without hesitation," she recalled.

She claimed the man instructed her to hang out with his friend called "John" in return for a large amount of money and said she was given a taser to put in her purse.

"John was huge, lumbering, towering over both of us," she said. "He had beady blue eyes, shortish but thick hair. I remembered him because his features were remarkable and unusual."

Taylor said she left the man's apartment with John around dawn and traveled by taxi to an inn in Cherry Hill, New Jersey. Once inside, she claimed John told her to put out cocaine on the bathroom countertop.

"He laid on the bed. I tried to keep the conversation going so I could avoid sex with him," she recalled. "We did not have sex. I was half naked and walking around frequently trying to avoid his touch.

"John instructed me to tell him about my young friends. He asked me who my youngest friends were, specifically their names and ages; he went into pedophilic fantasies about young girls and boys."

After leaving the hotel room, Taylor said they took a cab to an ATM where John withdrew $1,500 and instructed the driver to take them to a townhouse/apartment complex.

She recalled the apartment had no furniture, which "startled" her, and there was a television that was held up by two milk crates with a porn DVD menu on the screen.

John told her to break out lines of cocaine in the kitchen while he went upstairs, but Taylor became alarmed when she heard a "human-sized scurrying" sound.

"I freaked out. I grabbed my bag, took out my taser and ran to the front door. He barreled down the stairs and blocked the door with his arms spread, the money in one hand," she said. "I held the taser to his neck as I yelled repeatedly for him to get out of my way and give me the money."

After fleeing the house, Taylor said she ran to a gas station to call a cab. Days after the event, she said John called, looking for her. She said her mother had answered the phone. Taylor never took the call or spoke to him again.

Taylor shook as she read from her testimony. "When I saw Rex Heuermann on Google News, I had a visceral reaction. I became panicked, distressed, and wept hysterically because I was quite certain that Rex Heuermann was the 'John' who I met that day in 2010."

Another witness, using the pseudonym Alice Poe, claimed she attended a party where a "huge" man was present and remembered him [Heuermann] looking angry.

"His size, face, demeanor, and attitude deeply scared me," she wrote. "I am certain that the huge man was Rex Heuermann. When I saw him on TV after he was arrested, I immediately recognized him as the man I have described."

Another woman, using the pseudonym Nanu Poe, said she was running on a trail in Virginia and saw a man in a camo jacket crouched down hiding behind a tree who she claimed resembled Rex Heuermann.

"He was staring at me in a way I knew I was in trouble," she said. After fleeing, she said she was so scared she wet her pants on the way home.

In their sworn affidavits, the women said they went to attorney John Ray because "they did not trust the Suffolk County Police Department."

CHAPTER SIX

Attorney John Ray challenges District Attorney Ray Tierney's steadfast statements that Asa and her children were out of town, state, or country when the murders occurred. Ray said that the police were given false alibis. For example, according to the police, photos as well as phone and financial records show that Heuermann's family was out of state during the time of Jessica Taylor's disappearance, that they were in Virginia from July 20 to July 27, 2003, according to Suffolk County District Attorney Raymond Tierney. Attorney John Ray said, "Rex Heuermann's family's alibi of being out of the state in Virginia is incorrect. They [Asa and her children] did not check in to a hotel until a few days later," that is, sometime after July 27, 2003.

In another example involving a timeline discrepancy between John Ray and Ray Tierney concerns the disappearance of murder victim Maureen Brainard-Barnes. Police documents supposedly include a credit card statement that shows Asa Ellerup checking into the Atlantic City hotel on July 6, 2007, and staying through July 20, 2007. But John Ray and his team personally spoke with the hotel manager and learned that Asa Ellerup did not check into the hotel until July 17, 2007, according to hotel computer records, which were checked twice.

John Ray would have you keep firmly in mind that the cheek swab samples collected from both Asa Ellerup and her daughter Victoria were a DNA match found on some of the remains of the homicide victims. The samples collected from Asa were taken on the evening of her husband's arrest, July 13, 2023.

What we need to understand is that DNA testing done decades ago has since been considerably refined. In the early 2000s, scientists were limited in developing and analyzing **nuclear** DNA test results. Nuclear DNA comprises 23 chromosomes, half from the mother and half from the father. It is used to identify relationships within a family and determine an individual's identity. In the 2010s, next-generation sequencing enabled *researchers to develop and analyze* **mitochondrial** *DNA.* Mitochondria cells are only passed down through the maternal line.

Summarizing the DNA test results are two forensic laboratories working independently of one another to determine from whom the recovered hairs found on or around each victim originated. The results form the basis of the Suffolk County bail application.

Regarding one of the Gilgo Beach victims, Maureen Brainard-Barnes had a female hair found on a buckle of the belt used to restrain her lower body. The leather belt had two embossed letters with either the initials WH or HM — depending on how you held the belt. That is, right side up or upside down.

Scribed in my second fictional/nonfictional accounting of the Gilgo Beach murders titled *Snuff Stuff* (written under the umbrella of New Journalism, which allows an author to combine fiction and fact), I interpreted the initials HM as assigned to **Heather Malone**. It makes for plausible speculation, especially when you consider the fact that Heather Malone lived with James Burke as his mistress, off and on, for considerable periods of time, suggesting that Burke would certainly have had access to her belongings. I am not implying that Heather Malone is a killer, rather that James Burke may be somehow involved in the LISK murders. Also, it is a fact that authorities proffered Burke at one point as a possible suspect in the investigation. Too, it has been substantially stipulated that James Burke operated a prostitution ring with Heather Malone as evidenced in that the Internal Affairs Bureau was pursuing those allegations relentlessly.

Also, the initials WH could be interpreted as standing for Rex Heuermann's grandfather, William George Heuermann, Sr. who died in 1964. More on that belt speculation later.

Nuclear DNA test results indicated that the hair found on the belt buckle more than likely came from Asa Ellerup; that is, Rex Heuermann's wife. The bail application states, "The hair is 7.9 trillion times more likely to come from an individual with the identical genetic profile as Asa Ellerup." Rather than go on quoting astronomical figures regarding such likelihoods from the nuclear DNA results, we will simply home in on the mitochondrial DNA percentages given in the bail applications. For example: 99.69%, 99.96%, 99.98% of the North American population can be excluded, but not so-and-so. You may likely come away with some interesting observations.

Referencing Megan Waterman, the bail application states that two female hairs were found in areas on and around Megan's body: One female hair was found outside the head area. Another female hair was found on tape in the head area. Mitochondrial DNA test results indicated that the first outside head area hair came from either Asa Ellerup or her daughter Victoria Heuermann. The second hair found on the tape in the head area was deemed unsuitable for testing. On the bottom portion of the burlap, with which Megan was covered, was a male hair that 99.96% of the North American population can be excluded — but not Rex Heuermann.

In examining Amber Lynn Costello, a single female hair was found on tape in Amber's head area, from which 99.98% of the North American population can be excluded — but not Asa Ellerup or her daughter Victoria Heuermann as determined by mitochondrial DNA test results. Although these facts support attorney John Ray's assertion that Asa and her daughter may be more involved than authorities believe, the evidence remains circumstantial at best. Consider the other victims, two of which Rex Heuermann has additionally been charged. Sandra Costilla was found with a male hair that was tape-lifted off a striped shirt from above her head, which 99.96% of the North American population can be excluded, but not Rex Heuermann. Additionally, a female hair was found on Sandra's right arm; 99.98% of the North American population can be excluded, but not WITNESS number 3, a woman who police say was living with Rex Heuermann in the Massapequa Park home at the time of Sandra's murder two months before Sandra's disappearance and death in the fall of 1993. Incidentally, Rex's mother had also left the home shortly before WITNESS number 3 moved out, suggesting that Rex had free reign to kill Sandra and transport her body out east to North Sea.

Moving on to the murder of Jessica Taylor, a male hair was found beneath Jessica's body; 99.96% of the North American population can be excluded, not Rex Heuermann.

District Attorney Ray Tierney would argue that the hairs belonging to Asa Ellerup and Victoria Heuermann were "transfer" hairs, explained via Locard's Exchange Principle. That is, when two items come in contact with each other, traces from both items are exchanged. Meaning that Rex Heuermann had unwittingly transported those hairs from his wife's and daughter's clothing, which were generated from their home in Massapequa Park to the crime scene. As the lead prosecutor in the case against Rex Heuermann, this is precisely the point Ray Tierney will argue at trial, vigorously maintaining that Heuermann's children were vacationing out of town, state, or country at the time of the murders and are not considered suspects.

This might be a good place for us to pause, reflect, review, and reconsider those questionable arguments on which John Ray and Ray Tierney adamantly disagree — with the hope that a definitive and satisfactory conclusion may be reached.

CHAPTER SEVEN

O n May 6, 2022, Suffolk County Police Commissioner Rodney Harrison announced the release of *all* information concerning the "Gilgo Four": Maureen Brainard Barnes, Melissa Barthelemy, Megan Waterman, and Amber Lynn Costello.

"As the Homicide Squad continues its tireless work on this investigation," Rodney Harrison stated, "we believe now is the right time to disseminate this previously unreleased information in hopes of eliciting tips from the public and providing greater transparency about the victims. Through our recent partnership with Crime Stoppers, increasing the reward in this case to $50,000 [from $25,000], our hope is that the public will review the information and come forward with any additional tips about the victims or a potential suspect or suspects."

Here is the information on the "Gilgo Four," plus what was collected on the other Long Island victims to date:

Maureen Brainard-Barnes

Maureen Brainard-Barnes was 25 years old when she went missing in 2007 and was living at 180 Prospect St. in Norwich, Connecticut. She is believed to have taken an Amtrak train from New London, Connecticut to Grand Central Terminal in Manhattan on July 6, 2007.

While in Manhattan, Maureen was staying at the Super 8 hotel, located at 59 West 46th Street. She was 4 feet 11 inches tall, working as an escort, advertising on Craigslist, Backpage and other websites. Maureen was known to advertise under the names Juliana or Marie. Her routine was to travel to Manhattan for a few days as a sex worker then return home to Connecticut. While in Manhattan, she would also stay at the Red Roof Inn on West 32nd Street, the Carter Hotel on West 43rd Street, and the Manhattan Hotel on 8th Avenue.

On occasion, Brainard-Barnes would travel with another female who worked out of a different room at the same location. They both may have used a male friend, who they would refer to as their cousin, to accompany them and offer a level of safety and protection. Brainard-Barnes traveled with her female friend the weekend she went missing; however, her friend returned home early and Brainard-Barnes stayed behind. Brainard-Barnes was last heard from on July 9, 2007 at 11:43 p.m. when she called a friend in Connecticut. Although she was known to work out of hotel rooms, on the night of July 9, 2007, she told her friend she would be going to meet someone outside of the hotel on an "out-call."

Brainard-Barnes was reported missing to the Norwich Police Department by a friend on July 14, 2007. The NYPD assisted the Norwich Police Department in the missing person investigation, eventually taking it over. Brainard-Barnes was found on December 13, 2010 on the north side of Ocean Parkway, near Gilgo Beach, during the search for Shannan Gilbert who had gone missing from Oak Beach.

Maureen is believed to be the first victim in what is known as the "Gilgo Four."

Melissa Barthelemy

Melissa Barthelemy was last seen at her residence, a basement apartment at 1149 Underhill Ave. in the Unionport section of the Bronx on July 12, 2009. She was 4 feet 10 inches tall and was 24 years old when she was last seen.

Barthelemy was a sex worker who advertised on Adult Friend Finder as well as other sites. She used the aliases Chloe, and VerySexyChloe. She had tattoos with the words "Blaze" and "Focus" on her back, and letters on her chest. She was also known to meet clients at bars, restaurants, and hotels on the West Side of Manhattan.

On July 12, 2009, the night she was last seen, Barthelemy told a friend she was going to see a man and would be back in the morning. This friend was aware she was a sex worker, but Barthelemy offered no other details. Her cellphone records show she traveled from the Bronx to Manhattan, most likely via taxi.

Barthelemy's mother had not heard from her or been able to contact her for a few days, so she reported her missing to the NYPD on July 18, 2009. The investigation showed cellphone activity in Manhattan, Freeport, Massapequa, and Lindenhurst. Hotels and motels in and near these neighborhoods were investigated.

After Barthelemy had been reported missing, her younger sister received a series of taunting phone calls from someone using

Barthelemy's phone: "Is this Melissa's little sister?" the male voice asked in one exchange. "Do you know what your sister is doing? She's a whore." These calls are believed to have come from the killer and were made from the area near the Port Authority Bus Terminal on 8th Avenue, and from near Penn Station. These areas were thoroughly canvassed immediately following the calls; however, due to the large amount of pedestrian and vehicular traffic, no leads were developed.

On December 11, 2010, Barthelemy's body was found on the north side of Ocean Parkway, near Gilgo Beach, during the search for Shannan Gilbert. Although Melissa was the first victim found of the "Gilgo Four," she is believed to be the second to be killed.

Megan Waterman

Megan Waterman, a 22-year-old, 5-foot-5-inch-tall mom of one, was last seen on June 6, 2010. Waterman, a resident of Scarborough, Maine, was a sex worker who advertised on Craigslist and Backpage. She used the names Lexxy and Sexy Lexi. She was last seen by her family boarding a New York-bound Concord Trailways bus in Maine, possibly with her pimp.

Waterman was staying at the Holiday Inn Express, located at 2050 Express Drive South in Hauppauge. Waterman was known to stay at other hotels and motels on Long Island, including the Extended

Stay America in Bethpage. She left the Holiday Inn Express at 1:30 a.m. on June 6, 2010 to meet a client. Waterman called her pimp, who was in Brooklyn at the time, to tell him she was going to a convenience store near the hotel.

Waterman was reported missing to the Scarborough Maine Police Department on June 8, 2010. Family members felt it was unlike her not to call them to check on her then 3-year-old daughter. The Scarborough Maine Police Department contacted the Suffolk County Police to assist in the missing person investigation.

Waterman's body was found on December 13, 2010 on the north side of Ocean Parkway, near Gilgo Beach, during the search for missing person Shannan Gilbert.

Officials also recently released a video of Waterman leaving a hotel in Hauppauge in 2010. They believe she met her killer that night.

She is believed to be the third victim in what is known as the "Gilgo Four."

Waterman's pimp was arrested on federal charges of Interstate Trafficking of Prostitutes on April 11, 2012 and was sentenced to three years in federal prison in January 2013. There is no information to suggest he had any knowledge or participated in any way in Waterman's murder.

Amber Lynn Costello

Amber Lynn Costello was 27 years old and lived at 1112 America Avenue in West Babylon, Suffolk County, when she was last seen by acquaintances in September 2010. Costello was a heroin addict who lived at the house with another female and two men, who were also heroin addicts. Costello, 4 feet 11 inches tall, was a sex worker who advertised on Craigslist and Backpage to support her and her roommates' heroin addiction. Costello used the names Carolina or Mia and had tattoos of "Kaos" on her neck, a butterfly on her lower back and the word "Margeret" on her leg.

Costello had moved to New York from Clearwater, Florida and had completed a 28-day drug rehab program but had relapsed not long before her disappearance. Costello and her roommates shared a cellphone. The other female roommate was also a sex worker supporting a heroin addiction, and the two male roommates would arrange dates with clients for the women. Costello did "in-calls" at her home as well as "out-calls."

When Costello would meet clients at her home, the two male roommates would often arrange a scam, during which, once a client had paid money, and before any sex acts occurred, they would confront the client saying Costello was their girlfriend and the client would flee.

Costello was last seen leaving her residence on foot on September 2, 2010 to meet a client who was picking her up at her house. Costello did not have her cellphone with her at the time, and she was never reported missing.

Costello was found on December 13, 2010 on the north side of Ocean Parkway, near Gilgo Beach, during the search for missing person Shannan Gilbert. She is believed to be the fourth victim in what is known as the "Gilgo Four."

Valerie Mack

Valerie was 24 years old and living in Philadelphia when she went missing. She worked as an escort, using the alias "Melissa Taylor." Relatives last saw her in the summer or spring of 2000 in Port Republic, New Jersey, but she was never reported as missing to the police, or so they say.

Rex Heuermann was indicted for Valerie's murder on December 17, 2024. On November 19, 2000, her partially dismembered body (torso) was found close to the Peconic River Sportsman's Club near a utility path on an adjacent parcel of woodlands off Mill Road in Manorville. On April 4, 2011, eleven years later, Valerie's remains (her head, hands, and right foot) were found within plastic bags by three hunters in the vicinity of Ocean Parkway near *Gilgo Beach, 47 miles away.* Jane Doe #6 was eventually identified as Valerie Mack.

It is fascinating to learn how authorities employ genetic genealogy as a tool. To gain a detailed understanding of how this exhaustive investigation began, let us first look into Valerie Mack's background:

Valerie was born on June 2, 1976, adopted at age nine in 1985. Prior to that, she was shifted among seven foster homes. Valerie's sisters are Danielle Wade and a second sister, Angela. Valerie was raised in south Jersey, near Atlantic City, close to marshland in the New Jersey Pine Barrens. She was involved in youth plays in Egg Harbor.

Valeries's life unraveled in 9th grade at age 14. She ran around with the wrong crowd, did drugs, skipped school, became pregnant, and left her kid with the father. Valerie bounced between Philadelphia, Pennsylvania, and southern New Jersey. She was arrested three times in Philadelphia for prostitution, also for drugs and loitering. Valerie returned home after an illness, working at a Dollar Tree store in Egg Harbor Township, New Jersey. Later, she left for New York with some guy. In 2000, her parents tried to file a missing person report with the New Jersey police. When the police learned of her background, working as a prostitute, they simply did not take the report seriously. Therefore, the information was never recorded.

Sometime later, the FBI got involved, and Valerie's profile was uploaded into a public database. Authorities made a connection to a male cousin of Valerie's living in Georgia. The cousin had received a commercial DNA testing kit as a gift, allowing him to submit a DNA sample to trace his family members. A DNA match led to a living relative, an aunt, of both Valerie and the cousin: Aunt Ellen Munnings of south New Jersey.

Authorities wanted to know if Aunt Munnings had any relatives with a daughter. The woman could account for most of her nieces but not all the daughters of her sister, Patricia Fulton, who had been dead for almost 18 years. Patricia Fulton was the biological mother of the adopted Valerie Mack. Bingo!

This is just the beginning of how the feds eventually confirmed the identity of Valerie Mack. Patricia Fulton had four other children before giving birth to Valerie Lynn Fulton. All five of her children had been placed in foster care.

Authorities then interviewed another daughter of Patricia Fulton, Tricia Hazen. DNA testing affirmed Tricia shared the same biological mother as Valerie; that is, Tricia and Valerie were half-sisters. Further genetic testing referencing Valerie's son, Benjamin, confirmed that he was, indeed, the biological son of Valerie Mack.

Unidentified Asian man

On April 4, 2011, the skeletal remains of a yet-to-be-identified Asian man were found along the same 1.18-mile stretch along Ocean Parkway as were five of the seven Gilgo Beach victims for which Rex Heuermann has been charged. The man was found approximately ¼ mile east of Megan Waterman and approximately ½ mile west of Jessica Taylor. It is estimated that the man was between 17 and 23 years old, dressed in women's clothing: bra, a Chrysantheme brand blue-ribbed short-sleeve shirt with a crew neck in size large, another shirt of Rafaella brand, and Bill Blass pants.

He was approximately 5 feet 6 inches tall with close-cropped hair and bad teeth; missing his top and bottom molars and an upper front tooth. Interestingly, court records show that Rex Heuermann had searched pornography featuring slender Asian men. Authorities believe that the individual was a transgender sex worker of southern Han Chinese descent. The cause of death was blunt force trauma.

To date, investigators have been unable to find a match to the victim's DNA in genealogical databases. Therefore, forensic artists and anthropologists have created a rendering of the man's facial features by first examining the contours of the skull then reconstructing the shape of the brow, chin, and nasal cavity. "They can then approximate what he looked like with flesh and skin," said D.A. Ray Tierney. Photographed on the next page are images of how the Asian male could appear as both a female and male in the hope that it will help identify the man.

Unidentified Asian man

"Peaches" & Her Daughter

On June 28, 1997, an African American woman's partial remains (torso) were discovered stuffed into a plastic bin in a wooded area at Hempstead Lake State Park, Lakeview, New York. She was monikered "Peaches" because of the heart-shaped tattoo depicting a bitten peach on her left breast. On April 4, 2011, police found the remains of a female toddler who was about 2 years old at the time of death. On April 11, 2011, both of "Peaches" arms and legs (severed below the knees) were discovered at Jones Beach State Park. Her head was never found. DNA testing in 2016 confirmed that "Peaches" was the mother of the 2-year-old child. It appears that genetic genealogy, an amazing forensic tool, has traced family members of "Peaches" to Alabama.

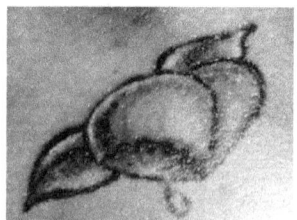

Peaches' Tattoo

Shannan Gilbert

Shannan Gilbert was a Craigslist escort who lived in Jersey City, traveling with her driver/pimp, Michael Pak, from New Jersey to meet a client, Joseph Brewer, at his Long Island home in the Oak Beach Association during the wee hours of May 1, 2010. Approximately two hours later at daybreak, Shannan ran hysterically from Brewer's home, dialing 911, stating "They're trying to kill me," knocking on neighbors' doors and pleading for help before vanishing. Nineteen months later, on December 13, 2011, police discovered Shannan's remains in a marsh approximately a ¼ mile from Joseph Brewer's home.

Here is a transcript of the 911 call received from the state police operator as Shannan runs from Joseph Brewer's residence, knocks on Gus Coletti's door, then Barbara Brennan's door before vanishing. Detective Lieutenant Beyrer of the Suffolk County Homicide section narrates. Later in the book, I will include a significantly enhanced 911 recording that John Ray acquired from J J.M. Cold Case Consulting agency. The recording well exceeds Suffolk County Police Department's copy of a copy by a considerable 3,639 words.

OAK BEACH, NEW YORK. FULL 911 CALL:

NYS 911 Operator: State Police Trooper Frye.

Shannan Gilbert: Yeah, there's somebody after me.

NYS 911 Operator: I'm sorry?

Shannan Gilbert: There's somebody after me.

NYS 911 Operator: Where are you?

Shannan Gilbert: There's somebody after me.

NYS 911 Operator: Ok, where are you?

Shannan Gilbert: There's somebody after me.

NYS 911 Operator: Where are you, ma'am?

Shannan Gilbert: I don't know.

NYS 911 Operator: Are you driving right now?

Shannan Gilbert: No, I'm inside the house.

NYS 911 Operator: I'm sorry?

Shannan Gilbert: I'm inside a house.

NYS 911 Operator: What house?

Shannan Gilbert: I don't know. Can you trace where I am?

NYS 911 Operator: I'm sorry?

Shannan Gilbert: Can you trace where I am?

NYS 911 Operator: No, I can't. What's your call back number you are calling from?

Shannan Gilbert: Huh?

NYS 911 Operator: What number are you calling from?

Shannan Gilbert: Somebody's after me. Please.

NYS 911 Operator: Are you in Nassau County or Suffolk County?

Shannan Gilbert: Um, I'm in Long Island.

NYS 911 Operator: Where on Long Island are you?

Joseph Brewer: Yeah, he wants to talk to you, the guy [Michael Pak, her driver] wants to talk to you.

Shannan Gilbert: No.

Joseph Brewer: Go ahead, talk to her.

Shannan Gilbert: No.

Joseph Brewer: *INAUDIBLE*

Shannan Gilbert: No. No. Stop, no!

Joseph Brewer: *INAUDIBLE*

NYS 911 Operator: Where in Long Island are you? Suffolk County? Nassau County?

Shannan Gilbert: Huh?

Joseph Brewer: *INAUDIBLE*

Shannan Gilbert: Alright.

Michael Pak: *INAUDIBLE*

Shannan Gilbert: Why are you calling me by my name?

Michael Pak: *INAUDIBLE*

Shannan Gilbert: Why?

NYS 911 Operator: What county are you on the line?

Shannan Gilbert: Stop!

Joseph Brewer: *INAUDIBLE*

Shannan Gilbert: Stop it, please.

Michael Pak: You ok?

Shannan Gilbert: Please stop.

Joseph Brewer: Alright. *INAUDIBLE*

Shannan Gilbert: Please can you shut the door?

Joseph Brewer: No, time to go.

Shannan Gilbert: Please.

Michael Pak: You ok?

Shannan Gilbert: Please.

Joseph Brewer: *INAUDIBLE*

Shannan Gilbert: Please.

Joseph Brewer: *INAUDIBLE* Come on, let's go. We'll all go outside. Come on, going outside, all of us. Come on, all of us, come on, we're all going outside. Come on.

Shannan Gilbert: No, please.

Joseph Brewer: *INAUDIBLE* Come on, please, come on.

Shannan Gilbert: Please.

Joseph Brewer: Please, come on.

Shannan Gilbert: Why?

Joseph Brewer: Please come out here.

Det. Lt. Beyrer's narration: Brewer and Pak continue to try and convince Shannan to leave the premises.

Joseph Brewer: I'll go upstairs, I'll go upstairs, you leave. Hey, look, I'm going upstairs, you leave. I'm going upstairs, you leave. Ok? You leave please.

Joseph Brewer: Take care.

Michael Pak: Take care.

INAUDIBLE

Michael Pak: Whoa, whoa. What's the matter? Are you ok?

Shannan Gilbert: What are you going to do?

Michael Pak: *INAUDIBLE*

Shannan Gilbert: What are you going to do to me?

Michael Pak: *INAUDIBLE*

Shannan Gilbert: Why?

NYS 911 Operator: Huh, I don't know *INAUDIBLE*

Shannan Gilbert: Why? *INAUDIBLE* You going to kill me?

Michael Pak: Are you crazy?

NYS 911 Operator: *INAUDIBLE* It's trying to, I think it's trying to *INAUDIBLE*

Michael Pak: No.

Shannan Gilbert: Why are you going to kill me?

NYS 911 Operator: *INAUDIBLE*

Michael Pak: Come on, you're freaking me out. Come on let's go.

Shannan Gilbert: Out in the middle of nowhere?

Michael Pak: Let's go back, let's go back to Manhattan, alright? We're in Long Island, near the water so, the ocean ….

Shannan Gilbert: Please stop.

Michael Pak: Come on, it's me, Mike. Come on let's go.

Shannan Gilbert: No. Stop it, please!

Det. Lt. Beyrer's narration: A second 911 NYS Operator joins the call.

NYS 911 Operator: Hello?

Michael Pak: *INAUDIBLE*

NYS 911 Operator: Hello?

Shannan Gilbert: Please.

NYS 911 Operator: What's, what's, what's the problem, what's the matter? What happened?

NYS 911 Operator: Hello?

Shannan Gilbert: Please get me out of here Mike.

Michael Pak: *INAUDIBLE*

NYS 911 Operator: Hello?

Shannan Gilbert: You're being sarcastic.

Michael Pak: About what?

Shannan Gilbert: About this…You are a part of this all along.

Michael Pak: I just met him just now…*INAUDIBLE*

Lt. Beyrer's narration: "Shannan then ran from Brewer's at 8 The Fairway to Gus Coletti's house at 17 The Fairway, a distance of two-tenths of a mile."

Background Noise:

NYS 911 Operator: Shannan.

Background Noise:

Shannan Gilbert: Screaming. Shannan knocks on distant neighbor's door of Gus Coletti.

Background Noise:

Det. Lt. Beyrer of Suffolk County Homicide narrates: "Shannan interacts with Coletti. He invites her inside his home."

NYS 911 Operator: Shannan.

Gus Coletti: What's the matter? Is somebody after you? Huh?

NYS 911 Operator: Hello. Hello.

Shannan Gilbert: *INAUDIBLE*

Gus Coletti: Are you alright?

Shannan Gilbert: I need help.

Gus Coletti: Don't get yourself hurt. Where are you going?

Shannan Gilbert: Shannan is breathing heavily.

Gus Coletti: Where are you going? What are you doing?

Lt. Beyrer's narration: "She then runs from Coletti's home, prompting Coletti to call 911. This is where Shannan's call ends. After Coletti's call, Shannan then runs another two-tenths of a mile to another home at 43 The Bayou, prompting a third 911 call made at 5:30 a.m. by Barbara Brennan."

SCPD 911 Operator: Suffolk Police what's the location of your emergency?

Gus Coletti: Yes, this, I live in Oak Beach in the Association. There's a young girl about 14 years old running around here screaming, and there's some guy trying to follow her.

SCPD 911 Operator: What's the address there?

Gus Coletti: I'm at 17 The Fairway.

SCPD 911 Operator: Alright. You have a description of the girl or the boy?

Gus Coletti: Pardon me?

SCPD 911 Operator: Alright. You have a description of the girl or the boy?

Gus Coletti: The girl is about 14 years old, blonde hair, very small. The boy I can't tell; he was in like uh…a Suburban.

SCPD 911 Operator: What color?

Gus Coletti: Uh, black?

Det. Lt. Beyrer's narration: "Michael Pak, Shannan's driver, was operating a black SUV."

SCPD 911 Operator: Did you happen to get a plate number or anything?

Gus Coletti: No, I didn't.

SCPD 911 Operator: Ok, telephone number you're calling from?

Gus Coletti: Phone number redacted.

SCPD 911 Operator: Are they still on The Fairway?

Gus Coletti: Uh, they just went past the gatehouse where the entrance is.

SCPD 911 Operator: And what's the name of the complex?

Gus Coletti: It's Oak Beach Association.

SCPD 911 Operator: Ok.

Gus Coletti: Out at, by Robert Moses.

SCPD 911 Operator: Alright, we'll get somebody over there.

Gus Coletti: I'll be watching.

SCPD 911 Operator: Oh, ok.

Gus Coletti: Bye.

Det. Lt. Beyrer's narration: Shannan Gilbert then knocks on Barbara Brennan's door, prompting a third 911 call.

SCPD 911 Operator: Suffolk police 875, what is the location of your emergency?

Barbara Brennan: 40…43 The Bayou. Some woman is knocking at my door.

SCPD 911 Operator: What town are you in?

Barbara Brennan: Oak Beach Association.

SCPD 911 Operator: What's the nearest corner street, ma'am?

Barbara Brennan: Ocean Parkway. She says she's in danger.

SCPD 911 Operator: Do you know her, or not?

Barbara Brennan: No, I don't. I'm not letting her in.

SCPD 911 Operator: She banging on your door now?

Barbara Brennan: Yeah.

SCPD 911 Operator: Did she say what kind of danger?

Barbara Brennan: No.

SCPD 911 Operator: Oh.

Barbara Brennan: And we live in a gated community.

SCPD 911 Operator: What's your name, ma'am?

Barbara Brennan : Barbara Brennan.

SCPD 911 Operator: Is there a name to that community?

Barbara Brennan: Uh, Oak Beach Association.

SCPD 911 Operator: Oak Beach Association.

Barbara Brennan: And I have an elderly mother here.

SCPD 911 Operator: Alright, I'll get somebody right over there, ok?

Barbara Brennan: Ok. Thank you.

SCPD 911 Operator: You're welcome.

Det. Lt. Kevin Beyrer's narration: "This (the video) shows drone footage shot from the ground showing the marshland. It was taken at the same time of the year and time of day as when Shannan went missing. These reeds can grow over 12 feet tall. They can disorient someone inside them, causing them to lose a sense of direction. One cannot tell where the highway is or the bay is. The reeds and brush can become impenetrable in places. There's a trench running east and west through the marshland. This was created to allow mosquito control. It is believed that Shannan followed this trench. Personal belongings of hers were found just north of the trench. Shannan's remains were found north of the trench about 158 feet south of Ocean Parkway, approximately three quarters of a mile from where she was last seen. There's been information received during the course of this investigation that other people may be involved in this incident. They have all been investigated, and there is no reason at this time to believe that anyone else is involved in this tragic series of events.

"The police responded to Coletti's and Brennan's 911 calls. Michael Pak, Joseph Brewer, and Shannan Gilbert were all gone. Gus Coletti provided a description of Pak's car, which was also gone. This created the possibility that Shannan had been driven out of the area, which caused delay in the initial search for her. The police department has thoroughly investigated this case for more than a decade. The official cause of Shannan's death is undetermined. This official classification means that there is insufficient or no evidence to determine or even to exclude a cause of death. The Gilbert family hired a private pathologist to conduct an autopsy. His determination is there is insufficient information to determine a definite cause of death, but the autopsy's findings are consistent with homicidal strangulation. That pathologist report will be made available.

"This case, including the 911 call and all of the other cases commonly referred to as Gilgo, in their entirety, were made available to the Behavioral Analysis Unit or BAU of the FBI. As part of BAU's review of the case, they retained the services of a psychiatrist to review Shannan's words and actions on the 911 tape, and also to review the facts of the case. BAU's opinion, based on their review of Shannan's case, the scene, the 911 calls, and the psychiatrist's review, is that Shannan Gilbert's death is not consistent with Shannan being the victim of violence or a violent offender. Significant differences between Shannan's death and the circumstances surrounding the other victims' deaths were also highlighted by the BAU.

"The Suffolk County Police Department is open to evaluate any evidence to be able to help us and all involved to determine an actual cause of death. However, based on the evidence, the facts, and the totality of the circumstances, the prevailing opinion is that Shannan's death, while tragic, was not a murder and most likely an accident."

Detective Lieutenant Kevin Beyrer

Jessica Taylor

Jessica was a 20-year-old woman working as an escort in New York City. Her torso was discovered on July 27, 2003 in a wooded area off Halsey Manor Road in Manorville. On March 29, 2011, Jessica's additional remains were discovered almost eight years later along Ocean Parkway in the Gilgo Beach area, 47 miles away. Jane Doe #5 was then identified as Jessica Taylor. Charging documents state that Rex Heuermann was linked to Taylor through DNA as male hairs were found on her body. Heuermann was charged with Taylor's murder on June 6, 2024.

Sandra Costilla

Sandra was 28 years old when she went missing. Her body was found November 21, 1993 by hunters near Fish Cove, a hamlet of North Sea, town of Southampton on Long Island's South Shore. She was found lying on her back, arms outstretched over her head, uncovered legs spread apart. Sandra had sharp force injuries to her face and body. Sandra, a native of Trinidad and Tobago (a dual-island Caribbean nation near Venezuela), lived in New York City. Charging documents state that Rex Heuermann was linked to Costilla through DNA as male hairs were found on her body. Heuermann was charged with her murder on June 6, 2024.

CHAPTER EIGHT

Below is a map indicating locations of victims, including dates the women's remains were found:

The next map focuses in on the location of Heuermann's house and storage units in proximity to where the bodies were found. The remains of an Asian male [Asian Doe], Peaches, and Peaches' 2-year-old toddler daughter have yet to be identified.

The events leading up to Rex Heuermann's arrest on July 13, 2023 involved the suspect discarding a pizza box containing pizza crust and a napkin. "The pizza crust is like a sponge," explained Ray Tierney. "It allows the saliva to seep into the dough," the Suffolk County district attorney elaborated. The sample gave investigators the genetic match that helped connect Rex Heuermann to the "Gilgo Four."

In fact, the first solid lead in the Gilgo Beach murder case came to light in the winter of 2010, when witnesses described to police a vehicle and an individual that the past administration failed to follow up on properly. The authorities could have had Rex Heuermann in their crosshairs as early as September of 2010, regarding the murder of Amber Lynn Costello.

Dave Schaller, Amber Lynn Costello's friend, roommate, and pimp, clearly brought evidence of this fact before the police on *more* than one occasion, referencing the past administration under James Burke, Thomas Spota, and Christopher McPartland.

That witness had not only given detectives a description of the truck and the man who was driving the vehicle that evening, he gave police a very accurate description of the stranger's distinguishing features: "Ogre-like looking," Dave Schaller had said. "Six-foot-four inches tall, weighing approximately 240 pounds." Schaller had reportedly told the detectives that he had exchanged blows with Amber's perspective client after coming home and pretending to be furious at finding Costello frightened and locked in the bathroom. "When the police told me she was dead, he [the client] was the first person who jumped into my head. I've been picturing his face for 13 years," Schaller told the *Associated Press*.

I first read that part of the story detailing the fight between the two men published in the *Associated Press* on July 23, 2023. The piece was headlined **Dave Schaller came face to face with alleged Gilgo Beach serial killer Rex Heuermann; 12 years later, his tip helped crack the case.** The fact that Dave Schaller had initially given a full description of both the vehicle and the ogre-looking man to the police shortly after Amber Lynn Costello's disappearance shows that Schaller's statement incredibly fell on deaf ears.

Addressing the matter following Rex Heuermann's arrest, Dave Schaller voiced his anger and frustration, explaining one of his last meetings with homicide detectives approximately two years after Costello went missing. "I gave them the exact description of the truck and the dude. I mean, come on; why didn't they use that?" Schaller had identified the first-generation Chevrolet Avalanche vehicle model from a line-up of photographs.

Suffolk County Legislator Rob Trotta, who had worked as a Suffolk County detective until 2013, said, "This was crucial information, and I don't know why they didn't share it."

Also reported via the *Associated Press* article: "Two high-ranking officials who worked closely on the case and attended briefings between 2011 and 2013 said they never heard anything about a witness statement describing the subject and his vehicle." Amazing! Amazing until you stop and realize you had a past administration hellbent on turning a blind eye regarding the investigation. To repeat, three men were disgraced and finally caught up in a web of conspiracy: former

Police Chief James Burke; former District Attorney Thomas Spota; and former Chief Prosecutor of the Anti-Corruption Bureau, Christopher McPartland.

Still, after Jimmy Burke's release from prison, the disgraced felon could not stay out of trouble. Burke found himself in handcuffs anew during an undercover sting operation at the Suffolk County Vietnam Veterans Memorial Park in Farmingville, Long Island. The Suffolk County Park Rangers' Targeted Response Unit took Jimmy into custody for soliciting a male operative for a sexual encounter. A true embarrassment for the macho former police chief. Again, please refer to my first nonfiction book titled *The Long-Awaited Arrest of Long Island Serial Killer Rex Heuermann ~ Past "Administration" to Blame* for a full accounting of Burke's, Spota's, and McPartland's criminal behavior.

CHAPTER NINE

Suffolk County Sheriff Errol Toulon Jr. told *Newsday* in early July, 2024 that his investigators spoke with 298 sex workers in Suffolk and Nassau counties' correctional facilities from the day of Rex Heuermann's arrest in July of 2023. They have culled 15 "credible" reports from those workers who likely have had encounters with Heuermann. Investigators are planning to interview sex workers in New York City's largest jail, located on Rikers Island (in the East River) in the Bronx, with reference to other encounters Heuermann may have had with these individuals.

Sheriff Toulon said that even if the incarcerated women do not have firsthand knowledge about Rex Heuermann, interviewing them could pay dividends in that they could lead investigators to other sex workers who may have pertinent information about the accused architect from Massapequa Park, Long Island. Toulon added there is a "strong possibility" some of the reports that were forwarded to the Gilgo Beach Task Force by the Human Trafficking Unit included relevant information, but he declined further comment, saying he was reluctant to discuss the ongoing investigation.

Toulon's staff of investigators have been deemed experts on this subject matter and will ultimately decide what evidence is relevant and could be used against Rex Heuermann at trial, who has been charged in the deaths of Megan Waterman, Melissa Barthelemy, Amber Lynn Costello, Maureen Brainard-Barnes, Jessica Taylor, and Sandra Costilla. Suffolk County District Attorney Ray Tierney has stated that Heuermann is also a suspect in the murder of Valerie Mack and will likely be charged. Toulon created the Human Trafficking Unit in 2018 after officials realized that many of the incarcerated women in Suffolk County jails in Riverhead and Yaphank were victims of trafficking.

Sheriff Toulon referred to Rex Heuermann, incarcerated in Suffolk County's Riverhead jail, as "The most unique individual I have seen in my 42 years in corrections. I've seen a lot of high-profile people. Heuermann is the most unique I've ever come across. Usually, a person will start to see the four walls of their cell closing in on holidays, birthdays, anniversaries, et cetera. Now he has six [now seven] charges, and still the walls are not closing in on him. At least not outwardly in his demeanor." His behavior has not changed. "He is stoic," Toulon maintains, "no matter what is reported against him or what occurs in court. I've never seen Heuermann laugh or smile," the sheriff added.

Rex Heuermann is segregated from the jail's general population because authorities are concerned that a fellow inmate might attack him to boost "street credibility" or avenge a sex worker's death. Therefore, Heuermann is not permitted to socialize with other inmates and largely keeps to himself. "Mr. Heuermann has been very compliant," Toulon stated. "When he first came into our custody, I personally spoke to him. He said we would not have a problem with him and, almost a year later, he has held true to his word."

Heuermann keeps to his 60-square-foot cell, which has a bed, toilet, and a sink. It is tidy and clutter-free. He spends much of his time reviewing discovery documents and reading fiction. Heuermann's regular visitors include his attorney Michael Brown, the defendant's estranged wife Asa Ellerup, and a third person whom Sheriff Toulon declined to name. You will learn the reason why in a subsequent chapter.

Suffolk County Sheriff Errol Toulon, Jr.

CHAPTER TEN

We are slowly beginning to focus in on a three-ring circus found among Michael J. Brown, the attorney representing Rex Heuermann; Robert A. Macedonio, the attorney representing Heuermann's estranged wife, Asa Ellerup; and Vess Mitev, the attorney representing Rex Heuermann's adult children Victoria and Christopher.

Attorney Michael Brown for Rex Heuermann

**Attorney Robert Macedonio for Asa Ellerup,
Rex Heuermann's estranged wife**

Attorney Vess Mitev for the Heuermann children Christopher and Victoria

Attorney John Ray is more than subtly suggesting the possibility that Heuermann's wife and daughter could somehow be involved in the killings, based on circumstantial evidence as Asa's and Victoria's hair were found either on or around several of the victims' bodies.

Covering a spot-on opinion piece scribed by Greg Blass (a six-term Suffolk County legislator), dated October 17, 2021, the man addresses the corruption prevalent in Suffolk County politics regarding Jimmy , Thomas Spota, Christopher McPartland, along with a couple other peripheral characters of, well, questionable character. Namely, former Suffolk County Executive Steve Bellone, and Timothy Sini, the latter of whom served as Suffolk County interim district attorney, deputy police commissioner, and police commissioner.

Steve Bellone ~ former Suffolk County Executive

Timothy Sini ~ former Suffolk County interim DA, deputy police commissioner, and police commissioner

Greg Blass' article is important because it asks and answers the question as to how Jimmy   could possibly stop the FBI from investigating him and Suffolk County corruption:

Greg Blass ~ *RiverheadLocal* Opinion

October 17, 2021

Was L.I. serial killer investigation stymied in coverup by corrupt Suffolk cop and DA? We need a special prosecutor to probe investigation

One of Suffolk County's most shameful episodes stands for sure to be the 10 Gilgo serial murder victims. More than a decade has passed since their bodies were left over time along Ocean Parkway, in the vicinity of Gilgo Beach and Oak Beach, Long Island. Many, if not all of them, were sex workers who advertised on Craigslist. And the Suffolk County Police have concluded that they were the victims of a single serial killer.

Much has been published about these unsolved crimes. At least one book – a compelling one – has been written by Robert Kolkor, entitled "Lost Girls" Then there's Billy Jensen's TV series about the murders, "Unraveled: The Long Island Serial Killer." The podcast, "Unraveled," delves into these women's terrible fate as well.

There lingers, however, a parallel mystery about Suffolk law enforcement's investigation of these murders, especially in its early stages. This mystery centers around the conduct of some of Suffolk's officials. One state senator has become so concerned about this that he has publicly called for a state investigation of Suffolk's investigation. More on that in a moment.

For now, consider some background: The Gilgo Beach killer, as investigators have dubbed him, is believed to have murdered between 10 to 16 people over the last 30 years. Their remains were found over a period of months during 2010-2011.

The disappearance of Shannan Gilbert, last seen running and screaming through the area, prompted a search by the Suffolk Police. While combing the area, police recovered four victims' remains (the "Gilgo 4") in December 2010, within a quarter-mile of each other. Six more were found during March and April of 2011.

A year after the discovery of the "Gilgo 4," the body of Shannan Gilbert was located. Accidental drowning caused her death, as the police tell it. An independent autopsy, however, determined "possible homicidal strangulation."

Then, in June 2011, Suffolk Police offered a $25,000 reward for information leading to an arrest in these cases. On Nov. 29, 2011, they announced their conclusion that one person, "almost certainly from Long Island," was responsible for all 10 murders.

At some point when this serial killer investigation got underway, the FBI joined the case, as well they should have. But while the FBI agents and their experts were knee-deep in their work, figuratively and literally, the new Suffolk Police Chief of Department, James Burke, inexplicably booted them out, according to reporting by the *New York Post*. Such a turn of events in this unsolved, notorious case was not known to the public, but it was well known within the department, and to its civilian "oversight."

It did gain brief mention in *Newsday*, ever so shy about delving into the antics of Suffolk's current power elite, but not till years later. That a police chief can remove the FBI from a murder investigation in itself boggles the mind. It's something to do with "initial jurisdiction" and other bureaucratic gibberish, and who calls the shots. Why would he do this — and why did his civilian superiors allow it?

Burke's booting the FBI happened in his heyday. At the top of his sordid game, he was as close as ever with his mentors, then-Suffolk District Attorney Thomas Spota, himself recently convicted, and Suffolk County Executive Steve Bellone, who appointed Burke chief of the department. It is well known that DA Spota and certain police union bosses urged Bellone to appoint Burke police chief, while diverse sources, including other police, warned against it.

During what many describe as Burke's "reign of terror" as chief, he was in touch with Bellone almost daily. He boasted to other top county officials of driving the county executive around in a police vehicle during night shifts to "inspect" police performance. They were as tight as a drum.

Burke and the Suffolk PBA, to whom Bellone is answerable, gave the OK for Bellone to bring in current D.A. Timothy Sini as Suffolk's deputy police commissioner. He was later made commissioner.

This prodigious foursome, Bellone, Spota, Sini and Burke (add Spota's chief assistant, Christopher McPartland, convicted along with Spota, to make it five) ran Suffolk law enforcement as their personal fiefdom, oiled with huge — really huge — bundles of Suffolk PBA PAC cash, regularly and involuntarily collected from rank-and-file police officers' paychecks.

These rank-and-file officers were intimidated by Burke's strong-arm tactics, including illegal surveillance of police officers whom Burke disliked. Did Sini, Spota and Bellone know this was going on? Considering the way things worked in Suffolk law enforcement, it is hard to believe they did not. As the Spota corruption trial brought out, along with over a thousand pages of documents collected by federal prosecutors that the trial judge released, most Suffolk police officers were pawns to these self-assured, self-absorbed power brokers. (*See prior column*: Documents in ex-Suffolk DA's corruption trial reveal county politics at their sordid worst May 16, 2021 Link: https://riverheadlocal.com/2021/05/16/documents-in-ex-suffolk-das-corruption-trial-reveal-county-politics-at-their-sordid-worst/).

When it came to the disruption of the FBI's role in the spectacular case of then-recent Gilgo serial murders, you can bet that Spota, Bellone and Sini knew about it when Burke did it. How could they not?

But then Burke got caught up in another one of his excesses — beating a handcuffed prisoner suspected of stealing his personal duffel bag. That's where things started to hit the fan. Spota was implicated (and later convicted) in covering up the episode and obstructing a federal investigation. As for Burke, he resigned in October 2015, as he was sure to face charges.

Suddenly, Sini and Bellone found themselves in damage-control mode. They had to time things very carefully. So, while Burke was out, they waited till they were sure he was out for good. That came with Burke's indictment on federal conspiracy and civil rights charges, handed down by a grand jury on Dec. 9, 2015.

The very next day, Sini, still Bellone's police commissioner, already angling in the shadows with the PBA to be Spota's replacement as DA, holds a news conference. In a cynical move, he proclaims that investigating the Gilgo serial murder case was a "priority." To prove this, he proudly announces that he was "bringing the FBI into the case." Thus, he creates a new narrative — never a word about the FBI's earlier involvement in the investigation and how Burke removed them from the case during Sini's watch. Note that Sini was both PD deputy commissioner and commissioner for 18 months of Burke's ignoble tenure.

And no one says a word.

This new narrative avoids discomforting questions: Why were the feds at first helping with the probe of a horrible crime, then shown the door? Who else was in on this decision? What was the reasoning behind it? How cold has the evidence, and the case, consequently become? And as for Burke, Spota, and McPartland's downfall, have things really changed in Suffolk County politics?

Enter State Sen. Phil Boyle of Bay Shore. At a June 28 news conference with the Gilgo-Oak Beach area as a backdrop, he publicly called for the NYS Attorney General to probe the Suffolk PD's Gilgo investigation, especially its initial stages, when the FBI was in, then out.

Sen. Boyle lodged a written request to the NY AG to focus on what exactly happened to Suffolk's Gilgo investigation, from the time Bellone was elected county executive on Nov. 5, 2011, to Dec. 10, 2015, when the FBI "rejoined," (as Boyle accurately put it) the probe. Stating that there were "far too many questions," Boyle posed a simple one for AG Letitia James: Did the Suffolk PD, at that time, do everything that could be done to get justice for these victims and their families?

AG James, for her part, has all these months sat on the senator's request, giving no official response at all. Is this surprising? She really has no interest in rocking the boat in her party by slapping subpoenas on Suffolk officials and their records, especially while Sini seeks re-election as Suffolk DA this November.

Even on the day of Sen. Boyle's news conference, AG James told *Newsday*, through a spokesman, that she simply cannot get involved. Catch the clever shell game in her statement: "In order for us to step in as a prosecutor to review the case, we'd need a referral from the Suffolk DA or Executive Office." Really?

Is there a way to reverse this sad state of county affairs? Could there be some path toward accountability?

Whatever role they had in letting the Gilgo case turn cold, Bellone and Sini could do a great public service by asking for a special prosecutor for the entire matter of the Gilgo case and how it has been handled. The county legislature should join. It means standing up to special interests, but the time is so right. Taking this path would go a long way to earning the deepest gratitude, and restored faith, of the people.

No matter who they were — no matter what their past — no one deserves to die as these victims did. No family should suffer this cruel mortification all these years without closure. And no county government — either through their elected or appointed officials — should carry on like this. Let them welcome the AG probe and pledge their cooperation. Better yet, let them and our county legislators join in call for a special prosecutor, to assure justice for those who perished so horribly.

****

Greg Blass is a former Suffolk County Family Court judge, six-term Suffolk County legislator, and commissioner of Social Services.

CHAPTER ELEVEN

During July of 2022, undercover detectives clandestinely collected empty bottles from a recycling container outside the Heuermann home in Massapequa Park. Investigators used those bottle samples to create a genetic profile of the Heuermann family: Rex Heuermann, his wife Asa Ellerup, and their two grown children Victoria and Christopher. However, they needed a direct sample from their prime suspect, Rex Heuermann, which they eventually secured. Test results conducted from human hairs found either on or around the bodies of three of the victims were linked one way or another to Rex Heuermann, his wife Asa, *and* their daughter Victoria. But then we are right back to whether those hairs belonging to Asa and Victoria were indeed "transfer hairs," or were mother and daughter somehow involved in assisting Rex.

Again and again, District Attorney Ray Tierney stated that Asa Ellerup and her daughter Victoria were vacationing when Rex Heuermann murdered those victims. But as I mentioned earlier, John Ray and his team personally spoke with hotel personnel and learned that Asa Ellerup and her children had not checked into hotels in question until later dates. As a reminder, see page 31 for those specific places and times. Someone has got it wrong.

It is not hard to understand why some folks distrust the police, especially with what had transpired referencing the past administration under Jimmy Burke, Thomas Spota, and Christopher McPartland, the latter of whom was considered the architect of lies when it came to creating cover-up stories. The following is but one example of horrific fabrication by the trio involving the severe beating of 26-year-old handcuffed prisoner Christopher Loeb within a holding cell at police headquarters in Smithtown, Long Island. It led to the downfall of Suffolk County's "dirtiest of the dirty, highest of high-ranking uniformed individuals — former Chief of Police James Burke," states Michael Edison Hayden, noted writer of the following article. We will read what unfolded in Hayden's own words:

March 15, 2016 ~ Vice.com Online Article

The Strange Rise and Violent Fall of Long Island's Dirtiest Police Chief

Former Suffolk County Chief James Burke's recent conviction on civil rights charges opened a window into a lurid cop culture of illegal wiretapping, cover-ups, sex addiction, drunk driving, and blackmail.

By Michael Edison Hayden

On December 14, 2012, cops arrested a 26-year-old named Christopher Loeb outside of his mother's house in Smithtown, New York, slammed his thin body to the ground, and started roughing him up. When his mother Jane arrived, the officers relented and drove him to the Suffolk County Police Department's fourth precinct in nearby Hauppauge, where they chained him to the floor. Loeb was kept in the dark about his arrest and denied access to a lawyer, but it soon dawned on him that the treatment might have something to do with a black duffel bag he'd recently stolen from the backseat of an unlocked black 2008 GMC Yukon. A heroin user who dabbled in burglary to support his habit, Loeb had found things in the bag that might have belonged to a police officer: handcuffs, mace, and a gun.

But he also found things that pointed to something much darker, according to a friend of Loeb's who spoke to him after the incident — like porn that appeared to him to feature prepubescent boys.

According to court documents, James Burke, then the chief of police for Suffolk County, derived pleasure from presiding over the continued abuse of Loeb at the police station. He told fellow officers with an air of wistfulness later on that it reminded him of his "old days" coming up with the force; he jokingly called the cops who aided him in subduing Loeb his "palace guards." One of these men allegedly told Loeb he was going to rape his mother during the beating, and Burke even threatened to murder Loeb with a "hot shot," or a fatal overdose of heroin that might later be arranged to appear self-inflicted.

Immobilized but conscious of the fact that Burke was the owner of the bag with the alleged porn stash, Loeb called the chief a name. Newspapers typically soften the word to "pervert," and the feds say Loeb was mistaken, but in Loeb's telling of the story, as documented in a video interview recorded for *Newsday*, he called Burke a "pedophile."

According to Loeb, when the chief heard that word, he exploded with rage, driving his thick fingers into the young man's face.

"He used to tell people that he wanted to become a cop so he could get away with breaking the law." — according to a high school acquaintance of James Burke.

In subsequent weeks, Burke pressured his colleagues to cover up the abuse. One cop later told the US attorney's office that if it were discovered by Burke that he had spoken to the FBI during the investigation, he would be a "dead man."

On February 26, after a lengthy FBI probe, Burke pleaded guilty to federal charges of violating Christopher Loeb's civil rights and knowingly conspiring to conceal evidence of it. But according to former police officers, local politicians, lawyers, and Suffolk County residents with whom I spoke about the case, Burke's conviction likely represents only the first domino to fall in what could become one of the more surreal federal probes of local law enforcement in American history.

It involves allegations of illegal wiretapping, cover-ups, sex addiction, drunk-driving cops, and blackmail. It involves a super PAC funded by the Suffolk Police Benevolent Association that critics say uses mandatory donations to cement a wall between cops and the people they are paid to protect. And it involves Tom Spota, the longtime Republican-turned-Democrat District Attorney of Suffolk County, who fathered Burke's rise to power through a close friendship that began after they met during the high-profile trial of a bizarre murder case.

Robert Trotta, an outspoken ex-cop who is now the county legislator from Suffolk's 13th District, has been struggling to pass bipartisan legislation to reform the police for more than two years. He compared the atmosphere of paranoia and fear officers experience there to that overseen by the KGB during the Cold War.

"I had to get out of the police department," he tells me from his office. "That way I could be free to talk about what is going on there."

"Suffolk is so dirty," concurs Peter Fiorillo, a retired New York City cop who has lived on Long Island since the 1960s. "Every place has corruption, but on a scale from one to ten, it's an 11."

From the outside, it seems strange that Burke was given so much authority. How could a man who in 1993 carried on a sexual relationship with Lowrita Rickenbacker, a convicted prostitute and drug dealer who'd been arrested multiple times in the very precinct where he acted as supervisor, become, in 2012, the top cop on a force of over 2,500 officers?

Described by those who knew him as a sex-obsessed narcissist, Burke — a squat, sharp-talking middle-aged bachelor with a vulgar disregard for social niceties — could also be charming when he wanted to be. He carried the reputation of a cop's cop, and his natural intelligence helped compensate for his lack of a college education. Three former officers with whom I spoke described him as an inspiring public speaker, and the Internal Affairs report into his relationship with Rickenbacker describes Burke's reputation as that of an "extraordinary street cop" with an intimate knowledge of "local street people."

It has been documented by Internal Affairs that Burke lost his gun on one outing with Rickenbacker, whom he knew then as Lowrita Fields, and that the pair had sex in his patrol car. But based on conversations with others about the incident, Trotta suspects Burke may have been shaking down drug dealers for crack and using the contraband with his girlfriend while they had sex.

There are few law enforcement agencies where a man like Burke would be a candidate for a leadership role. But Suffolk County is the exception to a lot of rules.

The county's demographics render it uniquely positioned for the kind of corruption embodied by men like Burke, according to Bruce Barket, the attorney handling Loeb's lawsuit against the county. Tucked onto the eastern end of Long Island, it's home to 1.5 million people and is bordered only by Nassau County (and then New York City) to the west, the Long Island Sound, and the Atlantic Ocean. Other counties in the New York metropolitan area have borders that are frequently crossed by police and civilian vehicles, Barket notes, but Suffolk is an exception.

"To become what it is now," Barket says from his office in Nassau, "Suffolk County operated unobserved for decades."

At over 85 percent white and predominantly Catholic, the area is less than diverse, despite a robust Latino population dispersed throughout Long Island's East End. Communities like Smithtown, where Burke grew up, emerged largely through the phenomenon of white flight, where Caucasian families dealt with the specter of urban crime by fleeing from the five boroughs and heading toward the sea.

It's ironic, then, that Suffolk itself became known for a brutal murder case. On April 21, 1979, Joseph Sabina found his 13-year-old neighbor John Pius Jr. lying motionless in the yard of Dogwood Elementary School. Stones had been stuffed down his throat to asphyxiate him. The resulting trial was an odd convergence of the people who would run the county's law enforcement apparatus years later: The prosecutor assigned to the case was a young Spota, and Burke, then 14 years old, served as one of Spota's key witnesses. In the end, Smithtown locals Michael Quartararo, his brother Peter

Quartararo, Thomas Ryan, and [Robert] Bresnic — all high school–aged boys — were convicted of the murder.

Jesse Kornbluth, a journalist who chronicled the Pius case for *New York* magazine in a labyrinthine two-part 1982 story, describes Suffolk residents to me over the phone "as people who view New York City life as a kind of sinful Gomorrah." At the same time, he explains, people there are prone to ignoring the more psychologically horrific dangers that mutate along the quiet, tree-lined streets on which they live.

For some, the verdict in the Pius case did not bring any closure. One of those people is attorney Frank Bress, now a law professor at New York Law School in Manhattan, who defended Bresnic in a 1986 appeal.

"Burke was a low-level burglar and drug dealer as a kid," Bress says over a salad not far from his home in Westchester. "It made his testimony unreliable."

The lawyer ran a yearlong clinical program on Bresnic's appeal with eight of his students while he was teaching at New York's Pace University, immersing himself in what he perceived to be inconsistencies of evidence. Today, he believes the same thing he believed then: that all four boys were innocent. Theories abound about who might have committed the murder — some suggest it was Pius's father, or possibly a local drug dealer — and it is difficult to talk about the case without acknowledging a degree of doubt about the true identity of the killers.

Bress accuses Spota of dipping between his work as a prosecutor and as a civil attorney, handling the victim's

81

side of civil suits he himself prosecuted in criminal court. A yellowed file copy from the Bresnic retrial refers to Spota's "pecuniary interest" in trying cases. "I could see right away that Spota was dirty," Bress says now. "The way he conducted himself, moving between prosecution and civil cases like that was highly unethical behavior."

Bress's recollection of Burke as a small-time burglar and drug dealer was corroborated by an anonymous source that claims Burke mostly trafficked in small stuff, like marijuana and hallucinogens. Selling weed, the source notes wryly, was a slightly bigger deal back in 1979 than it is now, and he shares Bress's conclusion that Burke's criminal proclivities likely made him a malleable resource for the prosecution.

Even in those days, Suffolk cops had a reputation. According to Kornbluth's research, the department had a 97 percent confession rate for murder suspects, a number three or four times higher than most American homicide squads' best years — and there were allegations that officers would break all sorts of eggs to make that omelet. Examples cited by Kornbluth include a man who claimed that a thin telephone book was placed against his head before he was beaten with a slab of concrete, and another who said cops tied a slip of paper to his penis and then held it over a paper shredder, threatening to feed his member through the blades.

"None of what's happening is a surprise to me because Burke is the same guy then that he is now," the source who knew him in high school tells me. "He used to tell people that he wanted to become a cop so he could get away with breaking the law."

Burke was officially hired by the Suffolk County Police Department in 1986 as a 21-year-old. He was promoted to sergeant in 1991, when he was 26, and reportedly had Spota's ear. Two years later, Burke was having sex with a convicted prostitute inside his patrol car.

"Horny," says a gruff voice with a thick New York accent on the other end of the phone, when asked to describe the disgraced chief in one word. "*Horny* guy."

The voice belongs to a man I will call R, an ex-cop who met Burke as a student during a police-training course the former chief taught in the late 90s. The two hung out together, drinking and chasing women. At that time, Burke was being promoted from sergeant to lieutenant, and R describes him as personable and friendly, "the loudest guy in a given room." He also says Burke was a short guy with a Napoleonic complex and "a sex addict."

"He was once in a bathroom in a hotel room with other guys and there was definitely coke there. But drugs weren't his thing. Sex was," said R, a former New York cop.

"Burke used to take me and some of the other guys to Gossip, a strip club in Melville," R says. "Downstairs, in the private room, Burke and other cops used to fuck some of the dancers for money. Burke loved prostitutes, and he loved smoking cigars. He loved dipping his cigar in cherry brandy."

R cites a locally infamous bust at World Gym in Ronkonkoma in 2002, where officers were convicted for selling cocaine and steroids, as representative of the scene among Long Island cops at the time.

I ask whether he ever imagined his friend would go on to become chief.

"No way," he responds with a laugh. "I figured he'd just get hit with a DUI. But he was Spota's boy, and that was his hook."

Burke has since admitted to driving drunk and using the power of his badge to avoid paying a price. Court documents reveal that in 2011, he struck a state-owned vehicle, abandoned the scene, and failed to report the incident. He later concealed the crimes by surreptitiously paying thousands of dollars for repairs.

When asked about R's allegations of sex work, a spokesperson for Gossip informs me that the club was rebranded under new ownership in 2014 with an emphasis on "upscale and sophisticated" entertainment. But a dancer named Gia who worked at the old Gossip between 2003 and 2004 confirms R's description of the place as a "cop hangout," though she admits she would not know Burke's face from thousands of others because of the heroin she was abusing at the time.

Gia says she worked on Wednesday, Thursday, and Friday nights with two regular dancers named Tara and Hawaii, and that the trade of sex for money was commonplace in the basement of the club. She adds that empty "liquor cabinets" were used for sex work, and the ownership at that time, which she describes as "shadowy" and Russian, encouraged prostitution — and that one dancer at the club had a "Felix the Cat magic bag" filled with vibrators, nipple clamps, and other gear for female submissive S&M sessions.

Gia says cops were regular customers, but "different from the firefighters," who were usually looking for a gentler time. The police she knew, as a rule, were misogynists who liked it harder. And some of the cops, she claims, would bring "base" to smoke with the girls — a.k.a. crack cocaine.

"You have to understand that these were vulnerable girls with drug problems," Gia says. "They were raised to respect cops, and then when they see them breaking the law with drugs, or roughing them up, it can be really upsetting because it suddenly feels like the whole world is against you."

I ask Gia if she might introduce me to Tara or Hawaii to see if they ever encountered Burke.

"I can't," she says, her lips curling downward into a pout. "They're dead of a drug overdose."

Trotta's online bio once noted that his campaign was waged with "the goal of making county government more efficient," a polite reference to the vile culture he says he witnessed over 25 years as a Suffolk cop. He speaks from his office with a Long Islander's vowel-twisting accent, peppering descriptions of his homeland with words like "Gestapo," "unbelievable," "crazy," and "staggering." He says that beyond what's already known about corruption through local newspaper stories about Burke, police have created an unsustainable system where they receive massive paychecks to the tune of hundreds of thousands per year while the county plunges into deeper and deeper fiscal ruin.

Even after Burke was forced into retirement by the scandal surrounding Loeb, for example, he was still owed an eye-popping payout of $434,370 under the auspices of unused sick and vacation time. (Burke averaged an annual salary well over $200,000 in his final years on the force.) Trotta keeps the news clippings of Burke's public implosion taped to the wall above his toilet.

"The money that the cops are putting together right now is just stupid, staggering," he says, flipping through a set of stapled pages. "Look at how stupid this is."

The pages refer to financial disclosure reports of a super PAC called the Long Island Law Enforcement Foundation. Trotta claims that the county Police Benevolent Association (PBA) fills the coffers of the super PAC with mandatory paycheck deductions from officers, and that the money they collect is then spent on massive advertising blitzes to help friendly candidates. He further claims that these mandatory donations are illegal — and that they reinforce a culture of secrecy that enables men like Burke to rise unchecked. He believes the majority of cops are not behind these efforts, however, and that they emerged from corruption in the upper ranks of the PBA and county administration.

(The Suffolk County Police Department referred me to the PBA regarding inquiries into the super PAC. The PBA did not respond to multiple phone messages left at its office.)

When he was still a cop, Trotta served on a special FBI task force formed in 2010 featuring two other Suffolk officers, John Oliva and Willie Maldonado. The unit was charged with bringing violence under control in heavily Latino neighborhoods of Brentwood and Central Islip, where MS-13 — a Salvadorian gang — had gained a foothold, according to Robert Doyle, a retired detective sergeant who helped assemble the squad. MS-13 members, often identifiable by blue and white colors and sometimes their love of Alex Rodriguez jerseys (he sports the number 13), were believed responsible for a gory trail of unsolved murders that the county needed federal assistance to solve. (Gang members' ability to escape south to Latin America when pressured by local police presented unique challenges.)

Former Suffolk Police Commissioner Richard Dormer praises the work of that task force in a phone interview, saying they did a "yeoman's job," singling out in particular the skills of Oliva, the son of Cuban immigrants who gained reliable access to Spanish-speaking neighborhoods. But on the Friday before Labor Day 2012, with the probe still underway, both officers were abruptly transferred to peaceful, low-crime districts. Doyle now alleges that Burke and Spota moved the officers to eliminate a hovering FBI presence in the county. At around the same time, Burke was reported to be obstructing federal authorities from collaborating on the effort to catch the Long Island Serial Killer. (Spota's office referred numerous requests to comment for this story to the US attorney's office, which declined to comment.)

Doyle describes the reassignment of the officers as "having diamonds that you toss away in the coal."

The *New York Times* reported this February that federal investigators were examining the circumstances under which Officer Oliva's phone was tapped by Spota's office in 2014. The bug was said to be the work of Assistant DA Chris McPartland, who is described, ironically enough, as Spota's top anti-corruption lawyer. (Cops who knew McPartland, and feared his power, called him the "Lord of Darkness" behind closed doors.) Meanwhile, court documents reveal Burke ordered his officers to install a GPS in the Suffolk deputy police commissioner's car in an effort to blackmail him. And *Newsday* published a story on March 8 detailing how federal investigators believe Spota blocked their probe of Suffolk Conservative Party leader Ed Walsh, a former county sheriff charged with wire fraud and stealing government funds.

Both Trotta and Doyle are quick to note that Spota has run twice unopposed for office. In 2013, the most recent election, he was cross-endorsed by both the Democratic and Republican parties as well as the Independent and Conservative parties. Ray Perini, a Republican attorney who attempted to challenge Spota, was quickly stifled by members of his own party.

"They had the cops out working in force against me," Perini says over the phone with a chuckle.

When I visit Suffolk County police headquarters in Yaphank on a recent warm Wednesday evening, farms and empty fields engulf the isolated station. One cop car shoots across the open road and disappears onto the Long Island Expressway, flashing red and blue lights into the dissolving daylight. Inside, it feels like most of the station has gone home. One plainclothes officer behind the reception desk stares vacantly at a News 12

Long Island TV broadcast chirping about Spota's alleged efforts to protect Walsh.

Words like "corruption" and "ongoing" echo in the deserted lobby.

At 35, Timothy Sini is Suffolk's youngest-ever police commissioner. He had to adapt quickly to the atmosphere of mistrust that engulfs this end of the island: On first being appointed last November by County Executive Steve Bellone, he was greeted by a harsh op-ed in *Newsday* assailing his "zilch experience" and "weak credentials."

The cop has the kind of face that stays young, along with round, clean-shaven cheeks that undercut the gravity of his somber talk about reform.

"It's a humbling experience," Sini says of his first few months on the job. "But I see this as an opportunity to move the department forward in a much more positive direction."

Sini assures me he's done a top-to-bottom assessment of the department and that he's working hard to increase transparency. He's also planning for the county police to have an active social media presence down the road, and he wants a better relationship with the press. He adds that he has transferred more officers into Internal Affairs to help avoid more incidents that might stain the reputation of the county, and he says that as a former member of the US attorney's office himself, his relationship with federal authorities is stronger than that of any predecessor.

So far, at least, Sini's strategy seems to be bearing fruit: The FBI has rejoined the hunt for the Long Island Serial Killer, and federal agents are once again going after MS-13 members in the area. Still, it's impossible not to notice how questions about Suffolk's shady past are taking a toll on the new commissioner.

"I didn't know who James Burke was when I was an attorney," Sini says, his light, intelligent eyes tracing the distant corners of a tired-looking conference room.

"I do now."

When he steps into Judge Leonard Wexler's federal courtroom in Central Islip on the morning of February 26, Burke is dressed in prison grays with pants cuffed at the ankle. The emblematic mustache he wore throughout his career as a cop has been shaved off, lending him a softer, more fragile appearance.

He looks skinnier than in recent pictures, and he wears a vague smile across his face, perhaps at the recommendation of his lawyer, a broad-shouldered man named Joe Conway. (When I speak to Conway before the plea, he describes Burke as inquisitive in their meetings, always provoking thoughtful discussions about his own defense.)

Burke has been housed in Brooklyn's Metropolitan Detention Center, far from the inmates he helped put behind bars over three decades in law enforcement on Long Island. "People adapt," Conway tells me of his client's state of mind. "Right now, James is making the most of a bad situation. You know how it is."

For his part, Loeb is also secluded from the public as he receives treatment for an addiction he cannot seem to shake. Heroin problems are on the rise on Long Island, as they are across much of America, and Loeb is just one of many people scuffling with the disease. The man-made headlines again in December after a violent altercation between himself and two other people spilled out into the gated community where his mother lives. When I go there to try to speak with Jane Loeb, Christine, a security guard, tells me Chris's public battles with drug addiction took a toll on his mother, and that she's grown depressed and reclusive in the years following his abuse at the hands of Burke.

Jane does not even bother showing up to the disgraced cop's date in court.

Christine makes it out for the occasion, though. As does retired NYPD Officer Fiorillo, along with other members of the community determined to catch a glimpse of Burke up close — and perhaps gain some insight into how a culture of police corruption has festered for decades.

When I ask Christine what she thinks of Burke, she shakes her head in disgust, calling him "just a dirty, dirty dog."

"Why do people like Burke even become cops?" she asks. "Don't they want to help people?"

Michael Edison Hayden grew up on Long Island. His work has been featured in The New York Times, Foreign Policy, Los Angeles Times, The World Street Journal, National Geographic, among other publications.

CHAPTER TWELVE

Under the auspices of the newly created Task Force, District Attorney Ray Tierney widened the scope of the search referencing subsequent police investigations of suspect Rex Heuermann by homing in on direct witness testimony, burner phone interactions, cell phone/cell site information, text messages, social media records, e-mail accounts, and male/female forensic hair analyses evidence. The information has been collected in a semblance of order as pertaining to the first four victims, including two additional victims for which Heuermann has also been charged. They are part of what is referred to as the Suffolk County Bail Application — meaning the seven indictments. The following is a timeline.

July of 2007

On July 6, 2007, Maureen Brainard-Barnes left New London from Norwich, Connecticut by train. She was last seen in Manhattan and was contacted by burner phone. Court records show that between July 6 and July 9, 2007, there were 16 interactions via a burner phone. On July 9, Maureen's cell phone was traced to Midtown Manhattan, near the 59th Street Bridge at 11:56 p.m. On July 12, 2007, two outbound calls were made on her phone near the Long Island Expressway in Islandia, Long Island, N.Y. The calls had been made to check her voicemail.

July of 2009

Melissa Barthelemy was contacted by burner phone before last seen in Midtown Manhattan on July 6, 9, and 10, 2009. According to court records, Heuermann's wife, Asa Ellerup, traveled to Iceland on July 8, 2009. Melissa was last seen on July 9, 2009 in New York City.

According to cell site records, the burner phone was traced back to Massapequa Park and Midtown Manhattan on July 10. Later that evening, Barthelmy's phone was traced to Midtown Manhattan and then Massapequa Park. On July 11, 2009, at around 11:43 a.m., Barthelemy's phone was used to make an outbound call, checking her voicemail in Freeport, N.Y. On July 12, 2009, Barthelemy's phone was used to make two outbound calls, checking her phone in Babylon, N.Y. On July 17, 2009 to August 26, 2009, a man calls Barthelemy's family from her phone. The man admits to killing and sexually assaulting Barthelemy. Records show the calls were traced back to Midtown Manhattan. On August 8, 2009, Heuermann's wife returned to the United States.

June of 2010

Megan Waterman was contacted by burner phone and was last seen leaving Holiday Inn in Hauppauge, Long Island, N.Y. On June 4, 2010, Heuermann's wife traveled to Maryland, according to cell phone billing records. On June 5, 2010, Waterman was contacted by burner phone, which was newly activated according to court records. Waterman communicated with the burner phone up until June 6, 2010, when surveillance video showed her leaving the Holiday Inn in Hauppauge. This was the last time she was seen. According to cell site records, the phone was traced back to Massapequa Park, N.Y., which was in the vicinity of Heuermann's home at around 3:11 a.m. On June 8, 2010, Heuermann's wife returned to New York from Maryland, according to cell phone records.

September of 2010

Amber Costello was contacted by burner phone, last seen leaving home in West Babylon. N.Y. A witness describes seeing a pickup truck in front of Costello's home. On August 28, 2010, Heuermann's wife had traveled to New Jersey, according to cell phone records. On September 1, 2010, Costello was contacted by burner phone, which was located at West Amityville and Massapequa Park, according to court records. Costello received the calls at around 11:33 p.m. and 11:34 p.m. Shortly after, the burner phone traveled to West Babylon where Costello lived. Costello was contacted by the burner phone around 12:05 a.m., September 2, 2010. According to witnesses, when Costello's client entered her home, another man claiming to be her boyfriend pretended to be outraged after Costello received money from the client. Another witness (a neighbor) told police that the client said he was just her friend and to tell her "I'll give her a call" as he walked out the door.

Based upon interviews, that client was described as a large white male, approximately six-feet-four inches to six-feet-six inches in height, in his mid-forties, with dark bushy hair and big oval-styled 1970s eyeglasses. A witness said the client drove a first-generation Chevy Avalanche, which was parked in the driveway. Around 1:18 a,m., Costello received a text message from the burner phone which said, "That was not nice, so do I get credit for next time?" Court records show that the burner phone was in Massapequa Park. According to a witness, Costello was contacted by the same client later that day. "Amber told us that he," meaning the client, "wanted to see Amber again, but that he didn't want to come back to the house because of her boyfriend," the witness said.

Costello was contacted by the burner phone four times that night between 9:30 p.m. and 11:17 p.m. with calls being traced back to Midtown Manhattan, then Massapequa Park, then West Babylon. Costello, who left her phone behind, was last seen on September 2, 2010, leaving her home that night. A witness said they saw a dark colored truck pass the house coming from the direction Costello had walked towards. On September 5, 2010, Heuermann's wife returned to New York from New Jersey.

December of 2010

The remains of four people [dubbed the "Gilgo Four"] were found off a stretch of beach along Ocean Parkway.

On December 11, 2010, Suffolk County police officer John Malia was conducting a training exercise with his canine partner, Blue, along Gilgo Beach, when the dog found a set of remains belonging to Melissa Bartelemy. On December 13, 2010, police found the bodies of three other women. Each of the four victims were examined by a forensic scientist at the Suffolk County Crime Laboratory. A female's hair, different from the victims, was found on three of the four bodies. The hairs were sent to an outside forensic laboratory. A male's hair was also found on one of the victim's remains. The hair was unsuitable for DNA analysis at that time by the Suffolk County Crime Laboratory. Around this time, police were searching for 24-year-old Shannan Gilbert, a sex worker from New Jersey, who vanished in May of 2010 after leaving a client's home in Oak Beach.

July of 2020

On July 31, 2020, a DNA profile generated from a male hair found on one of the victims' bodies was submitted for further forensics analysis. Forensic scientists determined that the hair belonged to a male person in the mitochondrial haplogroup. Translated and simply put, it means that male person was part of a population who shared similar DNA. It was later established that Rex Heuermann fit that genetic profile, meaning 99.96% of the North American population can be excluded — but not Rex Heuermann.

March of 2022

In March 2022, Heuermann was identified as a suspect after detectives linked him to a pickup truck that the witness reported seeing back in 2010. Following the discovery of the Chevrolet Avalanche, which was registered to Heuermann, detectives began investigating cell phone records and other items according to court records.

Heuermann made purchases and calls in the same location where burner phones were used. Heuermann used his American Express Card in the same area where he used the burner phone to contact the victims. Heuermann also made calls from the same locations where he checked voicemails and called Barthelemy's family members.

Significantly, investigators could not find one instance when Heuermann was in a separate location from these other cell phones when such a communication event occurred. Heuermann's Tinder account linked to one of the burner phones. American Express records obtained by a subpoena revealed payments made by Heuermann to Tinder. According to records obtained from Tinder, Heuermann, who went by the name Andy in his Tinder profile, had links to a phone number which was connected to one of the burner phones. The burner phone was linked to an e-mail account created on January 15, 2011.

A search warrant on the e-mail account revealed selfie photos that appeared to be taken by defendant Rex Heuermann himself. A burner phone e-mail had searches related to the Long Island serial killer. Another burner e-mail account was used to conduct thousands of searches related to sex workers, sadistic torture-related pornography, and child pornography. The e-mail account was also used to search active and known serial killers, the disappearance of Maureen Brainard-Barnes, Melissa Barthelmy, Megan Waterman, and Amber Lynn Costello, along with a number of podcasts, documentaries, and articles concerning the Task Force investigating the murders.

July of 2022

In July 2022, forensic scientists determined each of the female hairs recovered on the three victims of Maureen Brainard-Barnes, Megan Waterman, and Amber Lynn Costello belong to a female in the mitochondrial grouping A1C2, court records show. On July 21, 2022, an undercover detective recovered eleven bottles from a trash can in front of Heuermann's home. The Suffolk County Crime Laboratory took swabs of the bottles and sent them to the forensics laboratory for DNA profiling.

January 26, 2023

Detectives recover a pizza box thrown in the trash can, which belonged to Rex Heuermann. The pizza box was sent to the Suffolk County Crime Laboratory for analysis, where a swab was taken from the leftover pizza crust.

February 24, 2023

Based on the investigation and evidence recovered to date, the DNA profile on hairs match the bottles linked to Heuermann's wife, Asa Ellerup.

March 23, 2023

The Suffolk County Crime Laboratory sent a swab from the pizza crust to another forensic laboratory. On April 28, 2023, a detective hand-delivered a portion of the male hair found on one of the victim's remains to a forensic laboratory for forensics testing.

May 19, 2023

Rex Heuermann was captured on surveillance video purchasing minutes on one of the burner phones.

June 12, 2023

A forensic laboratory determined the male hair found on of the victims and the swab from the pizza crust had the same mitochondrial DNA profile.

July 13, 2023

Rex Heuermann was arrested in connection to three of the four Gilgo Beach murders: Melissa Barthelemy, Megan Waterman, and Amber Lynn Costello. On July 14, 2023, he was charged with both first- and second-degree murder for their murders. In a superseding indictment, Heuermann was charged with second-degree murder of Maureen Brainard-Barnes.

June 6, 2024

On June 6, 2024, Rex Heuermann was charged with two additional killings, both for second-degree murder of Sandra Costilla and Jessica Taylor.

The following is what witness David Schaller (who was initially ignored by police) said during an interview with TMZ regarding Amber Lynn Costello's murder. The TMZ video, published July 15, 2024, titled "Gilgo Beach Killer: Strange & Suspicious TV Show," may be viewed on YouTube.

"My name is David Schaller. I was good friends with Amber Costello. I was out and she [Amber] calls me. Like the guy [suspect Rex

Heuermann] didn't want to take no for an answer and started grab-assing on her, you know, and was basically trying to pull her down, you know, to rape her. So, I came flying back to the house and go through the front door, and there's this giant in my living room. I was like, you gotta go, and he just shook his head, like 'Nope.' I punched him in the face, he went out the front door, I knocked him down the stoop, punched him in the chest a couple times, you know, he got up. I dropped a couple more punches on him; he hit me. Finally, I pick up a rake that I had and was going to smash him in the face with a rake. He got in his car and bounced. The second she went missing, the first person that came to my head was that guy. All they had to do [the police] was run Avalanches [model of Chevrolet vehicle] in Massapequa, and the case would be over."

**David Schaller ~ friend and roommate of
Amber Lynn Costello**

In that TMZ interview, there was a woman author in the group, Kalpana Pot, that related a story of a young runaway and sex worker who was in a motel room with both Jimmy Burke and Rex Heuermann. It is precisely these kinds of stories that interrogators such as Sheriff Toulon's team want to investigate. Imagine the implications if a solid connection can be made between Heuermann and Burke.

One of several important points the video posited was that Rex Heuermann is known to have murdered his victims as early as 1993, making him 29, pushing 30 years of age at the time. As a rule, does a serial killer start murdering at that late age? Do you refrain from being a serial killer during time spent in South Carolina or Las Vegas, where Heuermann had properties?

CHAPTER THIRTEEN

As the prosecution and defense prepare for trial, new challenges will be met, with the emphasis on the word 'new.' New DNA technology will be at the heart of the proceedings during pretrial hearings, known as a Frye hearing. Significant advances referencing the methodologies employed for testing evidence will be at the core of the matter. The groundbreaking methods of analyzing hair and other DNA evidence will be determined by Judge Mazzei, referencing their admissibility, before the start of the trial.

The new DNA methods are being used for the very first time in New York and will prove to be a battle between prosecution and defense experts. Rex Heuermann's defense team will argue and fight to keep disputable and questionably damaging DNA testimony out of the case. Conversely, the prosecution's team will argue and fight to keep such controversial testimony in, citing that the new forensic DNA methods have already been approved by other courts outside of New York State.

Judge Mazzei becomes the final authority after having to carefully weigh the elements of the *law* juxtaposed to the *facts* of the case. It becomes a curious balancing act between the two: law and facts. The fact of the matter is that there is an avalanche — to use that word once again — of evidence, both circumstantial and scientific, which points directly and indirectly to the Heuermann family.

Again, there is that discrepancy between District Attorney Ray Tierney stating emphatically that Asa Ellerup and her daughter Victoria are not accused of any wrongdoing, when, in fact, attorney John Ray challenges Ray Tierney's assertion that the mother and her two grown children had arrived at two of the hotels in question well after the dates to which Tierney ascribed. That discrepancy would indicate that Asa and her children could still have been in Massapequa

Park. It is a definitive distinction that should be cleared up, one way or the other!

Back to Judge Mazzei and D.A. Ray Tierney:

The prosecutor is going to have to try and convince the judge that the new scientific DNA evidence is on solid footing and accepted by the scientific community in its indictment of Rex Heuermann. It does not have to be an ironclad consensus among scientists as to the viability of new DNA methodology, but it must meet with common acceptance.

Having employed mitochondrial and/or nuclear DNA analyses, the prosecution's case will maintain (1) that the single female hair found on a belt buckle used to transport Maureen Brainard-Barnes is to be viewed by a jury as a transfer hair originating from Asa Ellerup — not that Asa was present at the scene of the crime; (2) that the female hairs found in and around Megan Waterman's head area are to be viewed as transfer hairs originating from either Asa Ellerup or her daughter Victoria Heuermann — not that Asa or Victoria were present at the scene of the crime; (3) also, that a male hair was found on the bottom portion of Megan Waterman's burlap and is to be strictly viewed as coming directly from Rex Heuermann — who was certainly present at the scene of the crime; (4) that a female hair found on a tape in the head area of Amber Lynn Costello is to be viewed as a transfer hair originating from either Asa or her daughter — not that Asa or Victoria were present at the scene of the crime.

Are these examples of selective reasoning by Ray Tierney to eliminate Asa and Victoria as suspects from the crime scene because he *believes* they were out of area at the time of the murders? Is attorney John Ray *wrong* in his investigation of exactly when Asa Ellerup and her children arrived at two of the hotels in question? In any event, Judge Mazzei has his work cut out for him.

Although it is unlikely, there is another potential issue referencing the DNA hair analyses. That being, the defense team could argue the "mishandling" of the older forensic hair evidence when James Burke ran the Suffolk County Police Department, which would tend to magnify the cloud of suspicion that has already been cast over Burke's "involvement" in the Gilgo Beach matter.

Judge Timothy Mazzei

On or about February 1, 2024, Forensic Laboratory # 2 issued a report concluding that the mitochondrial DNA profile developed from the male hair found underneath the remains of Jessica Taylor and the profile developed from Rex Heuermann's buccal swab are the same.

DNA analysis of a male hair found on Sandra Costilla's body concluded that it came from Rex Heuermann.

As the serial killer drama unfolds, Rex Heuermann has been indicted in the murder of a seventh victim — Valerie Mack. We touched on Valerie's background on pages 41 – 43. If he is charged, it will be interesting to note precisely how Ray Tierney's team will present the evidence for Mack's murder.

In *Newsday*'s Sunday July 14, 2024 Long Island Edition, the paper did a nice job of reporting on what the Heuermann family is experiencing since Rex Heuermann's arrest a year earlier on July 13, 2023. It begins by giving the reader a glimpse of what their daily life has been like as the accused killer sits in the Suffolk County Correctional Facility in Riverhead, Long Island.

Inside their Massapequa home, the family spends most of their time reading, watching television, or playing video games. There has been no employment since the day Rex Heuermann's Manhattan architectural firm closed, following Rex's arrest. His daughter Victoria had also worked at the firm, which is now defunct.

Although Asa and her family have signed a seven-figure (one million!) dollar deal with NBC Universal and its Peacock streaming service for a documentary series, Ellerup's attorney Robert Macedonio claims that it does not dramatically improve their finances. He went on to say that while the money in the deal is guaranteed, they will not receive full payment until after the series runs on the network. Macedonio concluded by adding that to date the family has only been paid a partial advance and, "Honestly, it doesn't go that far."

Note 1: It is reported that attorney Robert Macedonio has signed a $400,000 deal; attorney Vess Mitev representing Asa's adult children (Victoria and Christopher) has a $200,000 deal.

Note 2: Since the money is going to the accused killer's family, not Rex Heuermann himself, it is not subject to New York State's "Son of Sam" law, which prohibits a criminal from selling his or her story to the media for profit.

CHAPTER FOURTEEN

No date has been set as to when the series will premier. But when it does, the programming will air for a minimum of three hours. Most of the filming has already been centered on interviews with other people, of which I was one of the folks selected. Texas Crew Productions was commissioned by Peacock for the documentary. Executive Producer Jaime Lustberg requested that I be interviewed for the documentary since I had written my nonfiction book titled *The Long-Awaited Arrest of Long Island Serial Killer Rex Heuermann ~ Past "Administration" to Blame.*

A crew of five came to our home early on the morning of September 18, 2023 and spent two hours setting up cameras and lighting. Jaime conducted the interview, which lasted approximately two and a half hours. I was also interviewed by *New York Post* senior reporter Dana Kennedy for an article that she wrote about yours truly on the LISK investigation, which appeared in that newspaper on July 21, 2023. The following is her published piece:

Gilgo killings unsolved for 13 years because 'bad dudes botched the case'
By Dana Kennedy, *New York Post*
Published July 21, 2023

If only people had paid more attention to Long Island-based crime writer Robert Banfelder.

The 80-year-old author could have told anyone who listened years ago that the Suffolk County DA and the cops in charge of the Gilgo Beach serial killer investigation were bungling the case.

"They failed, they failed miserably," Banfelder told The Post Thursday, referring to some of the Suffolk County law enforcement officials that were part of the lengthy so-called "Gilgo 4" probe. "They thwarted everyone who was trying to help the investigation, especially the FBI. These are bad dudes who botched the case."

Last week, Rex Heuermann was charged with three counts each of first -and second-degree murder in connection with the deaths of Melissa Barthelemy, 24, Amber Lynn Costello, 22, and Megan Waterman, 27.

All three women's remains were discovered in the marshes along Ocean Parkway near Gilgo State Park in December 2010.

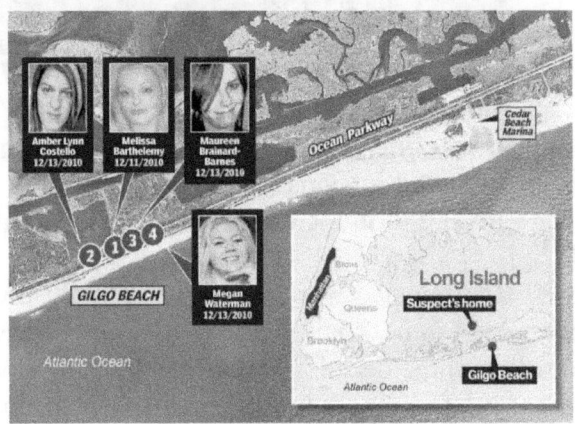

Map of where the remains of Amber Lynn Costello, Melissa Barthelemy, Maureen Brainard-Barnes, and Megan Waterman were found

Last week, Rex Heuermann was charged with three counts each of first- and second-degree murder in connection with the deaths of Melissa Barthelemy, Amber Lynn Costello, and Megan Waterman. He is the primary suspect in the death of Maureen Brainard-

105

Barnes. True crime writer Robert Banfelder said the investigations were bungled for years.

Long Island based crime writer Robert Banfelder wrote two [fiction] books about the Gilgo Beach murders and said he believed cops were bungling the investigation. Courtesy of Robert Banfelder

Banfelder, who's lived in the town of Riverhead, some 45 miles east of Gilgo Beach, for more than three decades, wrote two [fiction] books on the case: "The Long Island Serial Killer Murders – Gilgo Beach and Beyond," in 2020 and the sequel "Snuff Stuff" in 2022.

As recently as last year, he gave talks locally about what he called the case's "culture of corruption" involving the now-disgraced hierarchy of the Suffolk County Police department and DA's office: specifically, former police chief James Burke, former DA Thomas Spota and former Anti-Corruption Bureau Chief Christopher McPartland.

Burke was recently released after going to prison in 2016 for a cover-up involving his beating of a petty criminal who stole a bag of "sex toys" and pornography from his car.

Former Suffolk County DA Thomas Spota, seen here at his 2017 arraignment, is serving a five-year prison sentence for helping cover up former Suffolk County Police Chief James Burke's beating of a man who stole sex toys from Burke's car. *Newsday* **via Getty Images**

In 2021, Burke's longtime mentor Spota — who was disbarred a year before — and another ally, the top Spota deputy Christopher McPartland, were sentenced to five years in prison for their part in the cover-up.

Banfelder also blamed current County Executive of Suffolk County Steve Bellone for bungling the Gilgo case, pointing out that Bellone had been warned about Burke's past and character prior to hiring him.

"He dropped the ball," Banfelder said. "He hired Burke. But that was part of the problem. He hired a bad cop."

Former Suffolk County police chief James Burke was freed from prison in 2018 after being convicted of assault and obstruction of justice charges. *Newsday* **RM via Getty Images**

Not long after being appointed Chief of Police in 2011, Burke removed the FBI from the Gilgo murder investigations — because, The Post reported in 2015, he knew he was also being investigated for assaulting the thief who stole his sex toys.

"Burke never wanted us involved in this [serial killer] case because he knew we were investigating him," said a federal source.

Banfelder, because of his affinity for true crime, said he was well-aware of what he called the "corruption" surrounding Burke, Spota, and McPartland.

"They all go way back," Banfelder said.

**Banfelder's first book [a novel] about
the Gilgo Beach murders came out in 2020.**

Years ago, Banfelder had followed the strange case of a 14-year-old boy named John Pius who'd been found dead at an elementary school in Smithtown, LI, in 1979. Stones had been stuffed down the boy's throat to asphyxiate him. Spota was the young prosecutor assigned to the case and Burke, who was just 14 at the time, was one of Spota's key witnesses. (Burke was never implicated or charged in the crime.)

By the time Burke was the county's top police officer, they were way too cozy, Banfelder said.

"Spota had to follow certain guidelines in a legal sense," Banfelder said. "But Burke could do what he damn well pleased. And in a way this was all Jimmy Burke's stomping grounds, too. He was involved in prostitution and he was partying. There's no question about that."

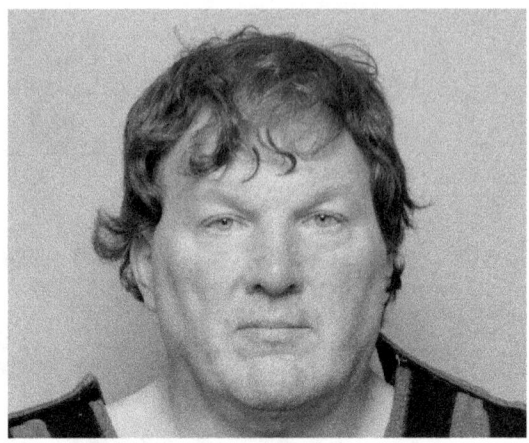

Rex Andrew Heuermann

Last week, Rex Heuermann was charged with three counts each of first- and second-degree murder in connection with the deaths of Melissa Barthelemy, 24, Amber Lynn Costello, 22, and Megan Waterman, 27.

The *New York Post* first reported in 2016 — and there have been similar accounts recently — that Burke attended parties with drugs and prostitutes in Oak Beach. not far from Gilgo Beach, according to John Ray, the attorney for victims Shannan Gilbert and Jessica Taylor. Ray also represented a prostitute who claimed a relationship with Burke, and per a separate source, Burke denied that relationship.

Banfelder feels sorry for the families of the dead women — who he said were dissed by many authorities because the victims were looked down upon as prostitutes.

"I feel emotional just thinking about all the time it took to make an arrest in these cases," he said. "It's shameful."

Long Island residents were frightened for years after the remains of murdered women were first found on Gilgo Beach in 2010 and 2011. Getty Images

Banfelder's second book [a novel] on the Gilgo Beach murders came out in 2022.

Banfelder honed his coverage of serial killers when he attended the trial of Long Island postal worker Robert Shulman who was convicted in 1999 of beating three prostitutes to death with blunt objects inside his Hicksville, LI, apartment between 1991 and 1996.

Banfelder was in court every day, he said, and got to know both the prosecutors and defense attorneys.

He started writing books in 1990 and has also penned hundreds of true crime articles.

As for Heuermann, he said, "He's going to be accused of murdering the fourth one. That's almost a given. And from there, they're going to go on to working at these other six victims and even beyond that."

****

Once authorities had Rex Heuermann in their crosshairs so to speak, I wrote two true crime stories on the Gilgo Beach and beyond murders. As mentioned in Dana Kennedy's *New York Post* article, the first book was titled *The Long-Awaited Arrest of Long Island Serial Killer Rex Heuermann ~ Past "Administration" to Blame*, published in 2023. You are presently reading my second true crime narrative on the subject, which I started on Father's Day, June 16, 2024. I feel this is important to emphasize because I am primarily considered a novelist. My two works of fiction (written under the umbrella of New Journalism) concerning the Gilgo Beach cases are appropriately titled *The Long Island Serial Killer Murders ~ Gilgo Beach and Beyond* and *Snuff Stuff*.

CHAPTER FIFTEEN

Initially, Asa Ellerup had visited her husband at Riverhead's Suffolk County Jail on a weekly basis since his arrest on July 13, 2023. Around the time that Rex was charged with the additional murders of Jessica Taylor and Sandra Costilla, Asa's visits have tapered off a bit. It may be because she had recently traveled to South Carolina in May of 2024, or the fact that, as attorney Robert Macedonio stated ". . . there already were strains in the marital relationship, and Heuermann's arrest was the 'final straw' leading to divorce."

Macedonio stated in *Newsday*'s TOP STORIES, dated July 14, 2024, that he does not see the family living long-term on Long Island, where trips to the supermarket are met with whispers and comments. Macedonio said he expects the family will remain in their house through Rex Heuermann's criminal case and eventually move out of state, likely to South Carolina, where Heuermann's brother lives and where Asa and her family have been spending time in the past year. Asa is now paying the taxes on 12 acres of rural property in Chester County, S.C.

Mr. Etienne deVilliers, who lives next-door to the Heuermann family in Massapequa Park, said in May of 2024 that Asa Ellerup had told him she plans on fixing up the house and moving down to Chester, South Carolina once the criminal case against her husband wraps up. He said the family expressed frustration with how long the case will take to get to trial. Etienne deVilliers went on to say, "Right now they're just kind of handcuffed." Interesting choice of words. "There's not much they can do."

Several years ago, Asa Ellerup had been diagnosed with skin and breast cancer. "I have up to three years and then the doctors will see if I am in remission," she said back in August of 2023. Macedonio had said that her health insurance was about to expire because it is tied to her husband's job as an architect.

Sandra Costilla was murdered by Heuermann in November of '93. He would have been 29 years of age. Given that most serial killers start murdering at approximately age 20, based on statistics cited by noted criminologist/psychologist Dr. Eric Hickey, there is the likelihood that Heuermann started murdering years earlier. In a later chapter, we will learn that Heuermann is being investigated for a murder as early as 1989, making him 25 years of age.

Let us first home in on the dismembering and decapitation of three of the victims:

Karen Vergata was last seen on Valentines Day, February 14, 1996, in the Heuermann home in Massapequa Park, according to eyewitness Ms. Lorraine Paulino (review pages 26 – 28). Two months later, on April, 20, 1996, Karen's severed legs were found in a plastic bag on Fire Island's Blue Point Beach. Fifteen years later, on April 11, 2011, her skull and several teeth were discovered at Tobay Beach. Tobay Beach is approximately 14 miles from the Heuermann home and 4 miles west of Gilgo Beach.

Valerie Mack's partially dismembered torso was found on November 19, 2000 in a wooded area near Mill Road, Manorville. Eleven years later, on April 4, 2011, her head, hands, and right foot were found in a plastic bag in the vicinity of Ocean Parkway on Gilgo Beach, 47 miles away.

Jessica Taylor's torso was discovered on July 27, 2003, off Halsey Manor Road (a half mile from where Valerie Mack's remains were found) in Manorville. Her hands had been dismembered below the elbows. A tattoo on the right side of Jessica's back was mutilated with dozens of razor-thin gashes. The tattoo was a red heart with an angel's wing that read "Remy's Angel." The Medical Examiner had to push the skin together to read the inscription. Eight years later, on March 29, 2011, in the Gilgo Beach area, 47 miles away from Manorville, Jessica's skull, hands, and forearm were found.

Next, let us focus on the dates chronologically in which several of these victims were first reported missing or last seen. That is, those women for whom Rex Heuermann had been indicted for murdering as well as those he is suspected of killing.

Karen Ann Vergata, age 34, was last seen on February 14, **1996**, running from the Heuermann home in Massapequa Park.

Valerie Mack, age 24, was reported missing by her adoptive parents, JoAnn and Edwin Mack, in the fall of **2000**. However, the police report was not taken seriously and therefore never filed by a local New Jersey police department because of their daughter's promiscuous history.

Jessica Taylor, age 20, was reported missing when she did not show up for her mother's birthday on July 25, **2003**.

Maureen Brainard-Barnes, age 25, was reported missing by a friend on July 14, **2007**.

Melissa Barthelemy, age 24, was reported missing by her mother on July 18, **2009**.

Shannan Gilbert, age 23, was seen running from her client Joseph Brewer's home in Oak Beach during the early morning hour of May 1, **2010**. Shortly thereafter, Shannan was pursued by Michael Pak (Shannan's driver) in his vehicle, presumably the last person to see her alive.

Megan Waterman, age 22, was reported missing by family members on June 8, **2010**.

Amber Lynn Costello, age 27, was never reported missing by her roommates. She was last seen on September 2, **2010**.

Now, ask yourself, is it likely that Rex Heuermann took a break from murdering young women in the years 1997, 1998, 1999, 2001, 2002, 2004, 2005, 2006, and 2008. Better yet, research the leading experts in stochastic (statistical) modeling referencing serial killers; namely, Simkin and Roychowdhury. The important takeaway here is the serial killer's intervals of time between committing murders, referred to as 'cooling-off periods,' which can vary between days or weeks or months. Rarely are we looking at a period of years. But there are, of course, exceptions. We will explore several of these people in a later chapter.

Ray Tierney's team is searching out of state for clues that may lead to other victims, particularly in areas where Heuermann and his wife had owned a time-share in Las Vegas, Nevada, and still own property in Chester, South Carolina.

In my first nonfiction book, exploring the Gilgo Beach murders, titled *The Long-Awaited Arrest of Long Island Serial Killer Rex Heuermann ~ Past "Administration" to Blame*, I covered seven victims whose cases in South Carolina and Nevada are being investigated with possible ties to Rex Heuermann. Let us examine one case, in particular, that stands out from the other six:

A pretty, petite, 5' 6", 110 to 120-pound South Carolina woman, Julia Ann Bean, had suddenly vanished on May 31, 2017, the day before her daughter Cameron Bean's high school graduation.

The last time Bean's daughter saw her mother was when they were going to get their nails done, the day before the graduation. Cameron said they were driven by a man she did not know. Cameron gave them both tickets to her graduation, which was to take place the following day.

"I gave her three tickets," Cameron Bean related in a text to *The U.S. Sun*, "just in case she lost one. I gave him [allegedly Rex Heuermann] two so he could bring her. He had introduced himself by a different name. He told me he has lake houses and big boats if I ever wanted to have a boat party. He offered to take me to a concert and told me he wanted to marry my mom. I never saw her again after that night."

In a statement to NBC News, Cameron said, "I saw her the night before my graduation. She didn't show up, which was definitely out of character for her." After her mom failed to show up for Cameron's graduation, stopped responding to text messages, and later missed holiday festivities, is when Cameron contacted authorities six months later, on November 8, 2017.

When Cameron Bean saw Rex Heuermann on the news following his arrest of July 13, 2023, she said she "had chills," stating that she recognized him right away. "That was the last man I saw her with personally." Later, when Cameron saw the truck on the news being hauled away by authorities from Rex Heuermann brother's Chester, South Carolina home, she believed it was the Chevy Avalanche driven by Rex Heuermann back in May of 2017.

A good friend of Cameron's, Heidi Kovas, says she had been talking about Julia Bean since the day she disappeared six years earlier. When Kovas saw the Gilgo Beach victims on the news, she said, "My jaw dropped. All of them [the victims] matched Julia. Everything. The blonde hair, the green eyes, the fact Julia was so petite." Kovas said that Cameron also suspected foul play right away, referencing the sudden disappearance of Julia Bean.

Above all else, Kovas wants to get answers for Bean's children to prove that Julia had never willingly walked out on them. "I'm not pessimistic at all," she said. "She has three children who were made to believe their mother had just walked out on them. Three really cute and sweet kids. One of her sons is a Marine, and he looks exactly like her. I've been in contact with him too, and all he kept telling me is how much this means to him, to have someone fighting for their mother. She messed up a lot and she was sick. But she did not walk out of their lives without saying goodbye. This wasn't her choice. And it really makes me angry" — as a woman who lost her way, too — "because at one point in my life, I turned my life around, and Julia could've too if she was given the chance."

Julia Ann Bean had left all her personal items at home the day she disappeared: wallet, keys, cellphone, money in her purse, and drugs left on the table. Kovas said that she believes her friend's mother Julia was perceived as a "problem" by police investigators because of Julia's troubled past. She said law enforcement knew Julia struggled with drug addiction, had prior criminal offenses, and was otherwise not worthy of their time.

Scott Bonner, an investigator with the Sumter County Sherrif's office in South Carolina, said they are investigating the potential connection to Rex Heuermann. The FBI is also involved in the investigation.

CHAPTER SIXTEEN

The following women may be connected to Rex Heuermann since he owned property in Las Vegas, Nevada and Chester, South Carolina, near where most of the women were found murdered. There are deed records for Heuermann at 5499 Tropicana Avenue West in Las Vegas. The condominium's time-share contract is from April 2005.

In 2012, Heuermann and his wife sold a Las Vegas time-share property for $51,000 to Wyndham Vacation Resorts. The property is part of Club Wyndham Grand Desert. It was purchased in 2004 and sold nine years later.

Heuermann was known to spend time in Nevada, including his attending a convention in 2017.

LAS VEGAS, NEVADA & VICINITY ~ POSSIBLE VICTIMS OF REX HEUERMANN

Jodi Marie Brewer

Brewer, Jodi Marie ~ On August 29, 2003, 19-year-old Las Vegas resident and sex worker Jodi Marie's torso was found wrapped in cloth and plastic, discovered across the state line in San Bernadino County, California. Jodi Marie went missing from the Harbor Island Club Apartments. The apartment is slightly over four miles from Heuermann's condominium. Her torso was found two weeks later near the California-Nevada border. It had been cut with precision via a surgical saw.

Victoria Camara

Camara, Victoria ~ On August 11, 2003, 17-year-old Victoria Camara resorted to sex work to earn a living for her baby girl and herself. Camara's body was found near a desert haul road in Boulder City, Nevada. The location is about 26 miles southeast of Las Vegas.

Jessica Edith Louise Foster

Foster, Jessica Edith Louise ~ On March 28, 2006, 21-year-old Jessica was last seen in Las Vegas, Nevada. Jessica's mother believes that her daughter became an unwilling victim of human trafficking. Jessica last had phone contact with her family while she was at home in the 1000 block of Cornerstone Place, North Las Vegas.

Lindsay Marie Harris

Harris, Lindsay Marie ~ On May 4, 2005, 21-year-old Lindsay Marie Harris disappeared from her home in Henderson, Nevada. She was last seen at a nearby bank making a deposit. Her rental car was found abandoned in the desert at the southern end of the Valley. Nineteen days later, on May 23, 2005, human legs were discovered in a grassy field off Interstate 55 in Divernon, Illinois. After conducting DNA testing, it was learned that both legs belonged to the same unknown person. Three years later, in May 2008, the FBI matched DNA samples of the *known* Illinois victim as Lindsay Marie Harris. Rex Heuermann is under investigation in Harris' murder. Heuermann and his wife had purchased the Club de Soléil time-share in Las Vegas, Nevada on April 23, 2005, 11 days before Lindsay Marie Harris disappeared.

Misty Marie Saens

Saens, Misty Marie ~ On March 12, 2003, 21-year-old Misty Marie Saens disappeared from her home in Henderson, Nevada. She was found dismembered, her torso wrapped in plastic bags and bed sheets. Misty's partial remains were discovered in the desert on a road leading to Red Rock Canyon National Conservation Area, just east of the Las Vegas Strip.

SOUTH CAROLINA ~ POSSIBLE VICTIMS OF REX HEUERMANN

Julia Ann Bean

See pages 116 – 118 for full details

Aallyah Bell

Bell, Aallyah ~ On November 26, 2014, two days before Thanksgiving, 18-year-old Aallyah Bell of Rock Hill, South Carolina disappeared after leaving her uncle's home in Rock Hill, where she was living with her godmother. The home is approximately 20 miles from Heuermann's vacant lots, where the immediate family owns property in Chester, South Carolina. Aallyah never made it back home.

CHAPTER SEVENTEEN

Rex Heuermann appeared in Riverhead Court with his defense attorney Michael J. Brown on Tuesday July 30, 2024, charged with two additional counts of murder for the killings of Sandra Costilla and Jessica Taylor. In sum and substance, the half hour conference amounted to Brown saying he would likely file a "motion to sever," having the trials separated from one another. Also, Brown is considering filing for a change of venue, though realizing that " . . . every county in our state knows about this [case]," he stated. "In fact, every country in the world knows."

The discovery evidence that the prosecution has turned over to the defense is, in a word, voluminous. "The newly turned over evidence includes 1,600 pages of lab reports, grand jury minutes, all of the raw data from the mitochondrial lab work, and 60,000 pages of documents seized from Heuermann's home and office in July 2023," said Assistant Suffolk County District Attorney Nicholas Santomartino to State Supreme Court Justice Timothy Mazzei. Mazzei set Heuermann's next court appearance for October 16, 2024, as "It would not be fruitful to conference the case again until mid-October."

Heuermann wore a black suit and a dark-blue tie. He glanced briefly at the audience, which included for the first time the family dog, Stewie, a scraggly black Labrador Chihuahua mix. The animal is certified and classified as an 'emotional support dog' for Asa Ellerup, who declined comment.

Attorneys Michael Brown and Robert Macedonio, representing Rex Heuermann and Asa Ellerup, respectively, said they did not think Heuermann had seen the dog because Asa and Stewie were seated in back of the courtroom.

CHAPTER EIGHTEEN

As there are several characters not thoroughly fleshed out, yet covered extensively in my first nonfiction account titled *The Long-Awaited Arrest of Long Island Serial Killer Rex Heuermann ~ Past "Administration" to Blame*, I want the reader to have a good understanding of what would be an otherwise unknown or obscure connection to one another. As a reminder, I have included in the <u>Cast of Characters</u> listed in the FORWARD, names along with a brief description of each person. This way, you will have a good grasp of the role each person played in the scheme of things. Too, it will help avoid repetitiveness if you are already familiar with a particular association between two or more parties. The connections among Jimmy Bissett, Shannan Gilbert, and Jimmy Burke are intriguing.

Shortly before Christmas in 2011, Jim Bissett, co-owner of the Long Island Aquarium and Exhibition Center, including the Hyatt Place Hotel in Riverhead, supposedly committed suicide in his vehicle at Veteran's Memorial Park in Mattituck, Long Island — a day or two after Shannan Gilbert's body was found by police. Some folks question whether it was, indeed, a suicide. Gilbert's phone number was purportedly listed in Bissett's cellphone directory. An undisputed fact was that Jimmy Bissett and James Burke were very good friends. Savvy folks were beginning to connect the dots. Coincidentally, the same initials referencing some of the key players presents a curious conundrum: **J**oseph **B**rewer, **J**ames **B**urke, **J**immy **B**issett, and **J**ohn **B**ittrolff, especially if one is of the belief that there are no coincidences. One can have a field day after summing up certain similarities in considering their prurient interests.

Jim Bissett

A year and a half after Jimmy Bisset's *supposed* suicide, Robert Lanieri, age 60, a food service executive for the Long Island Aquarium, committed suicide at his home in Jamesport, Long Island. He hanged himself. Yet another strange similarity.

Robert Lanieri

The following is a list of eight names of police personnel who either participated in the brutal beating of a handcuffed and shackled prisoner while in police custody at the Fourth Precinct headquarters in Smithtown in 2012, or stood by and allowed former Police Chief Jimmy Burke to continue pummeling Christopher Loeb for a period of over quarter of an hour: Detective Kenneth Bombace, Detective Thomas Cottingham, Officer Brian Draiss, Sergeant Michael Kelly, Detective Anthony Lito, Detective Christopher Nealis, Detective Kenneth Regensburg, Detective Keith Sinclair (see FORWARD as to their specific involvement ~ beating and/or cover-up).

Detective Lieutenant James Hickey was the government's star witness in the case against Thomas Spota and Christopher McPartland for covering up the Loeb assault. After receiving a federal subpoena to testify in the case, Jimmy Burke met up with Hickey alone in a restaurant parking lot. "I was very concerned he wanted to kill me if I testified," Hickey said of Burke.

Hickey was on the fringe of the "Administration's Inner Circle," as they cavalierly referred to themselves, that being the tyrannical trio: Burke, Spota, and McPartland; that is, up until the time Hickey turned tail and testified against the three in federal court, referencing the Jimmy Burke cover-up beating of Christopher Loeb.

Detective Lieutenant James Hickey

Next, we will take a close look at Dr. Peter Hackett, considered a wild card by several folks but never viewed by Suffolk County police as a suspect in Shannan Gilbert's disappearance in the eyes of the "past administration's" so-called investigation concerning the man. A week before Shannan's body was found by police on December 13, 2011, her clothing and other belongings (sling-type purse, ID, phone, lip gloss, tank top, jeans, and shoes) were recovered, scattered about as she ran into the marsh nineteen months earlier on the morning of May 1, 2010, pursued by Michael Pak via his black SUV.

A theory being bantered about by police in the early throes of that quasi-investigation to help explain away why Shannan Gilbert's belongings were found scattered along the marsh was that she had allegedly removed her clothing and discarded items while running scared, suffering from hypothermia as she disappeared deeper into the marsh. It is a strange behavior known as "paradoxical undressing." But keep in mind that the temperature was in the mid-sixties during that early morning hour.

Michael Pak was Shannan Gilbert's escort and driver that fateful night. Shannan had vanished into the marsh just 30 yards behind Peter Hackett's home and property, evidenced by her articles of clothing and other items found by police in the marsh ¼ mile from Peter Hackett's Oak Beach home. Hackett was being insulated by Jimmy Burke, Thomas Spota, and Christopher McPartland (monikered the architect of lies) from the onset. And with good reason as we will soon learn.

On the night of May 3, 2010, two days after Shannan Gilbert went missing, Peter Hackett had phoned Shannan's mother, Mari, and asked if Shannan had returned home. She had not. He told the woman that he ran a halfway house for troubled youths, took Shannan in that evening after she allegedly pounded on his door, gave her a drug to help calm her, and that she left. Hackett later said that he had never called Shannan's mother. Phone records proved otherwise.

After the police recovered Shannan Gilbert's body from the marshy area, Hackett was still not considered a suspect. One detective said of the retired Suffolk County emergency services doctor that, "He likes to get himself involved and has a history of injecting himself into media attention-grabbing events." Another detective echoed the same refrain, adding, "We believe that Peter Hackett called the mother as a show of support and to sincerely offer any assistance." That was Suffolk County's Chief of Detectives Dominick Varrone's take on the matter.

Interestingly, there is a strong connection between Peter Hackett and James Burke referencing the airline disaster near East Moriches back in the late nineties in which two hundred thirty people were killed. I am referring to the TWA Flight 800 crash to which both Burke and Hackett had been assigned. Years later, both men in separate interviews claimed that the most memorable moment of their career with the police was in dealing with the recovery of those bodies. The two had worked together closely. Doctor Peter C. Hackett of Oak Beach was and is still considered by several law enforcement personnel as the oddball oddity regarding the disappearance of Shannan Gilbert, perhaps working in concert with a group associated with Jimmy Burke.

Dr. Peter Hackett

Another fascinating true story, not speculation, is that we learn many things about Jimmy Burke. We learn that he ran a prostitution ring with convicted felon Lowrita Rickenbacker and later Heather Malone. We learn that the ring was comprised of both female and male prostitutes. We learn of his own proclivities in procuring prostitutes and consuming drugs at cocaine-fueled sex parties in the area where the Gilgo Beach bodies were found.

Even while serving time in federal prison for assaulting Christopher Loeb, Jimmy Burke is found with oxycodone in his foot locker. We later learn that Burke is a cross-dresser. We learn that he is bisexual. We learn that Thomas Spota, Jimmy Burke, and Christopher McPartland considered themselves untouchable. We learn that the trio used the power of their positions to threaten their perceived enemies with radical demotions and career-ending false criminal charges. We learn that Spota went to great lengths to protect a very troubled Jimmy Burke. We learn that a disgraced Jimmy Burke nevertheless receives an annual pension of $145,485.

Still, another remarkedly true story involving Heather Malone's husband, Guy Malone (one of the good guys in all of this), is excerpted from one of my earlier works on the Gilgo Beach murders titled *Snuff Stuff*. Here are the events unfolded via Frank MacKay's podcast interview with Guy Malone on January 23, 2020, discussing his wife, Heather Malone. The story began in January of 1999:

Heather Malone was a hairdresser who cut James Burke's hair. Guy Malone, an insurance salesman, and Heather lived in Smithtown. Burke lived very close by. Heather had asked her husband to go downstairs to get a paperback book from her purse. He does and finds a large gold police badge in her bag along with Detective Sergeant Burke's business card used as a bookmark. When Guy Malone confronted his wife, she used the customer/hair stylist relationship as her excuse for having those two items. Guy does not press the issue at that point in time.

Guy Malone later tells JVC's talk show host, Frank MacKay, on his nationally syndicated radio program titled *Breaking it Down with Frank MacKay*, that Heather is rarely home at night. Guy is home taking care of their five-year-old daughter, and that when Heather goes out in the evenings, she is dressed to kill. Very sexy. Hot. Tight black skirts, makeup, et cetera, et cetera. Guy and Heather's marital relationship is admittedly rocky to begin with. It seemed very odd that Heather would send Guy downstairs to fetch a book from her purse without her realizing that he would at least notice the large gold police badge, let alone the detective sergeant's business card used as a bookmarker. It seems like a setup from the get-go, as if she *wanted* him to find those items.

A week and a half later, Guy questions Heather about the detective's badge and business card. An argument ensues. The argument turns physical. She punches Guy with a powerful blow to his right temple, knocking him to the floor. He lost consciousness for a moment, inadvertently stepping on and bruising her toe when he got up. She calls the police; he is arrested and spends the night in jail.

Long story short, Guy's lawyer relates his client's side of the story and has Guy show the judge a good size bruise on the side of his temple. A thirty-day cooling off period is ordered by the judge. However, Heather had filed for an order of protection, and Guy was not allowed in his own home for forty some days. Folks who know Guy cannot believe what is happening to this decent fellow. Guy soon learns about a series of very detailed facts relating to Heather's affairs with other men.

So, Guy Malone hires a private investigator. Phone records over the course of a past year reveal many, many communications for the same number; ten to fifteen calls per day, every day, less than a minute long. The phone number goes through to a supposed nail salon of Heather's best friend. But Heather's best friend has no such nail salon business. Then to whom are these phone calls going? Guy learns that the number is an *unlisted* Page Net (short for Paging Network) phone number. The big question is, if it is a nail salon business, why is it an unlisted number? After spending eight hundred dollars for a further investigation because money talks and bullshit walks, Guy learns that the number is registered to a *Jane* Burke at address number 2 Sammis Street in Smithtown. Number 2 Sammis Street is *James* Burke's home address! That address is literally around the corner from the Malone residence.

Guy Malone had a good friend at Park's Bake Shop, King's Park, Smithtown; a hangout for the cops at the Fourth Precinct. Virtually everyone at the precinct knew about Heather Malone and Sergeant James Burke; Burke's *relationship* and his ties to prostitution. The expensive gifts Heather received from Burke were a Rolex watch, Louis Vuitton luggage (one piece costing eight hundred fifty dollars). The police officers knew Heather was untouchable, protected by Burke. Burke had given Heather eighteen hundred dollars to rent an apartment, covering the lease and security. The apartment had been rented *prior* to Heather and Guy's physical altercation and arrest, which she had said she rented *after* the fact. It was a lie and proved in court with documentation; that is, lease and rental receipt dates.

Sergeant Jimmy Burke had given Heather Malone a beeper to solicit clients for the purposes of prostitution. Burke now knows that Guy is on to him. Burke and Heather concoct a story of a second assault by her husband at the couple's five-year-old daughter's kindergarten graduation. Guy's second arrest results in a class B felony, which leads to a Grand Jury. In court, the daughter's teacher and two witnesses testify on behalf of Guy that the so-called 'attack' at the school never happened, and Guy was found not guilty. In a turn of events, Heather was found guilty again of lying before a Grand Jury. She is caught in a *big* lie.

Guy files for divorce. In a deposition, James Burke is brought in and questioned by Guy Malone's attorney. Burke denies any connection to prostitution. He is lying through his teeth while under oath. Who is representing Burke? Thomas Spota's law firm. Remarkably, the judge stops the show in mid-stream! He has, quote unquote, "heard enough" and rules in Guy's favor. Guy gets to keep the house. So, Guy's win is a Pyrrhic victory, hollow in the sense that he loses the opportunity through his attorney to question Burke and rip him apart, too, like he had his wife during an EBT (Examination Before Trial), referencing all of Heather's and Burke's lies and deceptions. Guy's attorney had over two hundred questions prepared on a yellow-lined legal pad. Ask yourself what went on behind closed doors for the judge to stop the trial; why stop the trial? The answer is that certain matters would have surfaced about police Sergeant James Burke that were best left alone as far as the powers that be were concerned.

Heather and her five-year-old daughter then lived with Burke for approximately seven years, off and on again for another three. The daughter, now in her late twenties, has nothing to do with her mother from the day she learned the truth. To this day, Guy Malone believes that the disgraced former Chief of Police James Burke has intimate knowledge of the Long Island Serial Killer murders — not that he is necessarily a murderer.

And those are just some of the highlights that you can hear for yourself. Simply check out JVC Broadcasting with Frank MacKay interviewing Guy Malone: 103.9 News Radio. Google the 45-minute, 19-second interview. It is surely an eye-opener.

Back in 1995, the Internal Affairs Bureau had already known about Burke's involvement with Lowrita Rickenbacker, a known prostitute who Burke had sex with while on duty, in uniform, and in his police vehicle, whereby he *loses* his service gun on more than one occasion, which she had taken then he later recovered. Lowrita Rickenbacker had the same beeper number that Heather Malone was later given.

Lowrita Rickenbacker

Rickenbacker's police record was sealed. Burke had been busted for prostitution and transferred from the Second Precinct in Huntington to the Fourth Precinct in Smithtown. It was all hush-hush. The public was not privy to any of this. Thomas Spota was Burke's attorney in these earlier matters. What were the consequences this time around for the detective sergeant referencing Heather Malone and

Jimmy Burke's prostitution ring? Burke is promoted to lieutenant. Guy Malone saw red. Internal Affairs kept everything under wraps; they did nothing. So, Guy later brought those pieces of information to light and handed the story to Tanya Lopez of *Newsday*, which was then verified by Lopez. The story ran in part; however, the full-length version got squashed. Guy also gave that and other subsequent information to John Ray, attorney for the Shannan Gilbert estate. John Ray was busy building a circumstantial case that named James Burke and Dr. Peter Hackett as possible suspects in the LISK (Long Island Serial Killer) murders.

Following these events, Heather Malone, maiden name Volino, was living in Warwick, Rhode Island at the time of my research, listed under numerous aliases and more than a dozen phone numbers. Does that not sound like a familiar pattern? She and another woman, along with Jimmy Burke had run a prostitution ring not only involving young women, but for the procurement of young boys as well, which helps explain why Burke would have pornographic videos of pubescent boys in his party bag that Christopher Loeb had stolen from the police chief's vehicle.

As an aside, Christopher Loeb was awarded a court settlement of $1.5 million. Jimmy Burke never believed he would end up behind bars. Thomas Spota and Christopher McPartland never fathomed their reign would end in ruination.

Christopher Loeb

CHAPTER NINETEEN

Law enforcement investigators from the days of London, England's Jack the Ripper in the late 1800s, right up to Rex Heuermann's July 13, 2023 arrest in Manhattan, serial killers have challenged authorities, caught the attention of the media, and captivated the public. As there is much misinformation out there concerning serial killers, what you can come to rely on is information that comes from the FBI's Behavioral Analysis Unit.

The topic of serial murder occupies a unique niche within the criminal justice community. In addition to the significant investigative challenges they bring to law enforcement, serial murder cases attract an over-abundance of attention from the media, mental health experts, academia, and the public at large. While there has been significant independent work conducted by a variety of experts to identify and analyze the many issues related to serial murder, there have been few efforts to reach a consensus between law enforcement and other experts.

To bridge the gap between the many views related to serial murder, the Federal Bureau of Investigation hosted a multi-disciplinary symposium in San Antonio, Texas in 2005. The goal of the symposium was to bring together a group of respected experts on serial murder from a variety of fields and specialties to identify the commonalities of knowledge regarding the subject.

I have highlighted and presented here what I feel are among the most relevant factors, among many, concerning serial killers; otherwise, we could be here forever and a day. Therefore, I focused in on a section of the study that often misleads the public: Myths.

Serial murder is a relatively rare event, estimated to comprise less than one percent of all murders committed in any given year. Much of the general public's knowledge concerning serial murder is a product of Hollywood productions. Story lines are created to heighten the interest of audiences rather than to accurately portray serial murder. This only leads to more confusion.

Myth: Serial killers are all dysfunctional loners.

Most serial killers are not reclusive social misfits who live alone. Many serial killers hide in plain sight within their communities. Serial murderers often have families and homes, are gainfully employed, and appear to be normal members of the community. Because many serial murderers can blend in so effortlessly, they are oftentimes overlooked by law enforcement and the public. Examples:

• Robert Yates killed seventeen prostitutes in the Spokane, Washington area during the 1990s. He was married with five children, lived in a middle-class neighborhood, and was a decorated U.S. Army National Guard helicopter pilot. During the time of the murders, Yates routinely patronized prostitutes, and several of his victims knew each other. Yates buried one of his victims in his yard, beneath his bedroom window. Yates was eventually arrested and pled guilty to thirteen of the murders.

• The Green River Killer, Gary Ridgeway, confessed to killing 48 women over a 20-year period in the Seattle, Washington area. He had been married 3 times and was still married at the time of his arrest. He was employed as a truck painter for 32 years. He attended church regularly, read the Bible at home and at work, and talked about religion with co-workers.

• The BTK killer (**B**inds, **T**ortures, **K**ills), Dennis Rader, killed 10 victims in and around Wichita, Kansas. He sent sixteen written communications to the news media over a 30-year period, taunting the police and the public. He was married with two children, was a Boy Scout leader, served honorably in the U.S. Air Force, was employed as a local government official, and was president of his church.

Myth: Serial killers are only motivated by sex.

All serial murders are not sexually-based. There are many other motivations for serial murders including anger, thrill, financial gain, and attention seeking.

• In the Washington, D.C. area serial sniper case, John Allen Muhammad, a former U.S. Army staff sergeant, and Lee Boyd Malvo killed primarily because of anger and thrill motivation. They were able to terrorize the greater Washington, D.C. metro area for three weeks, shooting 13 victims, killing 10 of them. They communicated with the police by leaving notes, and they attempted to extort money to stop the shootings. They are suspected of other shootings in seven other states.

• Dr. Michael Swango, a former U.S. Marine, ambulance worker, and physician, was a health care employee. He was convicted of only four murders in New York and Ohio, although he is suspected of having poisoned and killed 35 to 50 people throughout the United States and on the continent of Africa. Swango's motivation for the killings was intrinsic and never fully identified. Interestingly, Swango kept a scrapbook filled with newspaper and magazine clippings about natural disasters, in which many people were killed.

• Paul Reid killed at least seven people during fast food restaurant robberies in Tennessee. After gaining control of the victims, he either stabbed or shot them. The motivation for the murders was primarily witness elimination. Reid's purpose in committing the robberies was financial gain, and some of the ill-gotten gains were used to purchase a car.

Myth: All serial murderers travel and operate interstate.

Most serial killers have very defined geographic areas of operation. They conduct their killings within comfort zones that are often defined by an anchor point (e.g., place of residence, employment, or residence of a relative). Serial murderers will, at times, spiral their activities outside of their comfort zone when their confidence has grown through experience or to avoid detection. Very few serial murderers travel interstate to kill.

The few serial killers who do travel interstate to kill fall into a few categories:

- Itinerant individuals who move from place to place.
- Homeless individuals who are transients.
- Individuals whose employment lends itself to interstate or transnational travel, such as truck drivers or those in military service.

The difference between these types of offenders and other serial murderers is the nature of their traveling lifestyle, which provides them with many zones of comfort in which to operate.

Myth: Serial killers cannot stop killing.

It has been widely believed that once serial killers start killing, they cannot stop. There are, however, some serial killers who stop murdering altogether before being caught. In these instances, there are events or circumstances in offenders' lives that inhibit them from pursuing more victims. These can include increased participation in family activities, sexual substitution, and other diversions.

• BTK killer, Dennis Rader, murdered ten victims from 1974 to 1991. He did not kill any other victims prior to being captured in 2005. During interviews conducted by law enforcement, Rader admitted to engaging in autoerotic activities as a substitute for his killings.

• Jeffrey Gorton killed his first victim in 1986 and his next victim in 1991. He did not kill another victim and was captured in 2002. Gorton engaged in cross-dressing and masturbatory activities as well as consensual sex with his wife in the interim.

Myth: *All serial killers are insane or are evil geniuses.*

Another myth that exists is that serial killers have either a debilitating mental condition, or they are extremely clever and intelligent.

As a group, serial killers suffer from a variety of personality disorders, including psychopathy, anti-social personality, and others. Most, however, are not adjudicated as insane under the law.

The media has created a good number of fictional serial killer "geniuses" who outsmart law enforcement at every turn. Like other populations, however, serial killers range in intelligence from borderline to above average levels.

Myth: *Serial killers want to get caught.*

Offenders committing a crime for the first time are inexperienced. They gain experience and confidence with each new offense, eventually succeeding with few mistakes or problems.

While most serial killers plan their offenses more thoroughly than other criminals, the learning curve is still very steep. They must select, target, approach, control, and dispose of their victims. The logistics involved in committing a murder and disposing of the body can become very complex, especially when there are multiple sites involved.

As serial killers continue to offend without being captured, they can become empowered, feeling they will never be identified. As the murders continue, the killers may begin to take shortcuts when committing their crimes. This often causes the killers to take more chances and make mistakes, leading to identification by law enforcement. It is not that serial killers want to get caught; they feel that they cannot get caught.

CHAPTER TWENTY

In August of 2024, there aired a podcast with host Tony Brueski and his guest Shavaun Scott, noted psychotherapist and author of *The Minds of Mass Killers: Understanding and Interrupting the Pathway to Violence*. The broadcast is headlined "Hidden Killers" and was to address the titled question: Did Police Chief James Burke Provide Cover for Rex Heuermann's Crimes? Well, the question was certainly raised and touched upon but not explored in terms of those women who claim to have had contact with Burke and Heuermann collectively. In my research, I am looking for an *early* connection between then Police Officer James Burke and Rex Heuermann referencing the Gilgo Beach murders. There have been reports by more than one woman who claim that Burke and Heuermann were together in the same motel/hotel rooms with other partygoers.

Scott went on to discuss Victoria Heuermann's so-called fascination and appreciation for her artwork, depicting and enjoying torture and sadism (which John Ray had portrayed in his press conference), stating that "something is off there," Scott made perfectly clear. "Normalizing sadism and violence are unhealthy," she continued. "A young mind is mapping around sadism, violence, and sex." Not a good mix.

At the end of January 2024, news reporter Luke Kenton for the *U.S. Sun* wrote an article titled **Gilgo 'serial killer' Rex Heuermann 'partied with police chief at crack-fueled motel bash and terrified a young runaway.'**

Former Suffolk County Police Chief James Burke has long been accused of sabotaging the early stages of the Gilgo Beach investigation. Here is Luke Kenton's piece:

DISGRACED ex-Long Island police chief James Burke once partied with alleged Gilgo Beach killer Rex Heuermann decades ago at a drug-fueled motel gathering, a woman has claimed in a new affidavit.

During a symposium in New York on Tuesday night, attorney John Ray shared previously unreleased statements from several women claiming to have shared frightening and violent past encounters with Heuermann.

One woman, given the pseudonym Alice Poe, alleged in an affidavit provided to John Ray that she met Heuermann in 1993 at a drug-fueled party hosted by James Burke at a Budget Inn along Montauk Highway, in Patchogue, New York.

Then a young police officer who had recently transferred from the NYPD to Long Island, Burke would go on to become the Chief of Suffolk County Police in 2012, holding the position for three years before he was arrested for brutally beating a suspect who stole sex toys and porn from his car.

Burke has widely been criticized for cultivating a culture of rampant corruption within the Suffolk County ranks and accused of actively obstructing the Gilgo Beach investigation to conceal his own nefarious proclivities, which allegedly included patronizing sex workers and consuming hard drugs.

In 1993, Alice Poe was a 16-year-old runaway living at the Budget Inn while she finished high school.

Alice claims she was invited to a party one Friday evening by a young mother she befriended who also lived out of the hotel, per a copy of the affidavit obtained by *The U.S. Sun*.

Alice said the woman led her to an L-shaped room with two beds and little else that was being occupied by a group of men who were drinking heavily.

"There was one other white man who was there. He was the life of the party, talking to everyone. He tried to convince me to get mad at my boyfriend, who was not there," Poe's statement reads.

"This boisterous person was James Burke," she further claimed.

"I was told by someone at the party he was a cop, and that another one of the men was a cop.

"I have seen pictures of James Burke when he was a cop [...] I am certain that this talkative man at the party was James Burke."

Alice alleges that Burke was passing around a crack pipe to the other men at the party and goading them to smoke it, though she did not see him consume the drug himself.

At one stage, she claims the cop repeatedly attempted to force her to take a "hit of the pipe" but she refused, causing his demeanor to change from the life of the party to "hostile" and aggressive, the affidavit reads.

Later, Alice claims there was a knock on the door, and a "large man" she now believes to recognize as Heuermann entered the room.

The large man's presence caused a commotion among the other people already at the party, Alice recounted, and she took the opportunity to attempt to leave.

However, she claims that Burke ran and blocked the door to prevent her from doing so.

"I began to feel frightened and tried to think of a way to get out of the room that wouldn't appear like I was attempting to leave permanently," wrote Alice.

"I approached the man with the brown hair and asked him if I could have a cigarette and if he would come outside with me to smoke it.

"I planned to tell him I was going to go to my room for my cigarettes, once outside, because I didn't like his brand. He agreed and we went outside."

Once outside, Alice claims she encountered Heuermann, who was wearing a flannel shirt and leaning up against a wall of the motel, crouched at such an angle that she could not immediately see how tall he was at first.

"He was pleasant to me. He seemed nerdy to me. I had begun to relax," recounted Alice. "I asked the man where he was from. He told me they were friends from Long Island and liked to party.

"He told me that when they wanted to hang out, the men would tell their wives they had to take a trip for business purposes. He told me he wasn't married anymore. He said he owned a car dealership."

Alice claims she made a sarcastic joke that a car dealership owner would not need to go on a business trip, but the comment apparently failed to amuse the tall man.

"He began to look at me like he was angry. I told him I was going to my room to get cigarettes and began to walk past him," wrote Alice in the affidavit.

"He quickly stood up from his leaning position and encircled me with his arm, urging me toward the door of the motel.

"He was now standing very close in front of me, and I looked up at him. I could see that he was huge. I exclaimed, 'My God,' he was tall. I could see he was pleased at my shock.

"I tried to joke but he remained serious. I did not want to go back into that room."

To stall, Alice said she feigned interest in a nearby car and asked the tall man to show it to her.

"When he brought me to the car, we were in the light, and I could see him clearly. His size, face, demeanor, and attitude deeply scared me," she recounted in the affidavit.

"He no longer spoke nicely to me. I told him that if he would wait, I just needed to get my own cigarettes. I told him that I was scared because my room was far and in a dark area of the motel.

"I asked him to watch me and wait for me to return to keep him from suspecting that I was trying to get away. He let me go."

Alice said that, once out of sight, she ran back to her room terrified.

Later that night someone knocked on her door twice but she did not answer and she did not look outside. Alice said she never saw the man again.

Years later, in July 2023, Alice said she was watching the news when a report of Heuermann's arrest flashed on the screen.

She immediately recognized the hulking, 6-foot-6 married architect as the tall man who'd frightened her that night in 1993, the affidavit states.

Ray believes Alice's testimony establishes a concrete social link between Heuermann and Burke that speaks to a wider conspiracy at play in Suffolk County.

The attorney alleges that personal relations between the pair may have prevented Burke from properly investigating the Gilgo Beach murders when the bodies of slain sex workers Melissa Barthelemy, Megan Waterman, Amber Lynn Costello, and Maureen Brainard-Barnes were first discovered in 2010.

Ray represents the family of Shannan Gilbert another sex worker found dead near Gilgo Beach in 2011.

It was Shannan's disappearance on May 1, 2010 that led to the discovery of Barthelemy and the three other women.

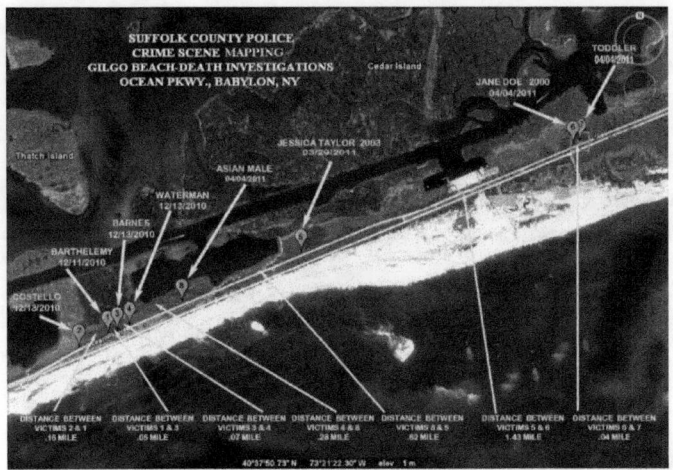

Eleven sets of remains were found along Gilgo between 2010 and 2011. Credit: Reuters

Police ruled Shannan's death an accident, although her official autopsy was inconclusive.

Ray and Shannan's family have long contested that ruling, insisting she was murdered and her death covered up by powerful locals who were friends with Burke.

Speaking at the symposium, John Ray said, "There's a lava that comes out of the volcano that exists in this case.

"And all I'm going to be able to present to you today is the first explosion of that volcano.

"But there is a volcano of truth, of fact, that has not yet been touched by the police, the district attorney, by the [Gilgo Beach] task force - by anybody.

"It's enormous. It stretches [...] all over society."

Attorneys for James Burke and Rex Heuermann have been contacted for comment.

A spokesperson for Suffolk County District Attorney declined to comment on the information shared at John Ray's symposium.

James Burke was appointed police chief during the crucial early stages of the Long Island Serial Killer investigation.

The hunt to find LISK began in late 2010 when the remains of missing sex worker Melissa Barthelemy were found along Ocean Parkway while searching for Shannan Gilbert.

Within two days, three more women would be found dead at the roadside, in similar positions to Barthelemy, bound with either tape or belts: Brainard-Barnes, Costello, and Waterman.

By mid-2011, seven more sets of remains would be found.

But the investigation quickly hit a wall - and the blame for the years of stagnation that followed has often been placed solely on the shoulders of Burke.

In addition to failing to follow up on concrete leads, Burke is accused of actively obstructing the investigation.

As chief, he blocked the FBI from assisting in the Gilgo Beach case.

His scandal-ridden reign ended in 2015 with his arrest on federal charges of obstruction and assault for beating Christopher Loeb, a heroin addict who stole a bag from his car containing sex toys and porn.

Burke pleaded guilty in 2016 to violating the civil rights of Loeb and orchestrating the cover-up of his crimes with the help of then District Attorney Thomas Spota and a handful of other officials.

After his conviction, numerous details about Burke's troubling past, corrupt antics, and alleged sexual exploits would come to the fore.

The allegations included frequent consumption of hard drugs, patronizing sex workers, cross-dressing, and a history of violent behavior.

Rob Trotta, who worked as a detective in Suffolk County for 25 years, told *The U.S. Sun* Burke's sordid escapades were an open secret among the department, years before his "long overdue" arrest.

During their first-ever meeting in the mid-1990s, Trotta claimed Burke asked him if he knew where he could get hold of a "snuff film," a violent pornographic movie depicting a real murder.

Trotta and a handful of his colleagues authored an anonymous letter to County Executive Steve Bellone in 2011, months before Burke's appointment as chief, urging Bellone to reconsider and highlighting a number of Burke's prior transgressions.

Mentioned in the letter was that Burke was known to frequent prostitutes, routinely threaten his subordinates, and in 1995, two years after his alleged encounter with Alice Poe, Burke was disciplined after having sex with a prostitute in his patrol car.

Trotta, who reluctantly retired a year after Burke's appointment, said he was unsurprised to see the wheels come off the Burke regime so quickly but he should have never been permitted to become a police officer in the first place, "let alone chief," he charged.

"The rumors were always everywhere," said Trotta.

"After I left the department and ran for office [...] on two occasions I was in a room with Steve Ballone and I told him, 'You've got to fire this guy. This guy's crazy.'

"And Steve Ballone looked me in the eye and said, 'I stand by him.'

"What message are you sending to the rank-and-file cops that you can go have sex with a prostitute in your police car and then you can still go on to be the chief of police? It blows me away," Trotta said.

Rumors, conspiracy, and innuendo have followed Burke around for years.

After his arrest in 2015, various local officials, including Trotta, State Senator Phil Boyle, and John Ray, all called for Burke to be investigated in connection with the LISK case, believing him to be a compelling suspect.

Those calls were renewed by Trotta and Ray last year after Burke was arrested for attempting to solicit sex from an undercover cop in a Long Island park.

Burke has never been formally accused or charged with any crimes related to the Gilgo investigation.

However, Ray likened Burke to Heuermann, insisting the two men appear to have been cut from the same deviant cloth.

Before Alice Poe's affidavit came to light, Ray also said he believed that Heuermann and Burke may have swum in the same social circles on Long Island.

The attorney theorized that any social ties between the pair could have drastically impacted the early stages of the Gilgo Beach investigation.

It would take until July 2023 for a breakthrough to come in the case, almost eight years after Burke's dismissal, when Heuermann was arrested outside of his Midtown Manhattan office.

The key to identifying Heuermann as a suspect came from an eyewitness account that had been sitting under the department's noses for years.

The account, shared by Amber Costello's roommate, described seeing the slain woman getting into a Chevrolet Avalanche with an ogre-like man on the day she was last seen alive.

Heuermann's arrest came after a months-long investigation, and he has since been charged with the murders of Megan Waterman, Amber Lynn Costello, Melissa Barthelemy, Maureen Brainard-Barnes, Jessica Taylor, and Sandra Costilla.

Police departments across the country are investigating Heuermann in connection with various cold cases, including in Las Vegas and South Carolina.

In September 2023, *The U.S. Sun* exclusively revealed that, additionally, Heuermann is being investigated in connection with the murder of Carmen Vargas, another sex worker strangled and discarded at the side of a road in Freeport, Long Island in 1989.

Carmen Vargas

John Ray closed his symposium by reaffirming his belief the investigation into Heuermann needs to be expanded and taken out of Suffolk County's hands.

John Ray said, "It is clear that the [Gilgo Beach] Task Force is not big enough, strong enough, organized enough, to handle all these cases that are multi-state.

"We have to get a much bigger look from the federal end. We need the FBI and the United States Attorney's Office to step in, which is why I started this case back in 2011."

Luke Kenton is a senior exclusives reporter for The U.S. Sun who specializes in news, crime, and features.

The two important takeaways from reporter Luke Kenton's article are that Alice Poe makes a direct connection between James Burke and Rex Heuermann — collectively; also, that another female sex worker, Carmen Vargas, was found strangled in Freeport, Long Island, N.Y. (South Shore of Long Island) in 1989 — for which Rex Heuermann is being investigated.

Let us do some simple arithmetic: In 1989 to the year Rex Heuermann was arrested in 2023 is 34 years. He is 59 at that time, making him 25 years years old when Carmen Vargas went missing. Do you recall the ages of when many serial killers begin murdering according to Simkin and Roychowdhury, and the FBI's Behavioral Analysis Unit? Early to mid-twenties. Could this be one of Heuermann's first kills?

Carmen Vargas was 29 years old at the time she disappeared. She was last seen getting into a vehicle outside her East Harlem apartment building. Two to four weeks later, her body was found dumped along the Meadowbrook State Parkway in Nassau County. Her legs were tied at the ankles; a towel and a rope were found around her neck. The following information is taken from historical documentation regarding Carmen Vargas:

Carmen was a petite 5' 1", 105-pound pretty woman with dark hair and brown eyes. She loved spending time with her nieces, babysitting, or taking them to the movies and the park to play handball. Carmen did odd jobs back then; she would clean people's homes or do their laundry to make money.

She was the youngest of four children, and her family were all born and raised in Harlem. In the 1980s, the heroin epidemic was just beginning. Cocaine was the drug of choice for white yuppies, but heroin was cheaper, more powerful, and its widespread use caught up with Carmen, especially after the death of her mother in 1986. She got embroiled in heavy drug use followed by sex work to support her addiction.

One day, she did not come home and was last seen by one of her nieces leaving her apartment and getting into a dark truck driven by a white man with glasses.

Carmen's sister and nieces searched everywhere for Carmen. They posted fliers and filed a missing person report with the 23rd precinct at 102nd street and 3rd Avenue, all to no avail.

On September 11, 1989, a motorist with his family on their way to Jones Beach pulled off alongside of the Meadowbrook Parkway, about a mile south of the Merrick Road exit, and discovered the remains of a female, dressed in a turquoise miniskirt with a white tank top and one gold crescent-shaped earring. The woman was petite, had brown hair tied in a ponytail held in place by a rubber-band. A towel had been draped over her face and tied around her neck. Her ankles had been bound. An autopsy revealed that the young woman experienced extreme violence to her face, and that she fought her attacker ferociously.

It was three years later when Carmen Vargas was officially identified and the family notified that the body found on a Long Island Parkway in 1989 was that of their beloved daughter, sister, and cousin.

On July 14th, 2023, the day following the arrest of Rex Heuermann, opened a Pandora's box of emotions, rage, sorrow, and determination for the Vargas family.

Believing that Rex Heuermann, the accused Long Island Serial Killer, might be responsible for the disappearance and brutal murder of their beloved Carmen Vargas, her nieces began a social media campaign to bring attention to Carmen's unsolved and cold-blooded murder.

There appears to be many similarities between Carmen and nearly all the female victims along Ocean Parkway: all were of petite, all were sex workers, several were bound at the head and ankles, and all were discarded along parkways.

In 1989, Rex Heuermann would be 25 years old, right at the prime age estimated by the FBI regarding emerging serial killers. Rex Heuermann began working in New York City in 1987 for architect Harvey Rothenburg, commuting to the city from Massapequa Park. By 1990, Heuermann is also working for Greer Construction in Freeport, Long Island.

CHAPTER TWENTY-ONE

Working backwards in time, months before Rex Heuermann's arrest in July of 2023, let us begin to connect another series of dots and fit together a picture of otherwise seemingly unrelated pieces of a jigsaw puzzle.

In May 21–23, 2023, two months prior to his arrest, Heuermann attended a convention in Las Vegas. The three-day annual ICSC convention (**I**nnovating **C**ommerce **S**erving **C**ommunity), held at the Wynn LVCC (**L**as **V**egas **C**onvention **C**enter), was comprised of brokers, deal makers, industry experts, analysts, and landlords. It was billed as the largest retail real estate trade show in the world.

A woman who chooses to remain anonymous (I will call her Jane) worked at the convention center serving coffee at a breakfast gathering to a boisterous group. Seated at the table was a rather large man who was obviously the center of attention. Jane casually asked the man his name. Members of the group laughed and jokingly replied that his name is T-Rex, short for the dinosaur *tyrannosaurus rex*. Rex had ordered a hot chocolate and nothing more was made of it. That was Jane's brief interaction with Rex in Las Vegas. Nothing sinister. Nothing strange. Yet, nothing short of a jaw-dropping recollection of the man's moniker (T-Rex), the nickname his group of friends had given him, coupled to a positive recognition when she saw Rex Heuermann on the news two months afterward following his arrest — the man whom she had briefly encountered as the man charged with four then two additional counts of murder.

Ironically, Jane had flown to New York, accompanying her husband on a business trip when she had first seen the news in their hotel room and saw a picture of Rex Heuermann, along with beige pants and dark belt he wore at the convention when she served him hot chocolate that day.

We know that Rex Heuermann and his wife own a time-share in Las Vegas, and that they had sold another time-share earlier in Las Vegas. Would the dates that Rex stayed in Las Vegas coincide with dates that women went missing or turned up dead? You will recall that Rex Heuermann was supposedly under surveillance for a year and four months before his arrest. Was Rex under surveillance while in Las Vegas during that time, or was he only under surveillance in New York?

In the case of Victoria Camara, Las Vegas authorities have tested Rex Heuermann's DNA with DNA taken from the Boulder City, Nevada victim mentioned earlier. Be reminded that Boulder City is only 26 miles from Las Vegas. To date, no results have been made public. I presume other promising DNA tests referencing Heuermann have been conducted. One of the more promising connections involving the disappearance of Julia Ann Bean may yet bear fruit. Time will tell.

Probing into Rex Heuermann's travels regarding several states, if not many states and certain areas within, would certainly give an investigator pause. We will be looking specifically into places where we know Heuermann traveled and/or likely traveled because of connections to immediate family, relatives, friends, and business associates.

It is interesting to note that Lindsay Marie Harris' partial remains were found in Divernon, Illinois, off Interstate 55. It may be a bit of a stretch (pun intended), but after disappearing from her home in Henderson, Nevada in May of 2005 — 15.5 miles from Heuermann's Las Vegas time-share at Club de Soléil — might Lindsay have been taken by Rex and driven to Divernon, Illinois where she was dismembered while making his way back east to Long Island? Divernon, Illinois is approximately two-thirds of the way en route to his home in Massapequa Park, Long Island.

Also of interest are four geographical locations surrounding the central part of Florida; that is, two areas on the west coast and two on the east coast that connect Rex Heuermann to those places. The connection being Rex Heuermann's relatives. William George Heuermann, Sr. of New Port Richey on the west coast of Florida was Rex Heuermann's grandfather who died the same year Rex was born. Therefore, we can take Rex out of the equation as visiting his grandfather, but not the grandfather's son, William Heuermann, Jr., Rex's uncle, who later lived in nearby Massapequa Park during Rex's childhood. Rex would be 22 years old when William Heuermann, Jr. died in 1986, but not before the uncle relocated to New Port Richey several years earlier. The point being is that Rex may have visited his uncle, William Heuermann, Jr., in New Port Richey.

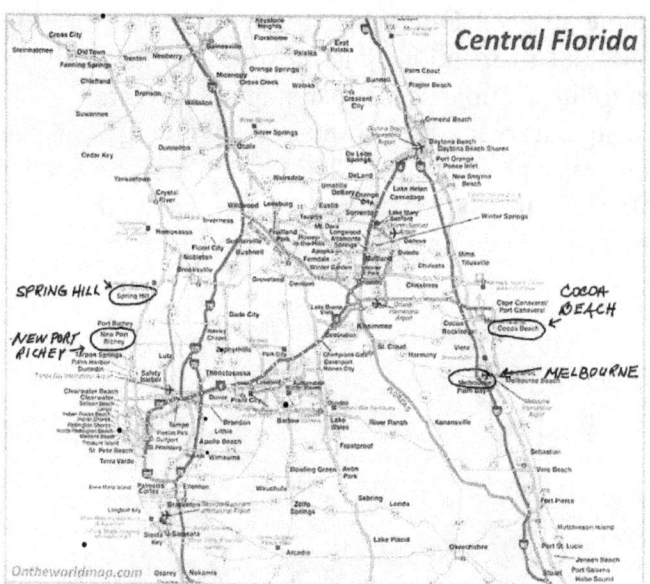

The map indicates where Rex Heuermann had relatives he may have visited in Central Florida.

Rex also had an aunt, Grace Heuermann Lichtenberg, living in nearby Spring Hill, Florida, a mere 20 miles north of New Port Richey. She lived to be 92. Too, Rex had a cousin, Captain George H. Heuermann of the Nassau County Police Department, who lived in

Bellmore, Long Island, just 4 miles from Massapequa Park before retiring and relocating to Melbourne, Florida on central Florida's east coast. At one point Rex Heuermann's mother was ill and reportedly living in Cocoa Beach, Florida, just 20 miles north of Melbourne. This four-point rectangular pattern (New Port Richey, Spring Hill, Cocoa Beach, Melbourne) is approximately a 3-hour drive from the west coast to the east coast across the central part of Florida. A piece of cake for someone who has spent many hours behind the wheel, for Rex had often driven long distances on business.

Rex had visited his mother in Cocoa Beach, Florida. Did he visit relatives in those other areas of Florida? More pointedly, did any women go missing and/or turn up murdered during such periods of time? These are questions investigators need to explore, now that we have a viable suspect. Obviously, the work ahead for authorities is voluminous, not to mention quite costly. The key will be peerless dedication to this complex case spanning many years.

A fascinating piece of information involving a contact of Rex Heuermann's is a priest named Alan Placa. Placa, residing at address number 10 The Fairway, Oak Beach, Long Island, lived next-door to Joseph Brewer.

Alan Placa
Number 10 The Fairway, Oak Beach, Long Island

Joseph Brewer
Number 8 The Fairway, Oak Beach, Long Island

You will recall from Chapter One that Joseph Brewer was one of Shannan Gilbert's clients. She disappeared from Brewer's home that evening in May of 2010, screaming for her life. Alan Placa was the first person to visit Rex Heuermann in Riverhead jail following his arrest.

Shortly after Rex Heuermann was settled in, Suffolk County Sheriff Errol Toulon, Jr., who presides over the Riverhead correctional facility, said that Rex Heuermann asked permission to meet on a weekly basis with his own personal clergyman. Sheriff Toulon thought it an odd request; however, the request was granted. When Alan Placa's name came up, Sheriff Toulon stated, "It wasn't a name I was familiar with until we did some research into this individual," evading the question of whether Heuermann's clergyman is, indeed, Alan Placa. Sheriff Toulon simply would not say.

In early 2002, a Suffolk County grand jury, convened by former District Attorney Thomas Spota, accused Alan Placa of sexually abusing children as well as helping cover up the sexual abuse of children by fifteen other priests. Placa had been part of a three-person team that handled allegations of abuse by clergy for the Diocese of Rockville Centre. A case of the fox in charge of the henhouse. Placa was instrumental in the development of diocesan policy regarding allegations of sexual abuse of children by priests as Placa himself became a target. Yet, in the end, Spota decided not to prosecute a single priest. It was the church that found Alan Placa guilty of sexual abuse and stripped him of his ecclesiastical duties in June of 2002. But in 2009, he was permitted by the church hierarchy to exercise priestly ministry in the Roman Catholic Church. However, he would not be given a diocesan assignment. His present status is that of a retired priest in good standing. Interestingly, Thomas Spota is a lifelong member of the Rockville Centre Church. Alan Placa had served as director for the Advocacy Office at Catholic Charities, a nationwide network from which Rex Heuermann of RH Consultants & Associates had received many lucrative jobs for decades as an architect and code expediter.

In September of 2024, *Newsday* reported that after a four-year battle, the Diocese of Rockville Centre had reached an agreement with hundreds of survivors of sexual abuse at the hands of clergy that calls for the church to pay out a total of just over $323 million. The agreement would benefit more than 500 people who have filed lawsuits against the diocese contending that they were abused by clergy when they were children. That would be an approximate average settlement of $646,000 per person as the result of deliberate indifference of the Diocese of Rockville Centre, for which these now men and women had suffered and endured as young children.

The diocese had declared bankruptcy on October 1, 2020. As part of the settlement plan, the diocese said that all its parishes will enter an abbreviated Chapter 11 to secure a release from liability. Therefore, not even one of Rockville Centre's 132 parishes will perish because of the stated agreement.

As an aside, on July 17, 2024, disgraced Suffolk County District Attorney Thomas Spota had been released from a federal prison in Connecticut, less than three years into his five-year sentence for his role in obstruction of justice referencing the Christopher Loeb case.

Another interesting tidbit of information concerning Alan Placa is that he claimed Shannan Gilbert had knocked on his door in Oak Beach on the early morning hour she vanished in May of 2010. Alan

Placa was Joseph Brewer's next-door neighbor. Placa's claim is that by Shannan doing so, it devalued his property to the tune of $60,000, so he applied for a property tax reduction. Placa was successful in securing that $60,000 tax bill deduction.

Incidentally, Alan Placa is a longtime friend of former New York mayor Rudy Giuliani. In fact, Placa is employed by his childhood friend as a consultant at Giuliani Partners.

There was another questionable practice involving a pedophile priest being investigated for embezzlement of hundreds of thousands of dollars from the House of Affirmation, a treatment center for priests with psychological and psychosexual problems. That priest transferred a condominium out of his name and into Alan Placa's name to avoid losing the condo. That condo is situated in Orlando, Florida, smack in that same central Florida area, still another place Rex Heuermann would have visited family members as mentioned earlier.

Getting back to Shannan Gilbert and the powers that be, it is important to keep firmly in mind that it was James Burke, Thomas Spota, and Christopher McPartland who created the narrative that Shannan died of a "misadventure," having accidently drowned by running into a marsh after fleeing Joseph Brewer's home that early morning hour. And it was their spokesman Detective Vincent Stephan who pushed that very narrative.

Rudy Giuliani

Adapted from a Shakespearian line in his play *The Tempest*, "Misery acquaints a man with strange bedfellows," is a fitting phrase for the figures we see connected to one another. Namely, Rex Heuermann, Alan Placa, Joseph Brewer, Thomas Spota, and Rudy Giuliani.

CHAPTER TWENTY-TWO

There is an intriguing new development involving convicted Manorville murderer John Bittrolff in the 1993 and 1994 killings of sex workers Rita Tangredi and Colleen McNamee, respectively. Bittrolff is seeking exoneration, looking to pin the two murders on Rex Heuermann. John Bittrolff has long been suspected of also killing Sandra Costilla, for which Heuermann was indicted on June 6, 2024. The three crime scenes are eerily similar in that all three women were found in wooded areas with their legs spread apart, hands above their heads, and each missing one shoe. Colleen and Sandra had their shirts pulled up over their faces. Woodchips were found on Colleen's and Rita's body.

Importantly, there were *unknown* hairs found on the bodies of both Rita Tangredi and Colleen McNamee.

Since Rex Heuermann has been officially charged with Sandra Costilla's murder, and because of the similarities found among the three women, one could likely assume that Heuermann might possibly be responsible for both Rita Tangredi's and Colleen McNamee's murders. But District Attorney Ray Tierney is not buying any of it.

"I've looked at those cases," Tierney said. "If I thought there was a problem with them, I would do something." He went on to say, "If we saw something that would give us pause, we would certainly share that and act accordingly."

Therefore, Tierney had flatly rejected appeals by Deputy Bureau Chief Lisa Marcoccia for the Legal Aid Society of Suffolk County to share forensic evidence from the Sandra Costilla crime scene, asking the D.A. to perform the same mitochondrial DNA testing used to charge Rex Heuermann, referencing previously *untested hairs* found at the Rita Tangredi and Colleen McNamee crime scenes. The point being that John Bittrolff was convicted with evidence taken from semen samples, proving that he had sex with the two women — not hair samples that could possibly include hairs from Rex Heuermann, his wife Asa Ellerup, and/or his daughter Victoria, be they transfer hairs or otherwise.

Marcoccia sent a second letter to Conviction Chief Craig McElwee, repeating her requests. Assistant District Attorney Guy Arcidiacono, deputy chief of the Appeals and Training Bureau, also denied the requests, writing that, "There is no basis on law or fact for providing you with these materials. As you are aware, Rex Heuermann has been indicted for the [Sandra] Costilla murder. Whether your client was ever investigated for the Costilla murder, it is evident he was not charged in that case. Neither the fact that he was not charged nor that Mr. Heuermann has been charged is exculpatory as to Bittrolff's murder convictions."

John Bittrolff with his defense attorney William Keahon

Back in May of 1994, the then head of Suffolk County Homicide, Detective Lieutenant John Gierasch, told *Newsday* that he believed that Rita Tangredi, Colleen McNamee, and Sandra Costilla may have been killed by the same person.

"They were all white, around 5 feet tall, and no more than 125 pounds," he explained. "The investigation definitely linked Rita Tangredi and Colleen McNamee. Additionally, we have reason to believe that Sandra Costilla may possibly be linked as well. We believe, based on the totality of the circumstances, they were most likely sexually motivated homicides." Sandra Costilla's cause of death was strangulation; Rita Tangredi's and Colleen McNamee's cause of death was blunt force skull and brain injuries as well as strangulation.

The jury trial of John Bittrolff was deadlocked three times before a guilty verdict had been reached. The trial was a *total* travesty:

Mr. Keahon, John Bittrolff's defense attorney, stated that the Suffolk County police destroyed a total of 148 pieces of evidence concerning the murder of Colleen McNamee in 2007.

Mr. Biancavilla, the prosecutor, acknowledged that fact, but added, "The evidence was mistakenly destroyed. We're not perfect," he said, calling the mistake "a speed bump or hiccup" along the way.

Mr. Keahon told the jury, "I'm unable to see that evidence now and have it analyzed. It's gone! Destroyed! And the prosecutor refers to that as a bump in the road."

The former director of forensic science at the New York Department of Criminal Justice Services (DCJS) stated that the Office of Forensic Science (OFS) made three catastrophic DNA identification errors and falsified a fourth certification document. The claims were made by Brian Gestring, a member of the state's Commission on Forensic Science. He said the errors exposed a "huge problem" with the forensic science work being done for the Department of Criminal Justice Services.

Gestring said that the falsified certification document involved the investigation of John Bittrolff, imprisoned for the murder of the two prostitutes, referring to Rita Tangredi and Colleen McNamee.

 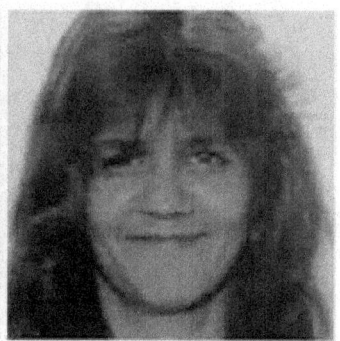

Colleen McNamee   **Rita Tangredi**

The three bodies were found within a 13-week time frame. The distance between Rita's and Colleen's body was about 8 miles apart; the approximate distance between their bodies and Sandra Costilla's body was approximately 32 miles.

To compound matters by adding fuel to the proverbial fire, two police officers were initially suspects when woodchips and/or shavings were found in one of their police vehicles. Wood shavings had been found in Sergeant Michael Murphy's police vehicle.

Sergeant Michael Murphy

During John Bittrolff's murder trial, the prosecution based its case on science and the use of DNA in its infancy. John Bittrolff's semen had been found on the Manorville's victims' bodies. Defense attorney William (Billy) Keahon based Bittrolff's case on the accusation of police corruption; that is, the destroying of evidence that would have likely implicated the two police officers in the murders of Colleen McNamee and Rita Tangredi.

Suffolk County Police Sergeant Michael Murphy of the Fifth Precinct had been a suspect since 1998, along with another police officer, Teddy Hart, in the double murder of Colleen McNamee of Holbrook, and Rita Tangredi of East Patchogue.

There were no crime scene photographs of woodchips or shavings found on Colleen McNamee and Rita Tangredi's body, nor the woodchips/shavings taken from suspect Sergeant Michael Murphy's police vehicle — as there should have been. The evidence had been destroyed. Officer Teddy Hart was later fired for making threats of violence toward women. Sergeant Michael Murphy [son of Thomas Murphy, department's chief of detectives at the time] was promoted to lieutenant. Sound familiar?

The Suffolk County Police Department destroyed the evidence in both those murder cases. The department also destroyed evidence that might have linked its then sergeant to both murders. The excuse for its destruction was that the evidence had not been properly identified as homicide evidence. This was testified to by Officer Linda Passarella, a 13-year veteran of the department's property bureau, during the murder trial of John Bittrolff.

Collectively, all these facts should certainly raise red flags. To begin to erase doubt from the minds of skeptics, it might prove prudent for District Attorney Ray Tierney to grant Deputy Bureau Chief Lisa Marcoccia her requests to have the D.A.'s forensic team perform mitochondrial DNA testing that was used to charge Rex Heuermann on the previously *untested hairs* found at the Rita Tangredi and Colleen McNamee crime scenes. Imagine if in so doing, those hairs were a match to Rex Heuermann or a family member as was the case in seven of the murders, thus far, for which Rex Heuermann has been indicted.

Is an innocent man, John Bittrolff, sitting in prison for another's murderous crime?

CHAPTER TWENTY-THREE

A discussion referencing the Gilgo Beach/Oak Beach matter was given by attorney John Ray and his legal assistant Lena Ajit via a podcast with Nick Bryan, titled "The Secrets of the Long Island Serial Killings," aired September 21, 2024, running just under 1½ hours. A second discussion was a 2-hour town hall presentation with John Ray, held at the Center Moriches Library, titled "The Gilgo Beach/Long Island Serial Killer," posted on October 1, 2024 via YouTube's *True Crime* Long Island channel:

Startling new information had come to light regarding Shannan Gilbert and a sex ring of surrounding players. It was learned that Shannan was a *high-end* sex worker commanding thousands of dollars per session, not a reported $300 for a 2- or 3-hour tryst referencing her rendezvous with client Joseph Brewer on the night of May 1, 2010.

Attorney John Ray, in his investigation, initially never understood why Shannan Gilbert and her driver Michael Pak would drive all the way from Jersey City to Oak Beach, Long Island (a round trip of 109.4 miles, which would normally take 3½ hours – 2 hours during off hours) for a paltry $300, of which Pak would receive a portion. It made absolutely no sense to John Ray.

Subsequent research by John Ray's legal assistant, Lena Ajit (a consummate investigator and computer expert) had revealed that a man by the name of Joseph Ruis operated a high-end 24/7 sex ring in the tri-state area, of which Shannan Gilbert was a part. Ray states that Shannan made a recorded $2,500 to $5,000 per session. Lena goes on to explain that back in 2009, Ruis was arrested for having operated a network named Lace Party Girls, a website which has a complete listing of women that the agency still offers its services. Ruis was also charged with running a cocaine ring.

Shannan Gilbert was under federal indictment the night she disappeared from Joseph Brewer's home. Shannan knew she was facing serious prison time. Joseph Ruis knew this, too. Had Shannan suddenly become a liability? What happened to the sum of money?

Lena Agit explained that "Shannan had a standing indictment as a co-defendant in the Ruis/First Professional Referral Services/World Class Party Girls case and was due in court a week or so after she disappeared on May 1, 2010." Michael Pak, too, worked for Joseph Ruis as his enforcer but was not charged in the indictment.

Interestingly, on May 1, 2010, the night that just happens to coincide with Walpurgisnacht ~ Walpurgis Night — the eve of May Day on which witches are held to ride to an appointed rendezvous — Shannan first receives a phone call in Jersey City at 12 o'clock midnight and makes the 2-hour trip with Michael Pak out to Joseph Brewer's residence on Long Island, from which Shannan flees in sheer fright. And it is somewhere around this time that things turn truly bizarre. Note that Shannan's mother, Mari, had a fascination for and was deeply involved with witchcraft. There may be the presence of a cult organization lurking in the background to help explain this mystique.

Mari had devoted herself to the practice of witchcraft (synonymous with black magic) for a period of 22 years before one of her four daughters, Sarra, murdered her mother with a knife, stabbing the 52-year-old woman repeatedly.

It is first necessary to make an important distinction between witchcraft and another practice. Voodoo. Voodoo is a religion. Witchcraft is about the craft itself, made more complicated by the distinction between black magic and its witches. Black witches signify the *evil* aspect of witchcraft, while white witches signify the *good* qualities.

Mari Gilbert lived in Ellenville, New York and attended witchcraft meetings in Middletown, 27 miles from her home, a convenient 32-minute drive. Mari was a self-proclaimed witch. Controversy surrounds whether she was a good witch or an evil witch. In any event, Sarra first beat her mother with a fire extinguisher then tried to drown her before stabbing her 227 times . . . Sarra's violence perhaps stemming from the times when Mari's boyfriend sexually abused Sarra as a child, resulting in more than one abortion.

Enough said.

What had gone on inside Joseph Brewer's home with Shannan Gilbert and Michael Pak that evening? What exactly transpired to prompt Shannan to make the 911 call? Following Detective Lieutenant Kevin Beyer's narration of the 911 tape, he makes no mention of the heated conversation between Gus Colletti and Michael Pak in the street outside Coletti's home during that early morning hour. It was about 5 a.m. This time, Gus Coletti had jotted down the license plate of the black SUV and went down his walkway to confront the driver:

"What are you doing here?" Gus barked.

"I'm looking for a young lady," the middle-aged Asian man with a head of dark black hair answered. "We were having a party, and she got up and left, so I'm trying to bring her back."

"You're not going anywhere, pal," Gus declared. "I've already called the police, and they're on their way here."

"You really shouldn't have called the police," the driver replied. "She's going to be in big trouble."

"So will you if you don't stay right here," Gus challenged.

At that moment, Shannan bolted out from beneath Gus Coletti's elevated boat that was parked on his lawn and where she had been hiding before running off, clearly terrified. Michael Pak sped off after her in his SUV. That was the last report of anyone seeing Shannan alive.

Is Michael Pak in someway connected to Shannan Gilbert's disappearance during that early morning hour? Did Pak finally catch up with Shannan in his SUV after having words with Gus Coletti? There are questions that need to be thoroughly investigated by the proper authorities, for things are obviously hidden in secrecy.

The criminal history relating to Michael Pak is sketchy. In 2009, Pak had been arrested in California on a felony charge for human trafficking, also for immigration and passport related offenses. He was sentenced to six months in federal prison, two years supervised release, and paid a $3,000 fine.

Back to Rex Heuermann:

Attorney John Ray states that he has several witnesses who claim they have had encounters with Rex Heuermann: one in Virginia, one in Florida, one in South Carolina, one in Philadelphia, one in New Jersey, one in upstate New York, one in Manhattan, and one in the borough of Queens, who now lives in Oklahoma. Ray has other witnesses as well.

Lena Agit points out it is interesting to note that Heuermann had apartments and other residences in his name in several places besides his office in Manhattan, home on Long Island, a time-share in Las Vagas, and property in Chester, South Carolina: Namely, North Carolina; Atlanta, Georgia; Smyrna, Georgia; Anchorage, Alaska; North Redding, Massachusetts; and, very interestingly, West Warwick, Rhode Island. If you recall, Warwick, Rhode Island is where Heather Malone (maiden name Volino), former wife of Guy Malone, worked as a procurer and call girl for Jimmy Burke before she disappeared to Warwick, using many aliases. It was business as usual.

You will recall, too, that Jimmy Burke was initially arrested as part of an undercover sting operation at the Suffolk County Vietnam Veterans Memorial Park in Farmingville, Long Island. The Suffolk County Park Rangers' Targeted Response Unit had taken Jimmy into custody for soliciting a male operative for a sexual encounter. What is of particular interest as Lena goes on to further explain is that the vehicle in which Jimmy was riding in the park had Rhode Island license plates.

Next, John Ray expanded on areas where Rex Heuermann secured hunting licenses, particularly in Anchorage, Alaska. Interestingly, Rex Heuermann's wife's half sister, Johanna Ellerup, claimed she did not know anything about what went on at the Heuermann household, including that she had no idea where her sister lived when in fact Asa Ellerup lived just five minutes away from Johanna. Additionally, we learn that Johanna is deeply involved in the study and practice of witchcraft. Sound familiar? Johanna's other areas of interest include cannibalism and human sacrifice. Johanna, a licensed pharmacist, kept apartments in Anchorage and Fairbanks, Alaska.

A 2024 murder trial in Anchorage involved Brian Steven Smith, convicted of killing two women in separate instances. Veronica Abouchuk and Kathleen Jo Henry. Smith was in to torturing women and making snuff films. He tortured, filmed, and murdered Veronica and Kathleen. Smith lived a five-minute drive from Johanna's residence.

American serial killer Robert Hansen, known as the Butcher Baker, was active in Anchorage, Alaska between 1972 and 1983. The similarities between Hansen and Heuermann are intriguing in that they were both hunters of women. Hansen literally hunted young women with a rifle after giving them a running head start, much like Richard Connell's character in his short story *The Most Dangerous Game.*

Johanna Ellerup has a few additional interests referencing the occult; namely, druidism (religion of the Druids — members of a pre-Christian religious order of the ancient Celts); esotericism (a form of black magic understood by only a few); Gnosticism (a group of ancient heresies stressing the escape from this world through the acquisition of esoteric knowledge, i.e., the spirit is *good*, but matter, including the physical body, is *evil*. Gnostics believe that we need to be delivered (freed) from the physical world before we can become truly spiritual; wiccan texts (books describing a form of modern paganism). Johanna Ellerup identifies herself as a Gnostic Christian, claiming to possess a secret knowledge about the nature of the universe.

The unconventional interests among several players we have been examining thus far, either prurient in nature or violently sadistic in scope, is often quite difficult to wrap one's head around.

A claim made by John Ray is that the timeline of events leading up to Shannan Gilbert's 911 tape is flawed, "a complete distortion," Ray states, skewed by the police having us believe that Shannan was *inside* Joseph Brewer's residence from the moment she arrived at Brewer's home and for several hours *before* refusing to leave his house. We are told that Brewer then got Michael Pak to help him forcibly remove Shannan from his house. John Ray asks us to consider that the opposite is true, that Shannan was initially involved in some sort of nefarious activity *outside* Joseph Brewer's home when she first arrived that evening, *before* seeking refuge *inside* his home. Ray is more that subtly suggesting that Shannan was engaged in some sort of cultish ceremony, temporarily escaping before making her 911 call.

Ray, who has listened to the 911 tapes many times, having subsequently obtained an exceedingly enhanced copy of the recordings through J. J. M. Cold Case Consulting, was able to decipher a number of sections that were previously unintelligible. For example, at 07:00. Shannan says, "I'm never gonna . . . again." At 07:17 Shannan says, "I never do. I never did." Those two phrases remain an enigma in that we do not know to what Shannan is referring. See those specified times listed accordingly in the following chapter.

CHAPTER TWENTY-FOUR

The following is an enhanced 911 phone call placed by Shannan Gilbert. It was split in two separate files by the providing agency, J.J.M., a consulting agency. The first recording lasted 01:24 minutes; the second recording ending at 21:06. For purpose of clarity, these two separate files have been combined into one file, lasting 22:40 minutes in duration, using a pre-existing overlap point between the two files for accuracy.

As stated earlier, this significantly enhanced 911 recording, which John Ray later acquired from J.J.M. Cold Case Consulting agency, far exceeds in both quality and content, Suffolk County Police Department's copy of a copy by a considerable 3,639 words. Therefore, Shannan's updated call is included here.

J.J.M. — consulting agency

COLD CASE CONSULTING

DATE OF RECORDING: May 1, 2010

TIME OF RECORDING: 4:51:55 a.m. EDT

LOCATION OF CALLER: Oak Beach, New York

IDENTIFIED PARTICIPANTS:

• Shannan Gilbert

• Joseph Brewer

• Michael Pak

• Gustav Coletti

00:00 – 911 OPERATOR: (begins in middle of sentence) …09, how can I assist you?

00:02 – (crosstalk from dispatch line)

00:03 – SHANNAN: (UNINTELLIGIBLE, Shannan sounds far from phone)

00:04 – 911 OPERATOR: Hello?

00:05 – SHANNAN: (UNINTELLIGIBLE, Shannan sounds far from phone)

00:07 – 911 OPERATOR: Hello?

00:10 - 911 OPERATOR: Hello? You're dialed into the 911 system. How can I assist you?

00:15 – SHANNAN: (to someone in the room with her) Why?

00:17 – MALE VOICE: (UNINTELLIGIBLE; cut off by dispatcher)

00:17 - 911 OPERATOR: Hello?

00:18 – SHANNAN: No.

00:20 - 911 OPERATOR: Do you need the police?

00:21 - SHANNAN: Yeah.

00:22 - 911 OPERATOR: Where?

00:24 – (sounds of 911 operator typing on a computer keyboard)

00:25 - SHANNAN: (UNINTELLIGIBLE)

00:27 - 911 OPERATOR: Where?

00:29 - SHANNAN: (UNINTELLIGIBLE; sounds like "You'd better take two" or "You'd better have two")

00:31 - 911 OPERATOR: Who's there with you?

00:34 - SHANNAN: Um…

00:36 – (Unintelligible ruffling noises from Shannan's line; sounds like someone shifting on a bed with springs.)

00:38 - 911 OPERATOR: Hello?

00:40 - SHANNAN: Yeah?

00:41 - 911 OPERATOR: What's going on?

00:44 - SHANNAN: (UNINTELLIGIBLE word) …there's somebody after me.

00:47 - 911 OPERATOR: What?

00:49 - SHANNAN: Somebody after me.

00:51 - 911 OPERATOR: Somebody is harassing you?

00:53 - SHANNAN: After me.

00:54 - BREWER: There's nobody after you. Come on, stop it.

00:54 – 911 OPERATOR: Who?

00:57 - SHANNAN: Can you trace where I am?

00:58 - BREWER: Your driver's out there. Your driver's right there.

01:00 - 911 OPERATOR: Let me talk to him.

01:03 - SHANNAN: Can you trace where I am?

01:06 - 911 OPERATOR: Let me talk to him.

01:07 - SHANNAN: I'm at the Jones Beach.

01:11 - 911 OPERATOR: You're at Jones Beach?

01:13 - SHANNAN: By the Jones Beach.

01:15 - 911 OPERATOR: All right, let me connect you to State Police. Stay on the line.

01:19 – 911 OPERATOR: (click)

01:20 - SHANNAN: (to someone in the room with her) Why?

01:20 – 911 OPERATOR: (dial tone; sounds of a number being autodialed)

01:27 – 911 OPERATOR: (phone ringing)

01:27 - SHANNAN: (to someone in the room with her) Why?

01:28 - 911 OPERATOR: You gotta talk louder to them.

01:30 - SHANNAN: (to someone in the room with her) Why?

01:31 – MALE VOICE: (UNINTELLIGIBLE; cut off by Shannan)

01:31 – SHANNAN: WHY?!

01:32 – 911 OPERATOR: (phone ringing)

01:34 - DISPATCHER: (click) State Police, Trooper... (UNINTELLIGIBLE; sounds like "Frye")

01:36 – MALE VOICE: (UNINTELLIGIBLE)

01:38 - DISPATCHER: State Police.

01:39 - SHANNAN: Yeah, there's somebody after me.

01:41 – (Unintelligible male voice continues in background, likely Joseph Brewer. The voice is speaking in a low, measured tone.)

01:42 - DISPATCHER: I'm sorry?

01:43 - SHANNAN: There's somebody after me.

01:44 - DISPATCHER: Where are you?

01:46 - SHANNAN: There's somebody after me.

01:48 - DISPATCHER: Okay, where are you?

01:52 - (Unintelligible male voice continues in background, likely Joseph Brewer. The voice is speaking in a low, measured tone.)

01:53 - SHANNAN: There's somebody after me.

01:55 - DISPATCHER: Where are you, ma'am?

01:56 - SHANNAN: I don't know. (adjusts phone)

01:58 - DISPATCHER: You're driving right now?

02:00 - SHANNAN: No, I'm inside a house.

02:01 - (Unintelligible male voice continues in background, likely Joseph Brewer. The voice is speaking in a low, measured tone.)

02:02 - DISPATCHER: I'm sorry?

02:03 - SHANNAN: I'm inside a house.

02:05 - DISPATCHER: What house?

02:06 - SHANNAN: I don't know. Can you trace where I am?

02:08 - DISPATCHER: I'm sorry?

02:09 - SHANNAN: Can you trace where I am?

02:12 - DISPATCHER: (Annoyed) No, I can't. What's your callback number you're calling from?

02:15 – BREWER: (UNINTELLIGIBLE)

02:16 - SHANNAN: Huh?

02:17 - DISPATCHER: What phone number are you calling from?

02:18 – (Unintelligible male voice continues in background, likely Joseph Brewer. The voice is now speaking in a more deliberate tone at a fast pace. It is likely that Michael Pak has just entered the home.)

02:22 - SHANNAN: Somebody's after me.

02:24 – SHANNAN: Please!

02:24 - DISPATCHER: Are you in Suffolk County or Nassau County?

02:28 - SHANNAN: Um, I'm in Long Island.

02:29 - DISPATCHER: Where on Long Island are you?

02:32 - BREWER: Yeah, he wants to talk to you. This guy wants to talk to you.

02:35 - SHANNAN: No.

02:36 - BREWER: You gotta talk to him.

02:38 - SHANNAN: No!

02:39 - BREWER (UNINTELLIGIBLE; sounds like "You have a freakin' problem, I think.")

02:44- SHANNAN: No.

02:45 – BREWER: You have to.

02:46 - SHANNAN: No, stop, no!

02:48 - PAK: Shannan, come on.

02:51 - DISPATCHER: Where in Long Island are you? You in Suffolk County? Nassau County?

02:54 – BREWER: (UNINTELLIGIBLE)

02:57 - SHANNAN: Huh?

02:58 - BREWER: Fuck off.

03:01 - BREWER: (UNINTELLIGIBLE; sounds like "Quick.")

03:02 – (heavy click sound; sounds like a dead bolt unlocking)

03:03 - SHANNAN: Why?

03:04 - BREWER: 'cause we've had it.

03:05 - PAK: All right, let's go. Shannan.

03:07 - (heavy click sound; sounds like a dead bolt unlocking)

03:08 - SHANNAN: Why are you calling me by my name?

03:11 - PAK: I gotta.

03:12 - SHANNAN: Why?

03:13 - BREWER: (UNINTELLIGIBLE; sounds like "It builds character.")

03:14 - PAK: Yeah.

03:14 - DISPATCHER: County, you on the line?

03:15 - SHANNAN: Stop!

03:16 - BREWER: All right, time to go.

03:17 - SHANNAN: Please. Stop it, please.

03:19 - BREWER: Pay attention.

03:21 - SHANNAN: Please stop!

03:22 - PAK: (chuckle)

03:22 - BREWER: (UNINTELLIGIBLE)

03:25 - SHANNAN: Please. Can you shut the door?

03:27 - BREWER: No, time to go!

03:28 - SHANNAN: Please.

03:29 – BREWER: (UNINTELLIGIBLE; sounds like "You're okay" or "You're good."

03:31 - SHANNAN: Please.

03:32 - BREWER: Please, out the door.

03:33 - SHANNAN: Please!

03:34 – (sounds of a door being rattled)

03:36 - BREWER: Go that way, please?

03:37 - PAK: (UNINTELLIGIBLE)

03:38 – PAK: Go, come on; let's go.

03:39 - BREWER: C'mon, let's go. C'mon, we're all going outside. Let's go outside.

03:41 - PAK: Yeah, let's go outside.

03:42 – C'mon, go outside. All of us.

03:43 – (sound of sliding door opening, possibly the door to the Brewer patio deck.)

03:44 - BREWER: C'mon, all of us. C'mon. We're all going outside. C'mon.

03:47 - SHANNAN: No, please.

03:48 – PAK: (UNINTELLIGIBLE)

03:50 - BREWER: We're all going. C'mon. Please, c'mon.

03:53 - SHANNAN: Please.

03:54 – (sounds of a door unlatching/unlocking)

03:54 – BREWER: Come on!

03:56 – PAK – (UNINTELLIGIBLE; cut off by Shannan)

03:56 - SHANNAN: Why?!

03:57 - BREWER: Just come out here. I wanna show you something; come here.

04:00 - SHANNAN: Why?!

04:01 - BREWER: You won't even know where that's at.

04:03 - DISPATCHER: County, are you on the line?

04:06 - BREWER: Come on!

04:07 – BREWER: Hurry up, I wanna show you something.

04:09 - SHANNAN: Why?!

04:09 - BREWER: I wanna show you this. Can you please just go look with me?

04:12 – BREWER: Please?

04:13 - SHANNAN: Why?!

04:14 - BREWER: Now look…

04:15 - SHANNAN: Why are you guys doing this to me?

04:16 - BREWER: What?

04:18 - SHANNAN: Doing this.

04:19 - DISPATCHER: What county you in, ma'am?

04:20 - BREWER: (UNINTELLIGIBLE)

04:21 - SHANNAN: Doing this!

04:22 - PAK: Hang up!

04:23 - SHANNAN: Why are you calling me by my name?

04:25 – MALE VOICE: (UNINTELLIGIBLE, chuckling)

04:28 – BREWER: (UNINTELLIGIBLE)

04:30 - BREWER: Please come here.

04:30 - SHANNAN: Please…

04:31 – BREWER: Please, give it to me here.

04:31 - SHANNAN: No, please.

04:32 – BREWER: Give it here.

04:32 – SHANNAN: No.

04:33 – BREWER: Please?

04:33 – SHANNAN: No, stop it, please.

04:35 – (a loud struggle for Shannan's phone is heard)

04:35 – SHANNAN: Stop it, please!

04:36 – BREWER: Time to go, (UNINTELLIGIBLE)

04:38 – SHANNAN: Please, stop it! Please stop it, no! Please, stop it!

04:44 - SHANNAN: Please, stop it, no!

04:45 - BREWER: All right, let me fix that. Let me fix that, please?

04:47 - SHANNAN: (hysterical) Please stop it, no! No, stop it, please! Please stop it! Please! No, what does that do to me?! What are you gonna do to me? Stop it!

04:56 - BREWER: (UNINTELLIGIBLE) Get her outta here!

04:58 – (struggling sounds cease at this approximate moment) 04:59 – (The sounds of Shannan running through the Brewer residence are heard. These sounds seem to indicate Shannan is wearing sandals/flip-flops and is running on a hardwood or linoleum floor. Male voices are heard in the background during this time.)

05:07 – PAK: Come on, we're trying to talk to you.

05:10 - DISPATCHER: (muffled) Ma'am?

[Note: At this point, the 911 side of Shannan's call becomes very muffled, possibly due to the dispatcher putting her hand over her microphone to speak with someone else at the center.]

05:11 - DISPATCHER: (muffled conversation over Brewer.)

05:12 - BREWER: (UNINTELLIGIBLE) I'll go upstairs. I'll go upstairs.

(UNINTELLIGIBLE) Look, I'm gonna go upstairs. 'kay? (UNINTELLIGIBLE) Take care.

05:23 - PAK: [amused](UNINTELLIGIBLE) What's the matter? Are you okay? (laughs)

05:28 - SHANNAN: What are you gonna do?

05:29 - PAK: You look a little bit hungover.

05:30 - SHANNAN: What are you gonna do to me?

05:32 - DISPATCHER: (UNINTELLIGIBLE)

05:37 - SHANNAN: Why?

05:38 - DISPATCHER: Huh?

05:38 - PAK: ...you don't give up...

05:40 - DISPATCHER: Well, I don't know; that didn't sound... (UNINTELLIGIBLE)

05:42 - SHANNAN: Why? What are you gonna do? You gonna kill me?

05:45 – PAK: (UNINTELLIGIBLE)

05:47 - DISPATCHER: (UNINTELLIGIBLE) I think it's Suffolk County...

05:47 - PAK: C'mon! (UNINTELLIGIBLE) You gonna kill me?!

 C'mon! (UNINTELLIGIBLE)

05:52 - PAK & DISPATCHER: (UNINTELLIGIBLE)

05:53 - SHANNAN: ...kill me?

05:54 - PAK: (laughing) No!

05:55 - SHANNAN: Why are you...?

05:56 - PAK & DISPATCHER: (UNINTELLIGIBLE)

05:58 - SHANNAN: Are you serious?

05:59 - PAK: C'mon! (laughs) You're freaking me out, c'mon.

06:01 - SHANNAN: Out in the middle of nowhere?

06:03 - PAK: Let's go back to, hold on, let's go back to Manhattan. All right? We're in Long Island. We're out near the water, the ocean.

06:10 - SHANNAN: Please, stop.

06:12 – BREWER: (UNINTELLIGIBLE; cut off by Pak)

06:13 - PAK: It's me - Mike! (UNINTELLIGIBLE; sounds like "You called the police, right?")

06:16 - SHANNAN: No, stop it, please.

06:17 - PAK: [frustrated] Oh, okay; fine, fine! All right.

06:21 - SHANNAN: Please, be my... (UNINTELLIGIBLE) ...you guys!

06:22 - DISPATCHER: (UNINTELLIGIBLE) ...on the water...

06:24 - SHANNAN: You guys...

06:25 - DISPATCHER: (UNINTELLIGIBLE)

06:26 – SHANNAN: I didn't do anything; I didn't do anything!

06:30 - DISPATCHER: (UNINTELLIGIBLE; answering a question from someone else in the center) ...631.

911...

06:31 - SHANNAN: God!

06:33 – (loud muffled interference)

06:36 – DISPATCHER: (UNINTELLIGIBLE, muffled)

06:40 – PAK: (UNINTELLIGIBLE)

06:42 - SHANNAN - Mike, do you feel that?

06:47 – PAK: (UNINTELLIGIBLE)

06:48 - DISPATCHER: Somebody named Mike is there.

06:50 - SHANNAN: Mike, why? Why?

06:51 – (interference noise ends)

06:54 - PAK: (UNINTELLIGIBLE)

06:56 - SHANNAN: Why?

06:57 - PAK: (UNINTELLIGIBLE)

06:58 – (interference noise returns)

07:01 - SHANNAN: Why, Mike?

07:03 - PAK: (UNINTELLIGIBLE)

07:06 - SHANNAN: For fun?

07:07 - PAK: (UNINTELLIGIBLE)

07:09 - SHANNAN: For me?

07:10 - SHANNAN: I'm never gonna… (UNINTELLIGIBLE) …again.

07:13 - PAK: (UNINTELLIGIBLE)

07:15 - SHANNAN: Why?

07:15 - PAK: You always do.

07:17 - SHANNAN: I never do, I never did.

07:18 – (interference noise ends)

07:19 – DISPATCHER: (UNINTELLIGIBLE, muffled)

07:20 – PAK: Yes, you did… (UNINTELLIGIBLE)

[**Note:** At this point, muffled conversations between at least one male voice and another party can be heard in the background. Due to Shannan's phone line not existing on a separate audio track in the provided recording, we cannot confirm whether these voices are emanating from another group of people inside the Brewer residence or inside the dispatch center.]

07:25 - SHANNAN: Mike, please.

07:27 – DEEP MALE VOICE: If you don't talk to her… [**NOTE:** Inconclusive if this is Brewer or a voice in the background of the dispatch center, but it does not appear to be Pak's.]

07:29 - SHANNAN: Mike, please.

07:31 – (UNINTELLIGIBLE male voice[s] in the background)

07:35 - SHANNAN: Please.

07:35 – PAK: Let's go! Let's go! C'mon!

07:37 - SHANNAN: Please.

07:38 - (UNINTELLIGIBLE male voice[s] in the background)

07:39 - PAK: (laughs) What? (UNINTELLIGIBLE)

07:45 - DISPATCHER: (UNINTELLIGIBLE) …I don't know what phone she's calling from, but…

07:49 - SHANNAN: You're gonna kill me…

07:49 - DISPATCHER: (UNINTELLIGIBLE) …coming from?

07:52 - (UNINTELLIGIBLE female voice in the background of the dispatch center)

07:54 - PAK: (UNINTELLIGIBLE) …gonna kill you.

07:56 - FEMALE VOICE IN DISPATCH: They're at a house somewhere.

07:58 - DISPATCHER: She needs help.

07:59 - PAK: That was when you were like, you know, "I gonna find my own way home."

08:02 - SHANNAN: (UNINTELLIGIBLE; asks a question that sounds like "Are you kidding me?", "Now you see me?" or "This is how you see me?")

08:02 - DISPATCHER: (UNINTELLIGIBLE) …in the house with the female. The female was the initial caller.

08:08 - PAK: (UNINTELLIGIBLE) …more dramatic, you know you hang up on me.

08:11 - SHANNAN: So, this was all set up?

08:13 - PAK: (confused) Oh, you… You set everything up?

08:17 - PAK: What are you talking about? I waited for you! You told me you were gonna find your own way home… (UNINTELLIGIBLE). You hung up and then I…

08:22 - SHANNAN: (interrupting) So, this was all set up?

08:26 - (UNINTELLIGIBLE female voice in the background of the dispatch center)

08:28 - PAK: You'd never do this before.

08:33 - SHANNAN: Was it all set up?

08:35 - PAK: Oh, you're joking with me, right?

08:38 - SHANNAN: Why?

08:39 - PAK: (laughing) I don't know. Why are you doing that?

08:42 - (UNINTELLIGIBLE female voice in the background of the dispatch center)

08:45 - SHANNAN: All right, I'll say I was lying. I was lying.

08:49 - PAK: I know.

08:50 - DISPATCHER: (muffled; to someone in dispatch center) It did?

08:51 - SHANNAN: Why?

08:53 - DISPATCHER: But it's a 631 number.

08:55 - SHANNAN: Why?

08:52 - DISPATCHER 2: Call 'em back. [**NOTE**: This is the first clear instance of the second dispatcher who eventually tries speaking with Shannan on the recording.]

09:02 – (the dispatcher line becomes unmuffled.)

09:03 - DISPATCHER 1: You can try talking to her, but she's not…

09:04 - SHANNAN: Please…

09:05 - DISPATCHER 1: I think she's got the phone down.

09:06 - SHANNAN: Please…

09:07 - DISPATCHER 2: Hello?!

[**NOTE:** This second dispatcher is very loudly breathing into the microphone, making transcription difficult.]

09:08 - PAK: (UNINTELLIGIBLE)

09:11 - SHANNAN: (UNINTELLIGIBLE)

09:13 - DISPATCHER 2: Hello?

09:14 - SHANNAN: Please…

09:16 - DISPATCHER 2: What's - what's the prob — what's the matter? What happened?

09:19 - (UNINTELLIGIBLE male voice[s] in background)

09:20 - DISPATCHER 2: Hello?

09:21 – PAK: (UNINTELLIGIBLE)

09:22 - SHANNAN: Please, get me out of here, Mike.

09:26 - PAK: (UNINTELLIGIBLE)

09:30 - DISPATCHER 2: Hello?

09:31 - SHANNAN: You're being sarcastic.

09:32 - PAK: About what?

09:34 - SHANNAN: About this. You were a part of this all along.

09:37 - PAK: (agitated) What are you talking about? I just met him just now.

09:40 - PAK: (UNINTELLIGIBLE; during this, the second dispatcher's loud breathing is prevalent, along with a background conversation between two or more people. The location of this conversation cannot be definitively determined now that the dispatcher's line is unmuffled.)

09:58 - SHANNAN: Mike…

10:00 – SHANNAN: Mike, please…

10:02 - SHANNAN: (UNINTELLIGIBLE); sounds like "I know who you are" or "I know what you want.")

10:04 - PAK: (UNINTELLIGIBLE) What do you want me to do?

10:06 - (UNINTELLIGIBLE male voice[s] in the background)

10:08 - SHANNAN: I just want to go home.

10:09 - PAK: Let's go.

10:13 - PAK: (UNINTELLIGIBLE)

10:17 - SHANNAN: (UNINTELLIGIBLE) Why?

10:18 - DISPATCHER 2: Well, we can give them…

10:20 - PAK: (UNINTELLIGIBLE)

10:23 – (UNINTELLIGIBLE female voice; cannot definitively determine if it is Shannan or Dispatcher 1.)

10:24 - DISPATCHER 2: (reading) 5 7 3 9 3 0 8]

10:28 - SHANNAN: Mike…

10:29 - DISPATCHER 1: Is that us?

10:29 - SHANNAN: What's going on?

10:32 - DISPATCHER 2: I think so.

10:33 - PAK: Did you ever see that movie with Johnny Depp?

10:35 - SHANNAN: What?

10:36 - PAK: "Fear and Loathing in Las Vegas."

10:37 - SHANNAN: Yeah.

10:37 – DISPATCHER 1: Extension eastern…

10:39 - PAK: You're acting like that movie, right, dude? (laughs)

10:41 – DISPATCHER 1: That's the number that came in.

10:42 - SHANNAN: Why are you sitting there like you're . . . (UNINTELLIGIBLE)? [Sounds like "Why are you sitting there like you're not responsible?"]

10:44 - PAK: (UNINTELLIGIBLE)

10:45 - DISPATCHER 2: Mhmm.

10:46 - DISPATCHER 1: Should I call it anyway?

10:48 - SHANNAN: Something's gonna happen to me.

10:50 - PAK: There's nobody outside!

10:53 - DISPATCHER 2: Yeah, you could call it…

10:54 - PAK: You're okay, right?

10:55 - DISPATCHER 2: ...but we're not gonna know where it is.

10:57 - PAK: ...Literal...

10:58 - DISPATCHER 2: County should call it.

10:59 - PAK: (UNINTELLIGIBLE)

11:02 - SHANNAN: Mike...

11:02 - DISPATCHER 1: (UNINTELLIGIBLE) ...county phone number?

11:04 - SHANNAN: Please...

11:05 - PAK: Shannan, come on. Let's go.

11:05 - DISPATCHER 1: (UNINTELLIGIBLE)

11:07 - SHANNAN: (UNINTELLIGIBLE) ...do this to me?

11:09 - PAK: Okay, okay, fine... Get out of here. What's with the phone?

11:12 - DISPATCHER 2: Oh, it does?

11:13 - DISPATCHER 1: Yeah.

11:17 - DISPATCHER 2: (UNINTELLIGIBLE) ...Suffolk? It's gotta be Suffolk, right?

11:20 - PAK: (UNINTELLIGIBLE)

11:23 - DISPATCHER 2: Hello?

11:23 - SHANNAN: Stop it. Stop it, Mike.

11:26 - DISPATCHER 2: Hello, where are you?

11:28 - SHANNAN: Huh?

11:29 - DISPATCHER 1: In a house on Long Island.

11:30 - DISPATCHER 2: Where are you?

11:33 - PAK: What is going on there?

11:34 – DISPATCHER 1: What's her name?

11:34 - SHANNAN: (UNINTELLIGIBLE)

11:35 - PAK: And where's the bathroom? (UNINTELLIGIBLE)

11:38 - DISPATCHER 2: What's your name?

11:39 - SHANNAN: Shannan Gilbert.

11:41 - PAK: (chuckles) God, who are you calling?

11:43 - DISPATCHER 2: What's your name?

11:44 - SHANNAN: Shannan Gilbert.

11:46 - DISPATCHER 2: Where are you?

11:49 - SHANNAN: I'm right um… I'm in Long Island.

11:53 - DISPATCHER 1: And Mike's there… (UNINTELLIGIBLE)

11:56 - DISPATCHER 2: And what's — what's wrong?

11:58 - SHANNAN: Huh?

11:59 - DISPATCHER 2: What happened?

12:01 - SHANNAN: These people are trying to kill me.

12:01 - PAK: Shut up. (laughs)

12:04 - DISPATCHER 2: Where are you? What's your address? (heavy breathing)

12:06 – PAK: (UNINTELLIGIBLE)

12:11 - DISPATCHER 2: What's your address? (heavy breathing)

12:15 – SHANNAN: (UNINTELLIGIBLE)

12:16 – PAK: (UNINTELLIGIBLE)

12:17 - DISPATCHER 2: What's your address?

12:18 – PAK: (UNINTELLIGIBLE)

12:19 - SHANNAN: No Mike, Mike stop. Mike no, Mike stop. Mike stop, Mike. Mike stop.

12:26 – PAK: (UNINTELLIGIBLE)

12:27 - DISPATCHER 2: Where are you? (continues to breathe heavily into phone)

12:28 - SHANNAN: Mike, Mike stop it! Mike stop!

12:31 - PAK: (UNINTELLIGIBLE)

12:32 - DISPATCHER 2: What's your name, Shannan?

12:34 – PAK: (UNINTELLIGIBLE)

12:35 - SHANNAN: Huh? Mike, Mike, Stop!

12:38 - PAK: Stop what?

12:38 - SHANNAN: Come here.

12:40 - DISPATCHER 2: Where are you? What's your address?

12:45 - DISPATCHER 2: Hello?

12:46 - PAK: You want me to call the police?

2:48 - SHANNAN: Yeah, call 911 and I want you to tell 'em the truth about this.

12:52 - PAK: What are we gonna tell 'em?

12:54 - SHANNAN: Tell 'em (UNINTELLIGIBLE)

12:57 - PAK: Oh my god… (laughs)

12:59 - SHANNAN: Mike, stop it – you have to file a complaint.

13:02 - PAK: Who?

13:02 - SHANNAN: Mike…

13:03 - DISPATCHER 2: Where are you?

13:05 - SHANNAN: Mike…

13:06 - PAK: (agitated) Oh, fine! Then why were… (UNINTELLIGIBLE)

13:06 – (sounds of a telephone dial tone, along with the dispatcher typing on a computer keyboard)

13:08 - DISPATCHER 2: Are you in a house?

13:10 - SHANNAN: Yeah… Mike, stop it!

13:13 - DISPATCHER 2: What town are you in?

13:15 - SHANNAN: In Long Island – Mike, it…

13:17 - DISPATCHER 2: Where?

13:18 - SHANNAN: Stop, Mike!

13:20 - DISPATCHER 2: Where in Long Island?

13:21 - SHANNAN: Stop it, Mike! Mike, stop it!

13:27 - PAK: Okay, find a ride.

13:28 - SHANNAN: (agitated) Hey, stop it! (shuffling noises)

13:35 - DISPATCHER 2: Where in Long Island are you?

13:40 - SHANNAN: I'm in… (UNINTELLIGIBLE)

13:41 - DISPATCHER 2: Hello?

13:43 – (shuffling noises)

13:47 - SHANNAN: They're gonna kill me.

13:51 - DISPATCHER 2: Where in Long Island are you?

13:53 - SHANNAN: I don't know. They want to kill me.

13:55 - DISPATCHER 2: Are you in a house?

13:57 - (shuffling noises)

13:58 - SHANNAN: Yeah.

14:01 - DISPATCHER 2: Are you in a house?

14:02 - SHANNAN: Yeah.

14:04 - DISPATCHER 2: Whose house is it?

14:06 - SHANNAN: I don't know.

14:09 - DISPATCHER 2: Who is Mike? What's his last name?

14:11 - SHANNAN: Be nice to me… (pleading, possibly to someone other than dispatcher.)

14:13 - DISPATCHER 2: Mike what?

14:14 – (UNINTELLIGIBLE male voice[s] in the background)

14:14 – (shuffling sounds)

14:15 - SHANNAN: (UNINTELLIGIBLE; sounds like "It's me.")

14:18 – SHANNAN: Please, can't you call? (pleading; possibly to someone other than the dispatcher.)

 14:20 – (UNINTELLIGIBLE male voice[s] in the background)

14:20 - DISPATCHER 2: How old are you?

14:21 – (shuffling sounds)

14:22 – (UNINTELLIGIBLE male voice[s] in the background)

14:25 - DISPATCHER 1: Let me…

14:28 - DISPATCHER 2: What's his last name?

14:30 – DISPATCHER 1: (UNINTELLIGIBLE)

14:33 - DISPATCHER 2: What's his last name?

14:35 - (shuffling noises; male voice[s] continue in the background. Shannan is possibly moving around the Brewer house at this point.)

14:41 - DISPATCHER 2: What's his last name?

14:42 - (shuffling noises; male voice[s] continue in the background.)

14:47 - DISPATCHER 2: Shannan?

14:48 - (unknown male voice[s] continue in background.)

14:55 - DISPATCHER 2: Shannan?

14:56 - (unknown male voices continue in background.)

15:02 – (sounds of a door unlatching/opening)

15:10 - DISPATCHER 2: Shannan?

15:11 - (unknown male voice[s] continue in background.)

15:24 - DISPATCHER 2: Shannan?

15:25 - SHANNAN: Yeah? (shuffling noises)

15:27 - DISPATCHER 2: What tow… What town are you in?

15:26 - (unknown male voice[s] continue in background accompanied by shuffling noises.)

15:35 - DISPATCHER 2: Hello?

15:36 - (unknown male voice[s] continue in background accompanied by shuffling noises.)

15:44 - DISPATCHER 2: What's Mike's last name?

15:46 – (unknown male voice[s] continue in background)

15:51 - DISPATCHER 2: Hello?

15:52 – (unknown male voice[s] continue in background)

16:06 - SHANNAN: They're gonna kill me.

16:08 - DISPATCHER 1: One of the guys said, "Let's go back to the city."

16:14 – (unknown male voice[s] continue in background)

16:16 - DISPATCHER 2: Where are you?

16:17 - (unknown male voice[s] continue in background)

16:23 - RADIO IN DISPATCH CENTER: 1034 Farmingdale in service…

16:27 - DISPATCHER 2: Where are you, Shannan?

16:28 – (shuffling sounds)

16:34 - DISPATCHER 2: Shannan?

16:35 - (unknown male voice[s] continue in background accompanied by shuffling noises.)

16:42 - DISPATCHER 2: Shannan?

16:43 - RADIO IN DISPATCH CENTER: (officer talking, unrelated to call.)

16:50 - DISPATCHER 2: Shannan?

16:52 – (Shuffling sounds coming from Shannan's line intensify, along with the sounds of her passing through a doorway outside and running down a wooden deck.) (**NOTE:** At no point do we hear Shannan "stumble" or "fall" and injure herself running down the deck, as has been previously reported/suggested by witnesses.)

16:56 – MALE VOICE: Get in here.

16:58 – (The sounds of Shannan's feet hitting the ground running are heard.)

17:00 – (Three loud sounds are heard in rapid succession, each appearing to be a hand or hands hitting the side panels or hood of a car. Shannan briefly continues running.)

17:03 – (Shannan stops running.)

17:04 - SHANNAN: (SCREAMS)

17:05 - MALE VOICE: No!

17:06 - SHANNAN: (SCREAMS)

17:07 – SHANNAN: SHUT UP! (SCREAMS)

17:08 - (Shannan resumes running.)

(**NOTE**: It is believed that Shannan's earring and jacket came off her body around this time as the result of what appears to be a struggle heard from 17:08 until 17:12, as both items were later found in close proximity to Brewer's deck and driveway.)

17:09 - UNKNOWN VOICE: Shit!

17:10 - (Sounds of Shannan running)

(**NOTE:** At no point from the time Shannan exits Brewer's house at 16:52 until the recording ends at 22:40 do any sounds of a car engine starting or running appear. Neither do any sounds of Michael Pak – or any other person, for that matter - following Shannan in a vehicle or calling out her name, as he has repeatedly insisted to the media and investigators that he had done during this time on the recording since 2010. In addition, neither police dispatcher acknowledges the screaming and apparent struggle that has just occurred.)

17:27 – (Shannan is still running. The sounds of birds chirping appear.)

17:33 - DISPATCHER 2: All right, she's not talking.

17:35 – DISPATCHER 1: I'm gonna put her… (UNINTELLIGIBLE)

17:37 – DISPATCHER 2: You do?

17:39 - DISPATCHER 1: I think this number… (UNINTELLIGIBLE) That's the number she's calling from? (UNINTELLIGIBLE)

17:45 - DISPATCHER 2: I think that... (UNINTELLIGIBLE)

17:51 – DISPATCHER 2: 9 3 0 8 is... (UNINTELLIGIBLE)

17:58 - DISPATCHER 2: Oh - did you call that one?

18:02 – (Shannan stops running at this approximate time; birds chirping loudly are heard in the background.)

18:06 – (All shuffling sounds cease, leading us to believe Shannan has set her phone down at an unknown location on the property she has stopped at – possibly 10 The Fairway or 12 The Fairway.)

18:07 – (An unintelligible conversation with at least one male participant is heard continuously in the background beginning at this point, leading us to believe that at least some of the previous male background voices heard on the tape were coming from the dispatch center, as Shannan is now outside running and these voices have continued.)

18:13 - (the faint sounds of Shannan knocking on a door or a window are heard.)

18:16 - DISPATCHER 1: Shannan?

18:20 - DISPATCHER 1: Hello?

18:22 – (Shannan retrieves her phone and begins running again. The previously mentioned male conversation continues at the same volume while Shannan is running, leading us to conclude its source as being the 911 dispatch center.)

18:27 - (Shannan stops running.)

18:33 – UNKNOWN DISPATCHER: (UNINTELLIGIBLE, muffled)

18:36 – (Shannan is heard knocking loudly on a door. At the same time, a police radio can be heard in the background of the 911 dispatch center along with the muffled and unintelligible sounds of an unknown dispatcher speaking.)

18:40 – UNKNOWN DISPATCHER: (UNINTELLIGIBLE, MUFFLED)

18:41 – (police radio sounds continue loudly within dispatch center.)

18:54 – (Shannan knocks again.)

19:00 - (Shannan begins to run again. She can be heard loudly breathing.)

19:01 – UNKNOWN DISPATCHER: (UNINTELLIGIBLE, muffled)

19:09 – UNKNOWN DISPATCHER: (UNINTELLIGIBLE, muffled)

19:20 - UNKNOWN DISPATCHER: (UNINTELLIGIBLE, muffled)

19:25 - SHANNAN: [startled] (SCREAM)

19:29 - DISPATCHER 1: (UNINTELLIGIBLE, muffled)

19:34 – DISPATCHER 2: Oh, I didn't… (UNINTELLIGIBLE)

19:36 - (Shannan stops running. She is heard loudly breathing.)

19:39 – DISPATCHER 1: What's the shield on the car?

19:42 – UNKNOWN DISPATCHER: 1, 9… (UNINTELLIGIBLE two numbers)

19:47 – (Shannan is heard loudly knocking on a door, most likely 14 The Fairway.)

19:58 - DISPATCHER 1: Shannan?

20:05 - DISPATCHER 1: I wonder if she has the phone in her pocket?

20:10 – (conversations within the 911 dispatch center are heard in the background.)

20:12 – (Shannan begins breathing loudly again.)

20:15 – (Shannan begins running again. The sounds of her moving are much more staggered and erratic this time and are marred by her loud breathing.)

20:42 - DISPATCHER 2: Shannan?

20:47 - DISPATCHER 2: Shannan?

20:50 - (Sounds of Shannan loudly knocking on what sounds like a glass window or the glass window of a door at 17 The Fairway, the home of Gustav Coletti.)

21:00 - DISPATCHER 2: Shannan?

21:05 - (door opens)

21:07 - COLETTI: What's the matter?

(Shannan does not answer.)

21:14 - COLETTI: Who are you?

(Shannan does not answer.)

21:17 – (shuffling sounds, Shannan begins breathing loudly again.)

21:21 - COLETTI: Somebody after you?

(Shannan does not answer, but is heard loudly breathing.)

21:25 - COLETTI: Huh?

(Shannan does not answer, but is heard loudly breathing.)

21:27 - DISPATCHER 2: (annoyed) Hello?

(Shannan does not answer, but is heard loudly breathing.)

21:30 - DISPATCHER 2: Hello?

21:31 - SHANNAN: You…

21:34 – SHANNAN: You… (UNINTELLIGIBLE)

21:36 - COLETTI: Are you all right?

21:37 - SHANNAN: I need help…

21:40 - SHANNAN: (UNINTELLIGIBLE) 21:41 - COLETTI: Don't get yourself hurt. What are you doing?

21:43 - (shuffling sounds, Shannan is still breathing loudly.)

21:48 - COLETTI: Wait a minute. Don't go away. Where are you going?

21:53 - DISPATCHER 1: Something like "Vopert"? V-O-P-E-R-T?

21:55 – (sound of a door closing.)

21:57 - (Shannan begins running again. Various shuffling and wind noises are heard, along with Shannan breathing.)

22:22 – (Shannan's line disconnects.)

22:23 - DISPATCHER 2: Hello?

22:27 - DISPATCHER 2: She didn't spell it, but that's what it sounded like.

22:40 - (beep, CALL ENDS)

Additionally, you can find other Internet searches for sites that have also posted Shannan Gilbert's 911 calls, either in transcript form or voice only. One example is titled "Gilgo Beach Murders: Listen to UNEDITED 911 calls Before Shannan Gilbert's Disappearance," posted by NBC New York on YouTube.

CHAPTER TWENTY-FIVE

Shifting gears to Nathan Adams' True Crime Patreon channel offers an interesting perspective. On September 18, 2024, Adams presented a video titled "Gilgo Beach Investigation Updates." It is a 1-hour 48-minute deep-dive probe into many subjects including the potential victims of Rex Heuermann, based on a plethora of geographical locations to which Heuermann has traveled, covering a span of 30-plus years. I will be focusing primarily on possible victims and their related proximities in accordance with Heuermann's travels. Keep in mind that Heuermann is presently being investigated by authorities for literally hundreds of unsolved murders. Several news outlets have used Nathan Adams' reporting in their own reports. He has worked in conjunction with law enforcement agencies to bring them information from the Gilgo Beach (and beyond) serial killer case that may be relevant to their unsolved homicides. We will begin with Stevie Bates.

Stevie Bates, a 19-year-old female award-winning architect student from Brooklyn, New York went missing in April 2012. "She was making a return trip home, traveling by Greyhound bus from Hot Springs, Arkansas to Manhattan," her mother had explained. On April 28, 2012, surveillance camera footage at Port Authority Bus Terminal shows Stevie coming up the escalator, alone, walking downtown on 8th Avenue from 42nd Street. That was the last time family and friends saw her. On September 18, 2020, eight years later, her skeletal remains were found wrapped in a blanket during an excavation at a construction site at 80-97 Cypress Avenue in Queens, New York — less than a mile from Rex Heuermann's RH Consultants & Associates, Inc., Manhattan office.

Laralee Spear, a 15-year-old freshman was reported missing after she failed to return home from DeLand High School. Approximately 90 minutes later, her body was found behind a home on Deerfoot Road that had burned down a year earlier. Laralee routinely walked home from her bus stop at South Spring Garden Avenue and Deerfoot Road, not far from where her body was found on April 25, 1964. DeLand, Florida is less than an hour's drive from Orlando where Rex Heuermann would have visited family members and where Alan Placa's priest friend had transferred a condominium into Placa's name — another place Heuermann could have stayed.

Michelle Otter, a 15-year-old schoolgirl went missing from Fort McCoy, Florida on May 7, 1998. Michelle has never been found. She was 4' 11", 95 pounds, with hazel-green eyes. McCoy, Florida is a 1¼ hour drive from DeLand, Florida where schoolgirl Larlee Spear's body was found in 1964. (see above).

Myrtle Rexroad, a 36-year-old 5' 10" 150-pound woman, her body was found off Old DeLand Road in DeBary, Florida on May 6, 1997. Old DeLand Road in DeBary is 12 miles from DeLand where Laralee Spear was found three years earlier. The disappearance of Michelle Otter, along with the murders of Laralee Spear and Myrtle Rexroad, occurred along the route from New York to where Rex would have visited his mother in Cocoa Beach, Florida.

Danielle Faith Goodling's body was found in the Bronx on April 20, 2021, presumed by police to be the victim of a drug overdose. Consequently, no DNA or fingerprints were taken. Interestingly, her cell phone number was listed in Rex Heuermann's PalmPilot, retrieved from his computer. Most interesting, taken from Rex's planning document, is the letter T, which according to District Attorney Ray Tierney stands for Target as in victim Target.

The next three victims lived in proximity to Boston, Massachusetts:

Latasha Beebe Cannon, a 17-year-old sex worker had been found three weeks after she went missing from the Boston area, murdered in a marshy area behind a Raytheon plant in Bedford, Massachusetts in

2001. Her body was partially clothed, and her throat had been slashed. Bedford is a small town located just 20 miles from Boston.

Melissa Doherty, a 19-year-old sex worker was also found with her throat slashed. On May 12, 2002, approximately one year after Latasha Cannon's body was discovered, the Andover Fire Department got a call. Melissa's body had been set on fire. Andover, Massachusetts is 25 miles from Boston.

Danielle Oliverio, a 25-year-old sex worker was found by firefighters in 2007 behind an Internal Revenue Service building in Wilmington, Massachusetts. She had been beaten and strangled. Danielle's body, too, had been set on fire. The Medical Examiner had said she was still alive when set on fire as there was smoke present in her lungs. Wilmington is 16½ miles from Boston.

One should be searching for any possible connection between Rex Heuermann and the Boston area referencing the murder of Latasha Cannon in 2001, Mellissa Doherty in 2002, and Danielle Oliverio in 2007. I thought I found a connection when researching and learning that Rex Heuermann had purchased a trailer home in North Reading, just 19 miles from Boston. That is, until I learned, as had Nathan Adams through a detective acquaintance, that Heuermann had *not* purchased the trailer home until some 20 years later.

Interestingly, there is a possible allusion to the Raytheon company, behind which Latasha Beebe Cannon's body was found in Bedford, Massachusetts in 2001. Raytheon is the famous military defense plant and supplier of aerospace technology. Rex Heuermann's father was an aerospace engineer who built satellites. Rex and his father did not get on well at all. Raytheon could represent a symbolic gesture, a venting by Rex, indicative of the contempt he had for his father, Ted Heuermann, who died mysteriously when Rex was 11 years old.

Additionally, there is the possible connection referencing the Internal Revenue Service building in Wilmington, Massachusetts, behind which Danielle Oliverio's body was found. Rex Heuermann battled with the IRS for years to the tune of more than $425,000, dating back to 2005.

Next, there are distinct connections among Rex Heuermann, his wife Asa Ellerup, Alan Placa, and Boston, Massachusetts. Monsignor Alan J. Placa, a civil lawyer, was counsel to at least one clergy-related treatment center. Namely, The House of Affirmation in Whitinsville, Massachusetts, a rehabilitation center for pedophile priests with psychological and psychosexual problems.

Nathan Adams directs our attention to Asa Ellerup's fascination with comic book events, commonly referred to as Comic-Cons. They included festivals and conventions held in Boston as well as places across the country such as in San Diego. Asa tweeted excitedly about these events and knew these locations well. That is how involved Asa was with these costumed gatherings, drawing crowds of thousands showcasing heroes, villains, and fantastic creatures.

Boston Comic-Con Convention

It would not be unreasonable to assume that Rex Heuermann accompanied his wife to at least one of these Comic-Con events held annually in Boston (only a 3½ mile drive from Massapequa Park, Long Island), or that he attended architectural design events and/or conventions in Boston, seeing as how he graduated from the New

York Institute of Technology before opening his own architecture firm, RH Consultants, in 1994. Boston is well known for its many architectural wonders and has a rich heritage that reflects the city's history and evolution. It would be surprising if Rex had not visited Boston both for business and pleasure. There are just too many coincidences to suggest otherwise.

Boston's Historic Faneuil Hall ~ built in 1742

Nathan Adams points to the June 1996 Boston murder of 20-year-old Swedish nanny (au pair) Karina Holmer as Rex Heuermann being a possible suspect. Karina was strangled, and the top half of her body was cut with a power saw. She was last seen leaving the Zanzibar Nightclub before being discovered in a dumpster behind the Boston State Transportation Building, the same building in the Back Bay neighborhood where Melissa Doherty and Latasha Cannon were seen. The bottom half (trunk) of Karina's body was never found.

Adams continues with another list of possible victims who were either found murdered or simply disappeared in the state of New York at the hands of Rex Heuermann. The victims were predominately from

New York City, Long Island, as well as upstate areas. Adams' reasonings for Heuermann being responsible are **threefold**, the True Crime reporter, Adams, presenting a plausible case. **One:** Heuermann fits a definite pattern; the locations from where the bodies were found or suddenly vanished in proximity to where he worked and/or traveled are too coincidental. **Two:** Heuermann had the perfect cover to commit these murders and/or kidnappings because he was not viewed as being out of place or time referencing job site locations. He was a prominent New York City architect, specifically a building-code expediter and zoning analyst expert, possessing an esoteric knowledge in cutting through the city's red tape and, therefore, in demand. **Three:** Heuermann was free to travel far and wide, and he did; from New York City, to upstate New York — not to mention cross-country drives as distant as Las Vegas.

Rex Heuermann did a lot of work in Brooklyn, New York. On October 10, 1991, 12-year-old **Tiffany Madia Dixon**, 5' 2" tall, 105 pounds, disappeared after walking her younger 8-year-old cousin to school. She saw him to the door of the school and began a four-block walk to her own school in Carroll Gardens, in the Bushwick section of Brooklyn at approximately 8:00 a.m. She never arrived and has never been seen since. Tiffany lived on nearby Hart Street.

Keep in mind that work-site permits are generally filed well <u>after</u> the start of a job site project, allowing time for a contractor to first consider and evaluate its undertaking.

Rex Heuermann began working for architect Harvey Ingersol Rothenberg in 1987 as an apprentice. Their offices were at 45 East 20th Street in Manhattan. Rothenberg lived on Carroll Street in the Park Slope section of Brooklyn, a street that leads directly into the adjacent Carroll Gardens neighborhood. On June 5, 1992, Heuermann filed a permit for the property at 689 Hart Street, just 600 feet away from Tiffany Dixon's family home.

On October 6, 1991, 16 pieces of grisly human remains were found piled in a heap within a weedy building lot at 236 8th Street in the Bushwick section of Brooklyn. The arms had been severed at the shoulders; head, hands, elbows, thighs, knees, and ankles were cut in two with a knife and chainsaw. Police believed they were the remains of Tiffany Dixon. The remains were later identified as 23-year-old Sandra Acosta, 4' 11", 98 pounds. She had been strangled. Her torso was never recovered.

Sandra Acosta and Tiffany Dixon had both disappeared a half mile from each other. Sandra lived on Douglass Street in Park Slope, a half mile from Rex Heuermann's boss' home. Sandra had last been seen at 185 Nevins Street, Brooklyn.

On March 3, 1992, a transit porter found two large bags filled with body parts near a stairwell at the Lafayette Avenue A Train Station in Fort Greene, Brooklyn. The dismembered woman was later identified as 27-year-old **Becky Detres**. Becky had worked on the corner of Classon Avenue and Fulton Street as a sex worker. She had been shot in the back as well as the head. In July of 1992, Rex Heuermann had filed a work permit for a building just 979 feet from that corner.

One year after the murder of Becky Detres, an unidentified woman was found bound and dead in a lot at Fulton and Cumberland Street in Brooklyn, a few hundred feet from where Becky Detres had been discovered. She has never been identified.

The locations referencing the remains of Sandra Acosta and Becky Detres, including the disappearance from where Tiffany Dixson was last seen, in relationship to their proximity referencing work permits for which Rex Heuermann filed, one could certainly note a pattern — not to mention the body of the unidentified female victim.

Again and again, Rex Heuermann worked in those vicinities over the course of years, often returning to the same job sites for additional work. These are areas that need to be thoroughly investigated and/or reinvestigated.

If a killer wants to thwart a murder investigation, it would be prudent to kill that person in a location other than where one plans on disposing the body. If one wishes to further hinder an investigation, one could deposit parts of the body in different locations. If one's desire is to baffle, befuddle and frustrate the police, one could simply change one's MO (*modus operandi*). Rex Heuermann is an experimenter and a game player, having likely practiced all the above scenarios. Rex presumably tortured and strangled most of his targets quite savagely as several of the women had ties to New York City, particularly Brooklyn, Manhattan, and Queens — all in proximity to those building sites where Heuermann was engaged in architectural work. In short, Rex Heuermann is a killing machine. Let us take a quick look at the locales.

Maureen Brainard-Barnes was living in Norwich, Connecticut, but she was staying at a motel in Manhattan when last seem, about one mile from Rex Heuermann's office.

Melissa Barthelemy was living in the Bronx when she disappeared. Her phone pinged in Manhattan near the Port Authority Bus Terminal shortly after she left home.

Megan Waterman was originally from Maine. At the time of her disappearance, she was living in Brooklyn, New York.

Amber Lynn Costello lived in West Babylon, Long Island.

Jessica Taylor was from Poughkeepsie, but was living in Manhattan.

Sandra Costilla lived in Queens.

Sandra Acosta was working as a prostitute in Brooklyn.

Karen Ann Vergata had recently been released from jail in February of 1996. She had been arrested more than a dozen times in Manhattan, Queens, and Brooklyn, most often for the possession of drugs and loitering for the purposes of prostitution. She was last seen at Rex Heuermann's residence in Massapequa Park, screaming and running naked from his home.

Shannan Gilbert worked for an escort service in Manhattan.

There are many more links to Rex Heuermann and a suspected list of murder victims comprised of prostitutes, innocent young schoolgirls, high school students, and college students. We have been dealing with the most likely victims. Rather than continue with a prodigious list of additional names, which tends to become more speculative rather than substantive, I will give an abridged listing of whose names and dates you have not seen on these pages. Hopefully, law enforcement will find the time and resources to *re*investigate these murders in connection to Rex Heuermann.

Laura Parker. Found murdered in 1994.

Barbara Breidor. Found murdered in a ditch in Atlantic City, Egg Harbor Township, West Atlantic City, New Jersey, along with three other women in 2007.

Molly Jean Dilts. Atlantic City Serial Murders, Egg Harbor Township, West Atlantic City, New Jersey, 2007.

Tracy Ann Roberts. Atlantic City Serial Murders, Egg Harbor Township, West Atlantic City, New Jersey, 2007.

Kim Raffo. Atlantic City Serial Murders, Egg Harbor Township, West Atlantic City, New Jersey, 2007.

Nancy Flores. A sex worker found murdered in Highbridge Park, Washington Heights, upper Manhattan. Her badly decomposed torso was stuffed into a plastic bag at 180th and 181st Street. June of 1997.

Valerie Lester. Red Bank, New Jersey woman's torso found decapitated in 1997. Tips of all fingernails missing. Identified in 2008 as sex worker Valerie Lester.

Sara Lepkofker. Sara disappeared from Brooklyn in May of 1997. In June of 1997, a woman's body was found in a sewage pump house in Red Bank, New Jersey. Her head, legs, and tips of her fingers had been cut off. In January 2008, the body was identified as sex worker Sara Lepkofker.

Jennifer Nichole Gaine. Found strangled and bound in a room at the Sherman Hotel, located at the corner of 47th Street and 8th Avenue in Manhattan ~ approximately two blocks from a hotel where Maureen Brainard-Barnes was staying before she disappeared in 2007. Jennifer Gaine was found in July 3, 1997.

Jane & John Doe. Four garbage bags filled with the body parts of two dismembered male and female victims were found in a parking lot behind the Borinqueen housing project on Moore Street in the Williamsburg section of Brooklyn: torsos, heads, arms, and legs of a Jane and John Doe. Estimated time of death occurred some six to twelve hours earlier on July 9, 1997.

Jane Doe. Two Brooklyn fishermen hooked a suitcase floating in Gowanus Bay near Bush Terminal, 20th Street and First Avenue. Stuffed inside the suitcase were two black garbage bags filled with human body parts, initially reported as one bag containing the balding head of a male victim. It turned out to be the head of a Jane Doe, July 10, 1997.

Eve Eskin Brown. On July 10, 1999, Eva left home in Plainview, Long Island to visit a friend in Freeport, Long Island, 14 miles away. On August 19, 1999, her car was found in Flatbush, Brooklyn. Sixteen months later, on November 15, 2000, her skeletal remains were found in a garbage bag during the construction of the Gateway Center Mall, near the Belt Parkway in East New York, Brooklyn. Her legs had been bound with rope. Rex Heuermann had filed a work permit just 16 days earlier, and only 2.7 miles from where Eva's body was found.

John Doe. The very next day, on November 16, 2000, the partial skeletal remains of an unidentified male were discovered at the same construction site.

Jacqueline Smith. Jacqueline disappeared from the Flatbush section of Brooklyn on August 7, 1999. She was 5' 7" tall, 130 pounds. Nineteen years later, on June 20, 2000, the torso of a woman was discovered in an overgrown weedy area within a plastic bag wrapped with tape at Rockaway Beach, Queens. It was the torso of Jacqueline Smith.

Andre Jamale Isacc. Andre Isacc (aka Sugar Bear), 6' 3" tall, approximately 250 pounds and worked as a female impersonator. He lived on De Sales Place in the Bushwick section of Brooklyn, New York. Andre disappeared in November of 2002. On December 17, 2002, Andre's partial torso was found in a housing project, covered in a bodysuit within a plastic bag a mile away from where Jacquline Smith's torso was found in Rockaway Beach, Queens. On January 26, 2003, Andre's skull was found 60 miles away, embedded in a frozen pond near Forge River, in Moriches, Long Island. He was shot in the temple with a Glock pistol. On April 10, 2004, Andre's arms and legs were recovered in a residential building site in Moriches.

Claribel Quinones. On July 3, 2007, Claribel's remains were found wrapped in a plastic garbage bag stuffed with newspaper and secured with duct tape in the basement of an abandoned house at 546 Lexington Avenue in Brooklyn. Claribel lived at 1065 Bedford Avenue, Brooklyn, directly across the street from Erica McDaniel who lived at 1084 Bedford Avenue.

Erica McDaniel. In 2013, Erica's skeletal remains were found stuffed inside a charred suitcase in an abandoned burnt-out building on Hull Street in Brooklyn, which is less than a mile from De Sales Place and where Andre Isacc (Sugar Bear) lived, and where Jessica Taylor's pimp Kahlil White once lived. Erica lived directly across the street from Claribel Quinones. Both Erica McDaniel and Claribel Quinones lived in the Bedford-Stuyvesant section of Brooklyn. Erica's relatives lived in Amityville and West Babylon, Long Island. Amityville is where Rex Heuermann had his self-storage units, just 7 minutes from is home in Massapequa Park. West Babylon is where Amber Lynn Costello lived and from where she was abducted. Erica's West Babylon relatives lived less than a mile from Amber's residence.

Jane Doe. Unidentified woman   February 15, 2012   Brownsville, Brooklyn laundry bag Watt Avenue and Bristol Street.

Tanya Rush. Thirty-nine-year-old Tanya Rush was last seen June 27, 2008 on Lavonia Avenue in Brownsville, Brooklyn. She was found dismembered, her remains dumped in a dark-colored suitcase found on a grassy shoulder of Newbridge Road exit ramp off the Southern State Parkway in Bellmore, Long Island, 4 miles from Rex Heuermann's house.

Wendy Robinson. Wendy Robinson went missing on August 12, 2005, half a mile from where Tanya Rush was last seen in Brownsville, Brooklyn; also, just half a mile south from where Erica McDaniel was last seen.

Demika Moore. On July 23rd, 2010, Demika Moore, age 25, was found beaten to death in an alleyway near 178-11 Leslie Road, Jamacia, Queens. Her hands were bound with duct tape. Ligature marks were on her wrists and arms, indicating that she had been tied up. Demika had 2 tattoos: Zoa (daughter's name) on her lower right arm, Libra on her left chest. She had disappeared six months earlier in January 2010. Nathan Adams asks the question of whether Demika Moore could have been kept alive during that six-month period. Note that Rex Heuermann's work-permit location for 176-06 Linden Boulevard, Queens, filed in 2000, 2001, and 2013, was less than a mile from where Demika Moore was found murdered near 178-11 Leslie Road, Jamacia, Queens.

Denise Hart. Denise was 43 years old and lived alone. She worked as a licensed practical nurse at a group home for developmentally disabled adults in upstate Schenectady, New York. She was last seen leaving work on November 11, 2007, then disappeared from her apartment at 15 Lafayette Street, just three blocks from Catholic Charities. You will recall that Catholic Charities is a national social services organization affiliated with RH Consultants & Associates through the Dioceses of Rockville Centre, Long Island, New York, for which Rex Heuermann received many lucrative job assignments over a period of decades. Denise was found brutally murdered six months after disappearing, her torso wrapped in plastic in a nearby village.

Here is an interesting takeaway reported by murderincorp.com: "Long Island serial killer Rex Heuermann's brother-in-law lived in Schenectady, New York and shows two residences during the time that the murder took place less than a mile from the group home where Denise Hart was last seen. In a 2018 deposition, Heuermann references travelling frequently with his wife and mentions having taken a recent trip to Upstate New York. One of Rex Heuermann's former employees also stated in a *New York* magazine article that Rex took frequent hunting trips upstate."

The points being are that both residences of Rex Heuermann's brother-in-law (Asa Ellerup's brother) in 2007 were less than one mile from Denise Hart's job at the group home at 1383 Keyes Avenue, Schenectady, just 2.4 miles from her apartment, and 15 miles from the location of where her torso was later found in the village of Menands, New York. Another point being that Heuermann is a hunter, and fall is hunting season. Rex is a hunter of deer and of humans. Upstate New York affords hunters excellent opportunities, especially deer hunting.

Virtually all the above-mentioned murders highlight not only proximity in relationship to one another (what Nathan Adams refers to as those six degrees of separation), but to certain similarities referencing how the victims were slain; namely, and mainly, the tortures and sadistic viciousness that Rex Heuermann displayed in subduing his prey. In Heuermann's own typewritten words retrieved from a device in the basement of his home in Massapequa Park: "hit harder" … "get more sleep to have more play time."

Addresses where Rex Heuermann lived for periods of time:

103 Main St, Trailer #4, North Reading, Massachusetts 01864

105 1st Avenue, Massapequa Park, New York 11762

1366 Huron Road, North Brunswick, New Jersey 08902

824 W. Osborn Road, Phoenix, Arizona 85103

1427 Main Street, West Warwick, Rhode Island 02893

7428 Beechwood Avenue, Beverly Hills, Michigan 48025

87 Columbia Street, New York, New York 10002

36 Ridgewood Way, Burlington, New Jersey 08016

5499 West Tropicana Avenue, #1012, Las Vegas, Nevada 89103

Methods and materials Rex Heuermann used on victims:

Strangulation

Decapitation

Dismemberment (head, hands, legs arms, feet, etc. (as many as 16 body parts)

Fire

Gunshot

Beating

Raping

Torturing

Hanging

Knife stabs

Power saw

Bodies wrapped in either plastic, burlap, or blanket

CHAPTER TWENTY-SIX

The Route 29 Stalker Case Thrown into Total Confusion

In 1995, Rex Heuermann's mother sold Rex their home at 105 1st Avenue, Massapequa Park, Long Island, New York, and eventually moved to 18 Zephyr Road in Palmyra, Virginia. Through the years, Rex often visited his mother, Dolores, driving 7½ hours, 378-miles from Massapequa Park to Palmyra. A few months after his mother moved into her new home, a series of murders occurred throughout the neighboring areas, the first three along Route 29 in Virginia.

Alicia Showalter Reynolds. Alicia Showalter Reynolds, a 25-year-old PhD pharmacology student at Johns Hopkins University in Baltimore, Maryland, went missing on March 2, 1996. Alicia planned on driving 150 miles from Baltimore, Maryland to Charlottesville, Virginia to meet her mother at a shopping mall. She had said good-bye to her husband that morning. Police found her car abandoned along Route 29 in **Culpeper, Virginia**, 50 miles from the shopping mall. On the windshield of the car, beneath a wiper blade, was a white paper napkin, a commonly used signal of car trouble. Police reported there was nothing wrong with Mrs. Reynolds' car.

The man had earlier used ploys of signaling motorists that sparks, or some such mechanical problem, were coming from beneath the target vehicle. A good number of people reported similar encounters. The police seemed to think that the man was on a practice run, testing, seeing what worked and what did not to lure women to stop their vehicle, get out, and have a look. Alicia was last seen by witnesses who reported seeing the woman looking under the hood of her car before getting into a dark pickup truck with a tall, white man who appeared to be assisting her. And there is the rub. Many witnesses (nearly two dozen folks, mostly women) to the man's ruse of directing their attention to supposed "car trouble" reported the individual stood 5' 10" to 6' tall, not the actual 6' 4" stature of Rex Heuermann. It is difficult to explain away the discrepancy, except to say we are dealing with another killer or killers.

We could spend a lot of time looking at three other possible suspects who have been considered prime suspects by law enforcement authorities in the Route 29 Stalker case. Namely, Richard Marc Evonitz (convicted serial killer), Randy Taylor (convicted murderer), and Darrell David Rice (imprisoned for murder then later acquitted). However, we are going to focus on a fourth person, Craig Arnold Heuermann; that is, Rex Heuermann's younger brother by two years. The likelihood of Craig being at least one of the Route 29 Stalkers, the one who witnesses saw assisting Alicia Showalter Reynolds with car trouble, will become abundantly clear. Craig Heuermann stands 5' 10" tall and looks exactly like his brother Rex. In fact, they look like identical twins, except that Craig is 6 inches shorter. I covered Craig Heuermann's violent display of temper in my nonfictional accounting titled *The Long-Awaited Arrest of Long Island Serial Killer Rex Heuermann ~ Past "Administration" to Blame*, which involved Craig's drug/alcohol abuse, and the death of a New York police captain. Craig was driving drunk and 'coked-up' when he crashed through the center median of the Southern State Parkway into the captain's vehicle, killing him in 1988. Craig is primarily unemployed and lives in Chester, South Carolina, a closer drive than his brother Rex if wishing to visit their mother in Palmyra, Virginia.

Two months after Alicia Showalter Reynolds disappeared, her body was found on May 7, 1996 in a wooded area near a logging area in rural **Lignam, Virgina**, approximately 11½ miles from her abandoned car. The Route 29 Stalker was surfacing in Virginia. Based on police reports, a composite sketch of the individual was eventually drawn up. After Rex Heuermann's arrest in 2023, a reporter for murderincorp.worldpress.com website first noted a very similar likeness between the composite drawing of the man dubbed the Route 29 Stalker and Rex Heuermann.

Top & Left: Composite sketches of Route 29 Stalker
Right: Rex Heuermann

Craig Heuermann was driven away from his home on Tuesday

Passenger Side: Craig Heuermann
Unknown Driver

The twin brother and younger sister of Alicia Showalter Reynolds believe an old state police sketch of the suspect looks just like the accused Gilgo Beach serial killer Rex Heuermann.

"When I saw the picture of Rex Heuermann, subtract 27 years from the way he looks now, it's the first time I've seen anyone look like any of the composite sketches that were done at the time of my sister's abduction," said her brother, Dr. Patrick Showalter.

Reynolds' sister, Barbara Josenhans, felt the same way. "The similarities are striking," Josenhans told PIX11 News. "The eyes and the cheeks, the face structure."

The fact that Rex and his brother Craig look identical, except for the six-inch height discrepancy, helps explain the difference; that is, if you accept that witnesses were seeing Craig Heuermann — not his brother Rex Heuermann. It makes for a good argument. Then again, there is a difference in hair color. A composite sketch of the Route 29 Stalker shows reddish hair. Craig and Rex Heuermann both have dark-brown hair.

Laura "Lollie" Winans & Julianne "Julie" Williams. The bodies of 26-year-old Laura Winans and 24-year-old Julianne Williams were found murdered on June 1, 1996. The pair were discovered at their campsite in Skyland Resort (basically in **Culpeper, Virginia**) after hiking through Shenandoah National Park. Their throats had been cut and their bodies wrapped with duct tape. The area is near where Alicia Showalter's car was found.

Thelma B. Scroggins. Thelma Scroggins, age 74, was found shot in the head four times in the living room of her home in **Lignum, Virginia** on July 14, 2005. Thelma lived directly across the highway from where Alicia Showalter Reynolds was abducted in 1996. Three innocent teenage boys were arrested for Thelma Scroggins' murder: Eric Weakley, age 15; Michael Hash, age 16; Jason Kloby, age 19. The trio became known as the "Culpeper Three." Jason Kloby was tried and acquitted. Eric Weakley was convicted of second-degree murder and spent almost seven (7) years behind bars. Michael Hash was sentenced to life in prison, spending twelve (12) years behind bars before his release.

The tragic part of this story is Eric Weakly had been railroaded by the police into signing a false confession, implicating Michael Hash and Jason Kloby. Eric Weakly had later recanted his confession, but not before the damage was done. The "Culpeper Three" were proven to be innocent thanks to The University of Virginia School of Law's Innocence Project Clinic. Though Jason Kloby had been acquitted at trial, his ordeal of having been charged in the first place was, indeed, unsettling. When interviewed, Jason said he is ". . . still perceived and treated by many people as someone who had simply gotten away with murder."

These deplorable police tactics of coercing false confessions from suspects are not uncommon and have been used in many high-profile, false-confession cases. Namely, the Memphis Three, the Norfolk Four, the Beatrice Six, and the Central Park Five. Nor are they uncommon in lower-profile cases such as the "Culpeper Three" case before you. Many of these cases involve, but are not limited to, relatively young people, who are more easily manipulated. Deprivation of food, drink, and sleep are just a few tactics police use to wear a person down and elicit a false confession.

One blatant travesty of justice I followed for many years was the incarceration of an innocent 17-year-old boy, Martin (Marty) Tankleff, who spent seventeen (17) years behind bars for allegedly murdering his parents. I covered the story in part in my nonfictional accounting of *The Long-Awaited Arrest of Long Island Serial Killer Rex Heuermann ~ Past "Administration" to Blame*. The story involved the nefarious tactics of police and law enforcement officials who knew they had the wrong person, yet allowed solid evidence that contradicted their presupposed notion to fall by the wayside.

Detective K. James McCready and Detective Norman Rein were Marty Tankleff's arresting officers. McCready had been cited by the State Investigation Commission (SIC) for perjury in another case. In this case, McCready was purportedly paid $100,000 to protect the real murderers of Marty's parents: Namely, Joseph Creedon and Peter Kent. Glen Harris was a witness and the driver of the car that brought Creedon and Kent that evening in 1988 to the Tankleff residence. Jerry Steuerman owed Seymour Tankleff nearly half a million dollars. Seymour had called in the note. Steuerman had orchestrated the murders. One law enforcement official who turned a blind eye to the truth and fought to keep Marty Tankleff behind bars was soon-to-be Suffolk County district attorney, Thomas J. Spota.

Police officers and law enforcement officials, especially the sordid likes of Detective James McCready, Police Chief Jimmy Burke, and District Attorney Thomas Spota, did tons of damage to promote distrust throughout Suffolk County, Long Island. They are the poster boys for corruption personified. Enough said? Not nearly, but we must draw a line in the proverbial sand someplace.

Anne Carolyn McDaniel. Anne Carolyn McDaniel, a slightly retarded 20-year-old woman, told housemates she was going to meet a mystery date on the night she disappeared, September 18, 1996. Anne lived at the President Madison Inn group home for disabilities in **Orange, Virginia**. Be reminded that Rex Heuermann did many jobs for group homes for the disabled. Be reminded, also, that Heuermann's stepson has mild disabilities. Plenty of things to talk about with Anne if polite conversation was on the killer's mind. Anne Carolyn

McDaniel's burned body was found by hunters four days later in rural **Batna, Virginia**, next to **Lignum**, **Virginia**, 5 miles from where Alicia Showalter Reynolds' remains were found. Anne was covered with brush that had been set on fire just 50 yards from a hunting cabin in the woods some 10 miles away.

Anne Carver Clapp. Anne Carver Clapp, a 19-year-old Fluvanna County Virginia woman, disappeared from the **Charlottesville, Virginia** area on September 15, 1997. She lived in **Palmyra, Virginia**, just one mile from Rex Heuermann's mother's home. Anne's skeletal remains were later found on a residential property in **Goochland, Virginia** in 2001.

Samantha Ann Clarke. Samantha Ann Clarke, 19 years old, was last seen in **Orange, Virginia**, the same town from which Anne Carolyn McDaniel disappeared in September of 1996. Samantha lived practically across a field from where McDaniel's house was located. To this day, Samantha Ann Clarke's body has not been found.

Sheryl Warner. Sheryl Warner was found murdered in her home on September 18, 2005 in **Culpeper, Virginia**. She was on the phone with a man claiming he had car trouble. Sheryl was found in her basement, shot in the head, hanging from the ceiling by an electrical cord. Her home was set on fire, which was across the street from where Alicia Showalter Reynolds' car was found in 1996.

Areas in Virginia from where victims lived, disappeared, and/or were found murdered: Palmyra, Lignam, Culpeper, Orange, Goochland, Charlottesville, Batna.

Other areas of significant interest referencing Rex Heuermann:

Christine Belusko. The remains of an unidentified female were found in **Staten Island, New York** on September 20, 1991. She had been handcuffed, brutally beaten with a hammer seventeen (17) times, and strangled before being burned in a vacant lot on the East Shore of the Island. The woman was identified 30 years later in April of 2021 as 29-year-old **Christine Belusko** of Morris County, New Jersey.

Christine, for decades, was referred to in the press as "The Girl with the Scorpion Tattoo" because of the image of the venomous arachnid on her buttocks.

Subsequent genetic genealogy tracking revealed that Christine Belusko had a 2-year-old daughter, Christa Nicole, whose whereabouts are unknown. Investigators do not know the father of Christine's daughter or where the child was at the time of her mother's murder.

The takeaway from Christine's disappearance is that Rex Heuermann had filed a building work permit for 317 Fingerboard Road, Staten Island, less than 2 miles away from the murder site and 1 month before Christine Belusko's brutally beaten and burned body was found.

1984 – 1985 Suffolk County & Nassau County Murders

West Hempstead, Hempstead Village, Lynbrook murders in Nassau County, Long Island are an approximate 4.5-mile distance from one another.

Lindenhurst murder in Suffolk County, Long Island is approximately 16 miles from the Hempstead/Lynbrook area.

Christine Clarkson. Christine was found murdered in **West Hempstead, Nassau County**, Long Island, New York on February 17, 1984. She was 30 years old, 5' 8" tall, 140 pounds. Christine was having drinks with friends at a local tavern. She left and began the few blocks walk home to her apartment when she was grabbed, brutally beaten with a blunt instrument, then dragged 150 feet into an alley between two factory buildings where she was raped and strangled. Christine's body was atop a pile wood and cardboard. Her apartment was 13 miles from Rex Heuermann's Massapequa Park home.

Laura Ann Parker. On May 23, 1984, 14-year-old Laura Parker disappeared from **Lindenhurst, Suffolk County**, Long Island, New York after walking home from school. On September 10, 1984,

Laura's body was found by children rolled up in a carpet 2 miles from Laura's home. Laura was among one of the first fourteen female victims in the Hempstead, Long Island area to either be found brutally murdered or gone missing — never to be seen or heard from again. Laura lived 16 miles from the Hempstead area.

Kelley Morrissey. At 9:30 p.m. on June 12, 1984, 15-year-old Kelley Morrissey went to buy cigarettes at a local gas station in **Lynbrook**, **Nassau County**, Long Island, New York. She met up with friends, then left to go to a video store. Kelley vanished that evening — never to be seen or heard from again.

Theresa Fusco. On November 10, 1984, 16-year-old Theresa Fusco went to work at the then popular skating rink, Hot Skates in **Lynbrook**, **Nassau County**, Long Island, New York. She had an argument with her manager who then fired her. Theresa called someone right after being fired then walked down the street toward the railroad tracks. Her nude body was found weeks later near the skating rink in a wooded area under a pile of leaves, having been beaten to death and sexually assaulted. Theresa's best friend had been Kelley Morrissey, who she had lost five months earlier.

Jacqueline Marterella. On March 26, 1985, 19-year-old Jacqueline Marterella from **Oceanside**, **Nassau County**, Long Island, New York, left her friend's house and walked to Burger King to start work. She never arrived. A month later, on April 25, her body was found naked and strangled on the 17th hole of the **Woodmere** Country Club, 4.3 miles from her home.

Jonie Jackson. Jonie Jackson, a sex worker with a long record of prostitution, was reported missing by her mother in January of 1985. In February of that year, an unidentified person, believed to be female, was found murdered in an alley in the village parking lot. The woman was later identified through dental records as 27-year-old Jonie Jackson of Dartmouth Street, **Hempstead Village**, **Nassau County**, Long Island, New York. Her badly decomposed body had been partially covered by a plastic garbage bag. Jonie's mother told police she had not seen her daughter since the end of September, but that it was not unusual for Jonie to disappear for long periods of time. Jonie had suffered severe head trauma; her skull having been fractured in multiple areas.

Dual-Related Jurisdictional Murder Discoveries ~ Nassau/Suffolk Counties

Peaches & her toddler. "Peaches," also known as Jane Doe #3, remains an unidentified black American female "Gilgo Beach" area victim. On June 28, 1997, the woman's dismembered torso was found in a green plastic Rubbermaid container, covered with a red towel and a floral pillowcase within **Nassau County's Hempstead State Lake Park, Lakeview**, Long Island, New York. Peaches' arms, and legs (severed below the knees) had not been found at that time. Her head was never found. Scant skeletonized extremities were later recovered by police in the spring of 2011 in the bramble of Jones Beach, on the same barrier island where Gilgo Beach is located.

Baby Doe. On April 4, 2011, Peaches' 2-year-old daughter was found in **Suffolk County**, left intact and wrapped in a blanket at the opposite end of Ocean Parkway, 10 miles apart. The child was found 250 feet from the partial remains of Valerie Mack. Peaches' daughter was wearing similar gold jewelry to her mother's: gold hoop earrings and bracelets.

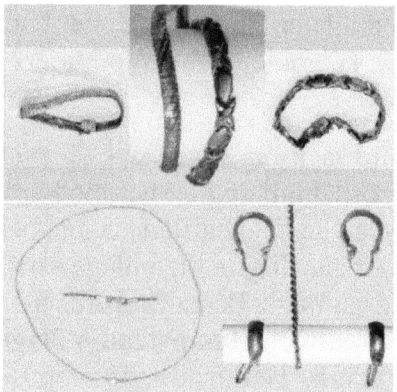

"Peaches" and daughter's similar jewelry

CHAPTER TWENTY-SEVEN

Taking a closer look at the brothers Rex and Craig Heuermann: Craig's Address is 1031 Rippling Brooke Drive, Chester, South Carolina. While jailed in the Suffolk County Riverhead Correctional Facility, Riverhead, New York, Rex sold his secluded Chester County, South Carolina retirement properties to relatives for $1. Craig owned two of four properties since 1997; however, he ran into financial problems, so Rex had helped his brother out by picking up the mortgages. The backstory is rather involved, suffice it to say that Asa Ellerup, now Rex's estranged wife, owns two of four parcels. Rex had planned on retiring to Chester, South Carolina with his wife Asa, building a home and living across the street from his brother Craig. Rex and Craig were going to buy up surrounding properties in the neighborhood and build a compound. That was the plan, foiled by Rex's incarceration. Property records show that Rex Heuermann bought a secluded 5-plus-acre property in the Mirror Lakes subdivision in Chester on July 28, 2021 for $154,351.

Rex Heuermann had also purchased 18 acres of land alongside a string of small, secluded ponds in Chester County. A neighbor, James Austin, who lives across a small pond from Rex Heuermann's then property said he heard the story of Craig's brother Rex planning to buy everyone out. "I'm not going anywhere," Austin had stated. He can see Rex Heuermann's property shrouded by a thick growth of trees along both the pond and the road on the other side.

Austin said Heuermann's brother Craig also has property in the subdivision but does not live there. He talked with Craig once, mostly about being MPs in the service. Austin said the Heuermann brothers kept mostly to themselves. His contact with Rex was seeing him riding by in the Avalanche. Stories about Craig Heuermann have circulated among the community, including one in which Craig hit a neighbor with a metal pole for mowing a lawn on a Sunday, the *New York Post* reported. Craig and Rex were also believed to have cut a small boat in half after warning the owner to get it off their property, Austin said. The boat had been there for decades, he added.

Craig Heuermann is a regular at Gene's Restaurant, located at 156 Gadsden Street, Chester, South Carolina 29706, in the heart of downtown Chester, 3.7 miles or an 8-minute drive from his home. "I know he's been in here, but I don't know who he was," restaurant worker Kim Toland said. Gene's Restaurant is a casual eatery with a homey ambiance, serving up classic comfort food for breakfast and lunch.

Some people said they had seen Rex Heuermann around town as well, a fact that after the crimes came to light, it became a bit unnerving for some folks.

"It makes me want to go home and make sure my doors are locked at all times," customer Susan Stepp said.

But that was not the opinion of everyone. One man who did not want to go on camera said he lives near where the Heuermann property is located, saying the brother Craig is a nice guy, and people should let the process play out before making judgments. "He's an all-around decent guy. Like I say, he don't bother nobody, he stays to himself. Just all-around good guy," the man said, adding that, "I'd like officials to bring out cadaver dogs to check the lake out near the suspect's property to make sure there's nothing out there that could be found later."

Craig Heuermann's Chester, S.C. Property

It is a matter of who you ask about Craig Heuermann's character. You would get mixed responses. Craig is in the habit of handing out business cards to those he sees in his area:

Craig Heuermann's mindset

Craig Heuermann was 22 years old in 1988 when he crashed through the center median of the Southern State Parkway, drunk and 'coked-up,' slamming into and killing a New York Housing Authority police captain in a head-on car crash, close to his brother Rex's Massapequa Park home on Long Island. The evidence showed that Craig Heuermann had a blood alcohol level of .20, twice the legal limit, and a blood cocaine level of .05 milligrams. He pleaded guilty to criminally negligent homicide and driving while intoxicated. The fact that Craig Heuermann received a three-year prison sentence, serving even less time, seems rather odd given the circumstances.

To conclude, Nathan Adams, among others, contends that Rex Heuermann has murdered in many of the places he has traveled. Adams throws out a number somewhere between fifty (50) to a hundred (100) people. Adams makes a strong case, and I concur. The trial (or trials) of Rex Heuermann, should there even be one, is going to be fascinating. We will never know how many people he murdered. But rest assured those whose lives Heuermann has taken suffered gravely, for Rex is the king of torture as stated in his planning document to "hit harder" and "get more sleep to have more play time." That certainly, and quite telling, says it all!

CHAPTER TWENTY-EIGHT

On December 17, 2024, it was reported in *Newsday* that Rex A. Heuermann was charged with the second-degree murder of Valerie Mack, bringing a total of seven victims for which Rex Heuermann has been indicted. I covered Valerie Mack's background in Chapter Seven, including a segment on genetic genealogy.

In a crowded Suffolk Riverhead courtroom that Tuesday, packed with media and family members of the alleged victims, Rex Heuermann gave an emphatic statement before State Supreme Court Justice Timothy Mazzei: "Your honor, I am not guilty of any of these charges."

Heuermann's utterance caused the assembled group to let out an audible gasp. It was the defendant's first pronouncement since his initial arraignment on July 14, 2023.

Defense attorney Michael J. Brown said he did *not* instruct his client to speak out in court, adding, "He's extremely frustrated," referring to his client's mindset to personally answer to the charges. "He has said from day one he is not responsible for these murders."

The Suffolk County Medical Examiner's estimated that Valerie Mack had been murdered between two and eight weeks before her remains were located on November 19, 2000. Court documents unveiled Tuesday revealed that the latest breakthrough came from a female hair found near Valerie's remains, which linked Heuermann's wife (Asa) or their daughter (Victoria) through DNA testing by two independent laboratories.

A single female head hair was found near Valerie Mack's left wrist.

Note: Victoria Heuerman would have been between 3 and 4 years of age at the time of Valerie Mack's murder, obviously indicating that the single hair would be a trace (transfer) hair.

The following chart, taken from the superseding bail application dated December 17, 2024, summarizes mitochondrial and nuclear test results from Forensic Laboratory #1 and Forensic Laboratory #2, both of which have been independently able to determine that the hair(s) recovered on or near the bodies of six of the seven victims are forensically tied to defendant Rex Heuermann, members of his immediate family, and an individual (Witness 3) with whom Heuermann resided.

The list of names is placed in chronological order referencing Rex Heuermann's indictments; i.e., Long Island Serial Killer victims Amber Lynn Costello (July 13, 2023), Megan Waterman (July 13, 2023), Maureen Brainard-Barnes (July 13, 2023); Jessica Taylor (June 6, 2024), Sandra Costilla (June 6, 2024); Valerie Mack (December 17, 2024).

Note: Melissa Barthelemy's name, one of the "Gilgo Four," is not included in the chart because no hair(s) were recovered on or near her body. Heuermann was also charged with her murder on July 13, 2023.

Victim	Designation In Bail Letter	Approx. Location- Hair Recovery	Mitochondrial DNA Results	Nuclear DNA Results
Amber Lynn Costelo	Female Hair on Costello	Tape In Area of the Head	99.98% of North American population can be excluded but not **Asa Ellerup Or Victoria Heuermann**	4.654×10^{63} times more likely to come from an individual with the identical genetic profile as **Victoria Heuermann**
Megan Waterman	First Of Two Female Hairs On Waterman	Outside Head Area	99.69% of North American population can be excluded but not **Asa Ellerup Or Victoria Heuermann**	2.374×10^{48} times more likely to come from an individual with the identical genetic profile as **Asa Ellerup**
Megan Waterman	Second of Two Female Hairs On Waterman	Tape In the Area Of The Head	N/A	2.778×10^{480} times more likely to come from an individual with the identical genetic profile as **Asa Ellerup**
Megan Waterman	Male Hair on Waterman	Bottom Portion of Burlap	99.96% of North American population can be excluded but not **Rex Heuermann**	1.408×10^{169} times more likely to come from an individual with

				the identical genetic profile as **Rex Heuermann**
Maureen Brainard-Barnes	Female Hair on Barnes	Buckle of Belt Restraining Lower Body	N/A	7.9 trillion times more likely to come from an individual with the identical genetic profile as **Asa Ellerup**
Jessica Taylor	Male Hair Under Taylor	On Surgical Drape Underneath Victim	99.96% of North American population can be excluded but not **Rex Heuermann**	1.837×10^{603} times more likely to come from an individual with identical genetic profile as **Rex Heuermann**
Sandra Costilla	Male Hair on Costilla	Tape-Lift Off Striped Shirt Above Victim's Head	99.96% of North American population can be excluded but not **Rex Heuermann**	4.347×10^{332} times more likely to come from an individual with the identical genetic profile as **Rex Heuermann**
Sandra Costilla	Female Hair on Costilla	Victim's Right Arm	99.98% of North American population can be excluded but not **Witness 3** (woman who lived with Rex Heuermann)	4.578×10^{1040} times more likely from an individual with the identical genetic profile as **Witness 3**

Valerie Mack	Female Hair on Mack	Inside Garbage Bags Containing Victim, Near Victim's Left Wrist	99.65% of the North American population can be excluded but not **Asa Ellerup or Victoria Heuermann**	1.31×10^{351} times more likely to come from an individual with the identical genetic profile as **Victoria Heuermann**

Ed Mack, the adoptive father of Valerie Mack, said back in June of 2024 that he believed prosecutors would likely charge Rex Heuermann in his daughter's death before the end of the year. And so they did on December 17, 2024.

Among the hair evidence collected, Valerie had a tattoo with her son's name on her left ankle that detectives believe Heuermann had removed. Additionally, Valerie had "two continuous ragged defects" corresponding to breast mutilation depicting pornographic images discovered on devices seized from the defendant's home.

Also recovered on a device was a document referencing Mill Road as a potential "dump site." Based on the Suffolk County Gilgo Homicide Investigation Task Force's training and experience, it is believed the "DS" heading in Rex Heuermann's planning document appears to be an acronym for "dump site," which is corroborated by inter alia (meaning among other things), the discovery of Valerie Mack at two separate "dump sites," one of those locations being the vicinity of Mill Road, which is listed as "DS-1, Mill Rd."

The same document listed "foam drainer cleaner" among the supplies Heuermann is believed to have used to help cover up his crimes. Investigators learned that he hired a plumbing company to check his mainline drain, paying $265.83 in November of 2000. The planning document also included items such as "acid, rope, tape, plastic bags, medical gloves" along with the mention of "removal of identifying marks."

After Tuesday's arraignment of Rex Heuermann on December 17, 2024, followed by a press conference given by District Attorney Ray Tierney, the D.A. turned the microphone over to noted California attorney Gloria Allred, representing family members of Melissa Barthelemy, Maureen Brainard-Barnes, Jessica Taylor, and Megan Waterman. In a show of support, the assembled families handed out roses to Edwin and JoAnn Mack. "We want her family [Valerie's] to know that they are not alone in their grief," Allred said of the Mack family. "We see you, we hear you, and we hope you will accept our condolences for your loss."

Attorney Gloria Allred (left) with several assembled family members of victims

Ray Tierney declined to comment on the remaining three unsolved Gilgo Beach cases; that is, the unidentified sets of remains: Peaches, toddler (daughter of Peaches) and Asian male.

With consideration to court dates, Judge Mazzei set January 15, 2025 for the defense to file motions for a hearing on DNA evidence as well as separating the Gilgo Four case from the others. Tierney has conceded that a hearing on the scientific standards used in the case(s) is necessary because the nuclear DNA methods used by outside laboratories to recover data from degraded hair samples has never been presented in a New York court. Prosecutors would oppose attempts by the defense to try the cases separately. Mazzei said that he intends to hold DNA hearings in either late February or early March. Consequently, no trial date for Heuermann has been set.

Prosecutors have also named Rex Heuermann a suspect in the death of Karen Vergata. It has been revealed that *all* of the horrific slayings for which the defendant has been charged and indicted were carried out in his Massapequa Park basement. Whether Heuermann will be indicted for Karen's murder, too, is up in the air. As it presently stands, an undetermined date before Heuermann goes to trial is possibly years away from the day he was arrested. Therefore, I decided to put this book out for publication sooner than later.

POSTSCRIPT

Robert Banfelder's body of works is inclusive of 11 novels, 2 nonfiction books on the Long Island Serial Killer case regarding Rex Heuermann, several reference works re Fishing, Hunting, Writing Well & Getting Published, Gourmet Cooking, plus hundreds of articles, scores of talks/lectures, editorials, and interviews. All books (paperbacks) are available on Amazon.

SOURCES

Adams, Nathan, True Crime with Nathan Adams videos on YouTube and his Patreon channel, "Gilgo Beach Investigation Updates," October 2024 and "Serial Killer Case Gets Even Worse," January 2025.

Blass, Greg, "Was L.I. investigation stymied in coverup to corrupt Suffolk cop and DA? We need a special prosecutor to probe investigation." RiverheadLocal Opinion Column, October 19, 2021.

Bryant, Nick, Podcast, October 4, 2024.

Celona, Larry, Joe Marino, Kevin Sheehan, Jorge Fitz-Gibbon, "Police conduct another search on Gilgo suspect Rex Heuermann's home," New York Post, May 20, 2024.

Chernoff, Alan, "Missing Woman Cried 'Help Me! Help Me!'", *CNN* Article, April 14, 2024.

DeStefano, Anthony M., "Gilgo Beach Killings: Accused killer Rex Heuermann sought to keep victims alive to enhance sadistic pleasures, investigators and experts say," *Newsday*, August 23, 2024.

DeStephano, Anthony M., Grant Parpan, " Feds: Gilgo Suspect Kept Victims Alive for Pleasure," *Newsday*, August 25, 2024.

DeStefano, Anthony M., "Who was Gilgo Beach victim Karen Vergata?" *Newsday*, March 4, 2024.

DeStefano, Anthony M., "Gilgo Beach Killings: New DNA technology's admissibility to be tested in case against Rex Heuermann, *Newsday*, July 11, 2024.

Finn, Lisa, "LI Serial Killer Symposium To Reveal 'Surprising New Evidence': Lawyer," *Riverhead Patch*, January 29, 2024.

_____ "Suffolk County Police Release New Information on Gilgo Four," www.forensicmag.com, May 6, 2022.

Fuller, Nicole, Grant Parpan, John Asbury, "Gilgo Beach Killings: Estranged wife of Rex Heuermann, Asa Ellerup, children, moving out of Massapequa Park home, attorney says," *Newsday*, November 20, 2024.

Fuller, Nicole, "Lab reports, computer data, police tips given to defense," *Newsday*, February 6, 2024.

Fuller, Nichole, Anthony M. DeStefano, "Gilgo Beach Killings: Prosecutors poised to rely heavily on nuclear DNA technology to prove case against Rex Heuermann," *Newsday*, February 8, 2014.

Fuller, Nichole, "Gilgo Beach Killings: Rex Heuermann's estranged wife, Asa Ellerup, says she has given him 'benefit of the doubt,'" *Newsday*, March 14, 2024.

Fuller, Nichole, Grant Parpan, "Gilgo Beach Killings: Investigators search wooded area in Manorville, officials say," *Newsday*, April 24, 2024.

Fuller, Nicole, "Attorney: Claims are 'reckless and defamatory,'" *Newsday*, June 14, 2024.

Fuller, Nicole, "Gilgo Beach Killings: Rex Heuermann's 'manifesto' became road map for investigators," *Newsday*, June 8, 2024.

Harris, Chris, "LI cops scour woods for clues in decades-old serial killer case – not tied to Gilgo slayings," *New York Post*, April 27, 2024.

Hayden, Michael Edison, "The Strange Rise and Violent Fall of Long Island's Dirtiest Police Chief," Vice.com Online Article, March 15, 2016.

Heldman, Caroline, "Long Island Murders: Sex Trafficking Ring Involved?" *MS. Magazine*, April 25, 2011.

Jones, Bart, "Clergy sex abuse survivors reach $323 million settlement with Diocese of Rockville Centre," *Newsday*, September 26, 2024.

Keane, Isabel, "Alleged Gilgo Beach killer's wife may have been in town during murder, attorney claims," *New York Post*, February, 4, 2024.

Kenton, Luke, "Gilgo 'serial killer' Rex Heuermann 'partied with police chief at crack-fueled motel bash and terrified a young runaway,'" *U.S. Sun*, January 31, 2024.

Kilgannon, Corey, "Gilgo Beach Serial-Murer Case Hangs on a Single Strand of Hair," *New York Times*, January 15, 2924.

Lans, Chanteé, "Suffolk County DA says it lacks resources to meet 'ambitious' deadlines in Gilgo Beach murder case." *Channel 7 Eyewitness News*, October 16, 2024.

Malaszczyk, Michael, Timothy Bogler, "Gilgo Beach Serial Killer Suspect Rex Heuermann Charged with Murders of Jessica Taylor and Sandra Costilla in Manorville and North Sea," *Dan's Papers*, June 14, 2024.

Offenhartz, Jake, "Dave Schaller came face to face with alleged Gilgo Beach serial killer Rex Heuermann; 12 years later, his tip helped crack the case," *Associated Press*, July 21, 2023.

O'Keefe, Michael, Rex Heuermann's house searched for a fifth day, several items taken from home of accused Gilgo serial killer," *Newsday*, May 24, 2024.

O'Keefe, Michael, Akiya Dillon, "Gilgo Beach Killings: Suffolk jail investigators turn over 15 'credible' reports of potential sex workers' encounters with Heuermann," *Newsday*, July 2, 2024.

Parpan, Grant. "Gilgo Beach Killings: Court appearance for alleged serial killer Rex Heuermann postponed, *Newsday*, January 14, 2025.

Parpan, Grant, "Gilgo Beach Killings: Cases against suspect Rex Heuermann should be tried separately, defense says," *Newsday*, July 30, 2024.

Parpan, Grant, "Gilgo Beach Killings" Defense says it wants to exclude DNA evidence against suspected serial killer Rex Heuermann at trial," *Newsday*, October 16, 2024.

Parpan, Grant, "Gilgo Beach Killings: Police search suspected serial killer Rex Heuermann's house in Massapequa Park," *Newsday*, May 20, 2024.

Parpan, Grant, "Gilgo Beach Killings: Search in Manorville expands to thousands of acres in the pine barrens, neighboring communities," *Newsday*, April 25, 2024.

Parpan, Grant, "Gilgo Beach Killings: Police expand search of human remains from Manorville to North Sea," *Newsday*, April 26, 2024.

Parpan, Grant, "Gilgo Beach Killings: Alleged Gilgo Beach suspect Rex Heuermann's family struggling to 'comprehend' renewed focus on the home, *Newsday*, May 22, 2024.

Parpan, Grant, "Gilgo Beach Killings: Police conclude second search of Heiermann's home, which is focused on basement," *Newsday*, May 26, 2024.

Parpan, Grant, "Gilgo Beach Killings: Lawyers for alleged Gilgo Beach serial killer Rex A. Heuermann want James Burke's FBI files," *Newsday*, April 17, 2024.

Parpan, Grant, "Gilgo Beach Killings: New details about remains of Gilgo Four revealed, document shows," *Newsday*, March 19, 2024.

Parpan, Grant, "Gilgo Beach Killings: Suspected killer Rex Heuermann facing new charge, multiple sources say," *Newsday*, June 3, 2024.

Parpan, Grant, "Lives of relatives turned 'upside down,'" *Newsday*, July 14, 2024.

Parpan, Grant, "Gilgo Beach Victim: New images, description released by Suffolk DA, *Newsday*, September 16, 2024.

Parpan, Grant, "Convicted Killer John Bittrolff wants to pin murders on Rex Heuermann," *Newsday*, September 16, 2024.

Parpan, Grant, "Gilgo Beach Killings: Rex Heuermann visited Manorville gun club day before victim Jessica Taylor disappeared, source says," *Newsday*, June 11, 2024.

Parpan, Grant, Nicole Fuller, "Gilgo Beach Killings: "Suspect Rex Heuermann had a 'manifesto' to plan and carry out killings, prosecutors said," *Newsday*, June 6, 2024.

Parpan, Grant, "Gilgo Beach Killings: Suspect Rex Heuermann indicted on 2 new murder charges," *Newsday*, June 6, 2024.

Parpan, Grant, "Gilgo Beach Killings: Alleged serial killer Rex Heuermann to be charged in two more killings," *Newsday*, June 5, 2024.

Parpan, Grant, "Gilgo Beach killings: Suspect Rex Heuermann, of Massapequa Park, charged with 7th in death of Valerie Mack, court papers show," December 27, 2024.

Sager, Monica, "Demonic Details Revealed about Rex Heuermann and Daughter: 'Human Devils,'" *Newsweek*, June 13, 2014.

Sedacca, Matthew, "BLOOD MONEY Gilgo 'killer' kin reap $1M," *New York Post*, November 2023.

Sheehan, Kevin, Olivia Land, " Gilgo Beach suspect Rex Heuermann nods as prosecutors read sickening planning document in court," *New York Post*, June 6, 2024.

Sheehan, Kevin and Jorge Fitz-Gibbon, "Accused Gilgo Beach killer Rex Heuermann kept *NY Post* article, other clippings about the murders: prosecutors, December 27, 2024.

Sheehan, Kevin, Isabel Keane and Larry Celona, "Gilgo serial killer suspect Rex Heuermann pleads not guilty in 7th murder charge — as lawyers claim he slaughtered victims in his basement," December 17, 2024.

Shivonne, Adeja, "Attorney: Evidence exists of Rex Heuermann's family involvement in Gilgo Beach murders case," *Fox News Digital*, June 13, 2024.

Spellman-Hoey, Peggy, "Christopher Loeb Indicted in Woman's Beating: DA," *Patch*, January 26, 2024.

TMZ.com video, "Gilgo Beach Alleged Serial Killer ID'd by Witness Dave Schaller in 2010," Undated.